"If thou beest he; But O how fall'n! how chang'd
From him, who in the happy Realms of Light
Cloth'd with transcendent brightness didst out-shine
Myriads though bright"

— John Milton, *Paradise Lost*

This book is a work of fiction. Names, characters, places, and incidents either are products of the author's imagination or are used fictitiously. Any resemblance to actual events or locales or persons, living or dead, is entirely coincidental.

Cover design by Richard Christiano. Photographs on cover and title page copyright © 2009 by Richard Christiano

Manufactured in the United States of America

ISBN-10: 1-4486-4452-6
ISBN-13: 978-1-4486-4452-0

GABRIEL'S FIRED

A NOVEL OF GOOD, EVIL, AND WORK

BY RICHARD CHRISTIANO

Saddle River Publishing

For Mom and Dad,
always the heroes of my story

TABLE OF CONTENTS

Chapter 1

GABRIEL'S TRUMPET BLOWS

No one who has been emasculated by crushing or cutting may enter the assembly of the Lord.

—Deuteronomy 23:1

"Oh, no. Please tell me this isn't happening. We do *not* promote people like you."

These were the first words I heard after moving into my former boss's office, spoken while my head was jammed so far into my lower desk drawer that I heard the echo. I was looking for orphaned paperclips. What I got was my "witty" friend and coworker, Kelvin James.

I sat up straight and grinned. "Nice. Thanks for the support."

Kelvin propped his lanky body against the door frame and looked around the room. His eyes always struck me funny; they looked normal enough most times, but when he glanced away they took on a weasellish quality that made you want to check his rap sheet.

"How long did that pig sit in here?" he asked.

"Nine years, I think."

He sniffed. "Smells it."

"Kelvin, if you don't have anything positive to say..." I broke off, laughing in spite of myself. There was no denying that Marty was a pig. He was an abrasive, slovenly man who was unloved at Cathedral; when he wasn't haranguing someone or other, he was creating silent clouds of halitosis around the people he spoke to peacefully. Fortunately for everyone—especially me—Marty was Random House's problem now. Thinking of him reminded me that I was Kelvin's supervisor now, and that—like it or not—I had to play Marty's role in my own way.

"So," I began, surprised by my own awkwardness, "Everything okay in the land of sports improvement titles?"

"I guess," he said. Shifty eyes again. He pointed to the bare wall behind me. "At least he took his ugly watercolors with him. I gotta go." With that, Kelvin retreated through the door again, and I was left alone once more. Did he sense what I was feeling; that after toiling with him in the editorial trenches for two years at Cathedral, I wasn't ready to play this role yet? Strange things happen when friends get promoted over one another, and I wondered if this new territory made him uncomfortable, too.

Returning to the drawer, I looked into the metallic void. Everywhere I've worked, it was common courtesy to leave the person inheriting your desk something... pens, loose change, Jolly Ranchers. Marty left me dust and air. Granted, our professional relationship was strained—as would be expected between a laid-back subordinate and a boss so engorged with Twinkies and an inflated sense of knowledge that he resembled a malevolent Buddha—but we'd never really argued, and I certainly wasn't expecting the scorched-earth farewell this desk exuded.

Sighing, I eyed the clock. Ten minutes left until the general staff meeting at 9:30. I was still wondering what was going through Kelvin's mind when Theresa Bowerman's head popped into view in the doorway. Long, curly brown tresses swung back and forth beneath her head, and her eyes bugged out a little when she saw me.

"Hi there," I said.

"Um, hey," said Theresa. She bit her lip and looked back down the hallway at something, and as her head turned I saw a flash of scarlet fabric on her shoulder. So *that* was why she was playing peek-a-boo.

"It's okay, Theresa. I know what's about to happen. No need to hide."

"I..." She bit her lip. "I just wanted to see if you were here yet." Now she smiled too... a little. She didn't smile often, and when she did it looked painful. "Some people want to know."

"Tell them I'd rather keep working. It's not like I haven't seen this 'general staff meeting' ruse before."

"Sorry," she said, maintaining that weird half-smile. "You know I can't do that."

I buried my face in my hands. "I know. But I had to try." When I looked up, she was gone.

Five minutes later, I made the right turn from my office and marched down the long hall towards humiliation. My first thought, when I woke up that morning, was that I'd need a tolerance for cheesiness I'd never had if I was to survive today without embarrassing the company or endangering my prospects for future promotion. Cathedral was what our CEO called a "high-personality institution," a term defined in our *Policies and Procedures Manual* as "a humanized company where innovative leadership practices spark creativity into every aspect of business." After two years in the trenches, I realized that this entailed only a bunch of young MBAs in the executive suites who tried to create an esprit de corps through an institutionalized series of hokey rituals. Nothing too bizarre, mind you—no animal sacrifices or public circumcision. Just mandatory events that weren't so much creative as half-assed attempts to substitute creativity for actual management. I've never been to business school, but I'm sure that corporate governance makes perfect sense when it's graphed on a chalkboard. The PowerPoint slides must be incredible. Yet — at least at Cathedral — these newly-minted whiz kids acted less like business wunderkinds than brats driving bumper cars. Chaos was a thrill, angry confrontation was part of the game, and if you got hurt, you were, like, no fun, man.

As I rounded the turn from the hallway I was greeted with the sight of all 130 employees of Cathedral standing in the cavernous main lobby. Two long rows of people, including most of my editors, wore bright red stoles that trailed from their necks to below their knees. Each of these silly garments had the Cathedral logo emblazoned in white. The two rows faced each other, with all heads turned towards me. Some smiled, some looked bored, and I looked momentarily at Kelvin scrinching his face up and lolling his tongue before shifting my eyes to the far end of the room, where the company executives looked like angels in their flowing white robes. They stood in a line that bridged the two rows of corporate cardinals, and at the center of the whole assembly stood the beaming figure of Charles Ting, President and CEO of Cathedral, Inc., wearing his Coke-bottle glasses and a replica of the pope's big hat, looking for all the world like Doofus Jesus. I wanted to run… somewhere, anywhere, far and fast.

"Well, Gabe, looks like we're finally walking down the aisle together."

The voice came from behind me, and I shot a startled glance over my right shoulder at Marcia Gold, Director of Cathedral's Public Relations department. Had she been there when I walked into the room? I didn't think so. She and I were the only ones in the lobby not dressed in costume, although the silken sash she wore over her dress gave her a vaguely military look, as if she were the ambassador from the Planet Saks.

"Marcia!" I said, mentally kicking myself for looking shocked in the presence of someone I despised. "What... I didn't know you were promoted too."

She gave me the classic Marcia simper: smug, reptilian, and oh so full of herself. "Charles thought it best to keep it under wraps until now. You know how he is," she said. Patronization coated each word like conversational lard.

I stared, tongue-tied and wondering what kind of maneuvering she did to engineer this. Somewhere in her early 50s, Marcia was now close to the apex of a career forged through unthinking imitation. She was the kind of woman who spent years watching the behavior of powerful male executives and learning all the wrong things. She was aggressive, manipulative, brusque, and never made any attempt to hide her status as a Charles Ting groupie. Short-haired and wearing her usual pearl necklace, she had the chilly patina of a blueblood. In short, she was a Komodo dragon with manners. And now she gestured toward the waiting rows of Cathedral staffers, irritating me further because, to the gathered assembly, it was clear that one of their rising stars was issuing direction to the other. I'd lost a silent competition before I knew I was competing.

And so we walked, side by side, between the rows of cardinals. I stole a glance at Kelvin, whose mugging had given way to open-mouthed horror. So he didn't know about this either. I closed my eyes, hoping to God that no one had a camera. People usually walked down the aisle in groups of four to seven at a Grand Ordination, since they were held only twice per year. The one saving grace I'd looked forward to at this ridiculous occasion—namely, standing before Charles as a lone hero—was gone. This wasn't even half my moment now.

As we approached the executives, I was surprised to see that Claire, one of my editorial assistants, stood among them. She was dressed in a white robe that was shorter than theirs, coming down to just below the waist, and since she was wearing tight jeans I knew that Charles, who stood one pace behind her, was a lucky man. A young staffer usually volunteered for the role of deacon, and my pleasure at seeing Claire nearly rescued the moment. Her long, black hair flowed smoothly over her shoulders, causing me to have another of my "If I was ten years younger and single" thoughts. And so it came to be that, at 9:30 a.m. on Monday morning, I was the guest of honor at a wedding where the priest was an eccentric geek, the bride was a giant lizard, the groom wanted to violate the living daylights out of the deacon, and most of the congregation didn't give a shit.

"Congratulations, Gabriel," said Charles, shaking my hand and taking a white-bound booklet from Claire.

"Thank you," I croaked. And as my hand closed around the white book he presented—ostensibly a Bible; in reality just a *Policies and Procedures Manual* with a white dust jacket—the sound of applause was drowned out by an awful braying. I looked up to see Bobby Ortiz from Accounting in the lobby mezzanine, holding his brass trumpet. After hours, Bobby was an enthusiastic if untalented jazz musician. His job here was merely to play two notes, one low and one high, each time one of the promoted staff was "ordained." He was in true form today, since what was supposed to be an ethereal accompaniment to the proceedings sounded like a hog being murdered. Fortunately, Marcia received the same treatment when she got her white book. Knowing I would regret it later, I shot her an evil smirk as the promotion she pushed so hard for was saluted with two-tone flatulence.

After another round of applause—now less enthusiastic, and accompanied by muffled giggling—Charles cleared his throat and waited until silence was restored. "I have one more announcement to make before everyone disperses," he said, his deep voice booming through the lobby.

Oh, no, I thought. *Now what?*

Charles waited for the anticipation to ripen before beginning again. "Enlightened leadership is hard to come by in the business world. It's not something you can really teach to people; more often than not, it seems to be an innate quality that every person either lacks or is born with. Good leaders make for good business, and as our company moves forward we will need people like Gabriel and Marcia to help ensure that excellence is manifested in everything we do."

I looked around the room. Blank looks reigned, and the boredom was tangible. I knew Kelvin was keeping his usual tally of business clichés, and as my eyes searched for him, I wondered what number he was up to.

"The best way," continued Charles, stepping forward to place a hand on Marcia's shoulder, "for a company to ensure its continuing success is to reward its best and brightest people with the most important responsibilities. So I am happy to announce that, effective this coming Wednesday, Marcia's group will now be called the Communications Division, and her executive oversight will extend beyond her wonderful Public Relations group to include our Web group, our software products group, and the book group, which is now ably lieutenanted by Gabriel here."

I twitched. *Lieutenanted?*

"I wish them continued success," said Charles, "and hope that you'll demonstrate your best wishes by giving them a big round of applause."

My heart sank as the clapping began. It was a joke. It was a travesty. I looked around for some sign that I'd misheard what Charles said. The cardinals were applauding politely, but their blank faces were unreadable. I looked at Jerry Lanville, the VP I thought would be my boss after today, but he avoided eye contact and clapped with a small, tight-lipped smile. Steeling myself, I glanced at Marcia, who was acknowledging the crowd with cute waves and displaying much more faux modesty than the situation required. Breaking out with sweat, I knew that if this was all a bad dream, the nausea was real.

As the assembly dispersed, people came forward to shake my hand and congratulate me. Most of the editors and the other people I knew had been standing towards the rear of the room, and as I chatted idly with the handshakers I glanced over their shoulders, looking for friendly faces to commiserate with. I didn't see any of my staff, and figured they'd bolted off to the book group's cubicles to bounce the shock off each other for a while. Lucky them, I thought.

Turning to Marcia, who had never strayed from my side as the neat formations of people broke up into babbling little groups and then into a nearly empty room, I swallowed hard and offered my hand.

"Congratulations, Marcia." I said with a sandy tongue.

"Thank you," she said.

I may as well have been talking to a robot. As we shook hands, I felt a wave of panic. Did she know how I felt about this turn of events? We'd never clashed, or even bickered, but I could remember a few occasions where I could have been more polite. I searched her eyes for some trace of amusement, some sign of acknowledgment that she'd won an ugly victory, but it was like looking into the eyes of an iguana. My only recourse—unless I preferred the unemployment line—was to behave as if working for Marcia promised halcyon days beyond measure.

"I look forward to working with you," I said, laying on as much cheese as I could stand.

"I wonder if you could stop by my office at three for a quick status meeting," she said. "Tell the editors. I'd like everybody there."

Before I could answer, she turned away and trotted after one of the departing VPs for some more gladhanding, leaving me alone in the lobby.

"*Kyrie eleison*," I said softly, clutching the faux-Bible and bowing my head.

* * *

Passing through the editors' cube farm on my way to my office, I could feel the eyes on me but said nothing. Thankfully, no one said a word as I rushed through, reached my office, and closed the door behind me.

Plopping down into my chair, I sighed loudly and stared at my computer screen. It was time I got myself a serious drinking problem, but since there was no booze at hand it would have to wait. Grasping my mouse, I called up CathMail and addressed a message to my editors:

3:00 status meeting in Marcia's office. Don't be late. Gabe.

While typing my name, I heard the chiming doorbell sound that CathMail emitted when a new message arrived. Scanning my inbox, I saw that there was neither a sender's name or a subject line on the new message. That was odd.

A knock sounded at my door.

"Come in," I said.

The door opened and Kelvin walked halfway in, with Theresa and Claire and the other editors crowded behind him. The stoles were gone.

"Um," said Kelvin, looking like a toddler who'd just soiled his pants. "We were just wondering if this was a good time to, uh, talk about... you know..."

I sighed again. "Look, guys, I'm feeling kinda blown away myself. I don't know what to make of it."

They stared at me bug-eyed. This was supposed to be my first attempt at leadership, and their expressions told me I was already blowing it. All of them shared my opinion of Marcia—she was a favorite target of our lunchtime harshing—so I figured they knew well enough what the implications were. They wanted something more comforting than information.

I rubbed my eyes and started again. "Okay, here's the plan. Today's Monday, and the Reign of Terror doesn't start until Wednesday. For now, just keep working on your projects the way you've been doing them. Your jobs haven't changed, and neither has mine. We've got next year's books all timelined out, so she can't do any real damage for a while. To be honest," I said, hating myself for the lie, "I really don't see this affecting us much. She's a Public Relations person. If we just do our jobs well, she'll probably leave us alone."

They appeared somewhat reassured. Kelvin still looked dubious, but Theresa's brows were no longer furrowed and Claire was actually wearing the ghost of a smile. I rummaged through my mental box of platitudes, and a few more calming gems seemed to calm things down enough for everyone to go back to their offices, one by one. Theresa was the last to go.

"Something on your mind?" I asked.

"The woman's a moron, Gabe."

I smiled. "She just made VP. That must take some intelligence."

"That just proves she's clever. Big difference."

I breathed deeply. "Yeah."

"And what does *lieutenanted* mean?"

"That I can't help you with."

Her hands balled up into fists. I couldn't help but smile. Theresa was best-of-breed when it came to editors, but when something made her angry… she behaved like this. And she got angry often. It suited her. "Marcia doesn't even know what editing is. She'll be signing off on our raises, and she's not even qualified to judge our work."

"We don't know that yet. None of us have worked with her directly before. Who knows, maybe we're underestimating her, and she'll turn out to be Boss of the Year."

Theresa just stared. So much for that.

"Look," I said, the flashing icon on my e-mail screen catching my eye, "I've got some things to do right now. All I'm saying is, let's give her a chance. She may surprise us. I think this 3:00 meeting will give us a chance to really see what she's like to work with. So let's wait until then before we lose our minds."

She bit her lip, thought hard for a moment, then exhaled hard. "All right." Turning to leave, she made it as far as the doorway before turning around again. "But Gabe?"

"Yeah?"

"Bring a helmet."

I waved her out with a laugh and swivelled my chair around to face the screen. Clicking on the authorless and subjectless message, I waited the few moments for my antique PC to call the text up.

To: Gabriel Marino
From:
Date:
Re:

YOU ARE IN GREATER DANGER THAN YOU KNOW. BE CAREFUL.

ARCHANGEL

I chuckled, then hit the delete key. Cathedral had its share of kooks, and apparently some were sociopaths. This one—whoever he might be—was both amusing and inventive. I made a mental note to switch Kelvin's computer wallpaper to something obscene.

The rest of the morning was spent between fitful spurts of editing and phone calls. Kelvin played dumb about the anonymous e-mail, forcing me to actually believe him for a change. A couple of friends outside the company had nothing to do with it either, although one of them said he'd given my e-mail address to a new sect of e-Mormons. This was a character who once joined me in an unfortunate college incident involving a lot of beer, two bear costumes, and a campus security blotter item involving a mooning at a women's lacrosse game during Parents' Weekend. If it wasn't him, it wasn't anybody.

Finally, unable to concentrate on the manuscript in front of me, and irritated by a page that had more dashes than an Emily Dickinson poem, I dropped my red pen and called Cathedral's Management Information Systems department.

"M.I.S.," a voice answered.

"Rajput?" I asked.

"Yes?"

"It's Gabe Marino, in Books. Can I ask a quick question?"

"A question."

"Yes. Is it possible for someone here to send an anonymous e-mail message to someone else? From one user to another, that is."

"Anonymous."

"Try to follow me here, Raj. E-mail. Is it possible to... I don't know, mask your identity... you know, block it somehow, when you send a message?"

"A message."

I banged the receiver against my forehead. Talking with Cathedral's tech guys was like trying to build a skyscraper with Lego blocks: It was impossible to construct what you wanted with the materials at hand. Tech people can have six Ph.D.s in Unix and still have the communication skills of a trained gorilla. And somehow, when I talk to them, I'm always the one asking for the banana.

Rajput thought for a moment. "Tech staff can do. And maybe... someone good. Very good. Knows a lot."

"Hmm. So, for example, if I wanted to do it myself, you think I could figure it out?"

"You? No way."

Well, *that* got communicated loud and clear. I looked at my watch; I'd wasted enough time, so I neverminded Raj and hung up the phone. It was time to lose myself in some work for a while. Technically, I wasn't supposed to line-edit manuscripts anymore, but I still had to carry the books I was working on until I could hire a replacement for my old position. I didn't mind. It was nice to immerse myself in someone else's thoughts and forget about Marcia for a while.

Unfortunately, the manuscript I'd chosen for distraction was a math book. Essentially, it was a primer on basic math for adults who spent their school years throwing spitballs and now wanted admission to grad school. Cathedral offered an amazing variety of products and services like this: Classes, tutoring, software, books... all of it fell under the rubric of remedial education, and our survival in the business world was built on the inability of the American public to grasp what they were taught. If your fourth-grader couldn't memorize her multiplication tables, we were there. If your high-school quarterback couldn't get into Notre Dame, we made sure he nailed the SAT score required by State... with plenty of free time to nail the head cheerleader if that was his thing. And if you grew bored with your career, we could make you a lawyer or a doctor or a geophysicist in seven easy steps. We were the consummate product of a quick-fix culture, where a pill or a 12-step program or a CD-ROM with cheesy animation made years of laziness and bad decisions just… go away. Our motto was, "In learning is life." It should have been "Duh."

I smiled down at the page before me, then marked it and set the manuscript aside. I wasn't exactly a paragon of education either. Sure, I edited books for a living and could whip out an essay on most subjects easily enough, but all math seemed like pointless mental gymnastics since Algebra II. Cathedral had a network of math teachers who taught classes on standardized tests, and I tapped them shamelessly for projects like these. Of course, I couldn't pay them anything from my budget – which was probably why they responded with open hostility. Yet they always did it, in a strained spirit of corporate teamwork that I always feared would snap. And once I was finished editing what little English there was between the mathematical hieroglyphics, I was happy to toss it on some propellerhead's desk and move on to more interesting work.

Looking at my watch, I saw that I'd spent hours grinding away at this. It was almost time for Marcia's status meeting. Rising from my desk and stretching, I felt the uneasiness creep back into the pit of my stomach and curdle. The time since the Grand Ordination had been quiet... no one had called, and the few people who came to my office didn't say anything irritating. I was calm, considering that the weather forecast for my career called for sleet and hail for the next 10 years.

Emerging from my office, I walked straight into Claire, who gave a little yelp as her left hip brushed against me. We both stopped, and for one long second the back of my hand was pressed against the warm place on her jeans where her thigh ended and her butt began. As a married man, I usually paid no mind to mini-collisions like these.

"Whoops, sorry!" I said, quickly pulling away. The beginnings of a hot flush began on my face as I made a spastic you-first gesture with my arm. The back of my hand felt conspicuously cool as it flopped in the general direction of Marcia's office.

"No problem," she said, smiling.

The hall was too narrow for us to walk side-by-side, so we made our way down to Marcia's office with Claire in front. That suited me just fine, for mostly bad reasons.

Marcia Gold had one of the larger offices at Cathedral, and as I walked in I noticed that there were several more chairs in front of her desk than usual. Kelvin and Theresa were already seated, talking quietly while Marcia sat behind her huge desk, listening, arms folded. Claire and I sat down. I watched Marcia closely for any sign of what was to come, but she seemed absorbed with something on her screen.

One of us was missing, and by the time my eyes found the empty chair and realized who it was, the sound of braying laughter from the hallway announced the arrival of Sally Tighe. Sally was the third editor in my group, and as she waved goodbye to someone in the hallway, I wondered how she and Marcia would get along. I'd never seen Marcia laugh, and Sally... well, she was unique.

Sally's entrance seemed to bring Marcia back to matters at hand. "Well," she said, smiling and meshing her fingers together in front of her. "What a nice little gathering we have here."

She seemed to expect an answer, so I cleared my throat. "Uh, yeah, we do parties and bar mitzvahs on request."

"Good one, Gabe," said Sally, rolling her eyes. "Guess that joke-telling webinar really paid…" She caught my not-now look, and watched with satisfaction as the other editors looked alarmed. Marcia continued to smile, but with tight lips.

"Well," said Marcia, "I won't keep you from your work very long. I just wanted to familiarize myself with the way you've been doing things, and," her smile widened, "also familiarize you with the way I do things."

Here it comes, I thought.

"First—and I can't emphasize this enough—I'd like to remind everyone that we are all professional staff here, and I expect everyone here to behave like professionals. At all times." Her smile was gone now, replaced by the look of a schoolteacher looking for the brat who threw the paper plane. She added emphasis to her last several words by flattening her hands against her desk and patting it in time with her speech.

I stole a look at my staff. No one was smiling now.

"Second, you all should know that I'm a very deadline-oriented person. Everything we do—every project, every component of every project—has to have a due date *and* a due hour attached to it. From now on, we'll have a formal meeting every Monday at 9:00 and go down the list of dates. Just to make sure we're not getting behind."

I saw a set firmness in Theresa's jaw and a crease forming between Sally's eyebrows. Kelvin was looking down at his lap. Claire's eyes were wide and locked on Marcia. I racked my brains for a way to tell Marcia this was unnecessary. Did she not realize she just told the most intellectual, professional group in Cathedral to sit up straight and eat their vegetables?

"Well, Marcia," I said, "I'm sure you'll be happy to know that in the past two years, not one of our titles missed its bound-book date. We're very proud of that."

"Wonderful!" said Marcia, raising her palms and leaning back in her chair. "That's really super. But let's keep in mind that there's always room for improvement."

None of us said a word. It took monstrous amounts of unpaid overtime to keep a line of 30 annual and another 15 biannual titles on time with the staff we had. There were hundreds of ways we could have sacrified the quality of these books to get them done faster, and with less work, but we never did. The urge to fix what wasn't broken wasn't a management sickness that Jerry Lanville suffered from. When our group reported to Jerry, we rarely heard a peep out of him save for the occasional compliment and pat on the back. But he wasn't our VP now.

Marcia cleared her throat. "Well. Now that we understand each other, why don't you all tell me what you work on? I can't wait to get started."

"Sure," I said. It could only get better from here. I explained how Cathedral's educational publishing system worked: We handled all editorial and layout for Cathedral's books, and our publisher, Greenlawn Press, took care of the printing and distribution. Each editor maintained a stable of authors who ground out annual updates of their titles. The companies split the profit down the middle, the system worked well, and by the time I finished, Marcia looked sleepy.

"Theresa works on professional improvement titles," I said. "You might have seen *Cover Letters for the Illiterate...* it's one of our bestsellers. What else are you working on, Theresa?"

Theresa glared for a moment, and my eyes dropped to the carpet. "Well," she began, frost encrusting each word, "My hottest project is a book for lawyers on how to ingratiate themselves with judges. It's called *Your Honor, My Pleasure*. Don't worry... it's on time."

I looked up at Marcia. There was no sign that she perceived the subtle sassing.

"Theresa's great at those," I said. "And Kelvin here does our sports and hobby books. I think your P.R. people just did a press release on Kelvin's latest, a guide to golf for people who have no time for practice. And now..."

"Yep," said Kelvin, smiling. "Where would the world be without *Who Needs Foreplay?"*

Marcia frowned. "Are these titles all so... irreverent?"

"It's our corporate brand," I said. "Our readership is young, and if you look at our sales figures, you'll see they appreciate the humor."

Her nose wrinkled.

"Sally, what have you got on tap right now?" I asked.

"Gee, Gabe, I've got so many I don't know where to start. How about Mary Bolin's manuscript for kids on how to deal with adults?"

Sally's grin was evil. We had no such book on our list, and by the time I figured out what she was up to, it was too late.

"Oh, how nice!" said Marcia. "I wish my daughters had something like that when they were little. What's it called?"

"*Don't Touch Me There*," said Sally, setting off giggling fits from Kelvin and Claire.

I sighed, watching Marcia's look of interest darken into something else. She leaned back in her chair again, looking as if someone held a sock under her nose. "I take it that was a joke," she said.

"We're a pretty high-spirited group," I said with as much good cheer as I could muster. "When you work hard together, you develop a camaraderie that sometimes goes a little out of bounds." I directed those last words at Sally. "We don't mean anything by it," I said. *Inhale, exhale, repeat.*

"Very well," she said. "Moving on to logistics, I'd like a detailed status sheet drawn up for next week's meeting, showing the phase that each of your books are in, and completion dates next to each phase. From now on, everything has a completion date and time, and I want to know in advance if it's going to run late. All unforeseen problems should be brought to my attention before they happen, not after. Claire, that will be your responsibility for every meeting."

Claire's eyes went wide. To her credit, and to my undying gratitude, she said nothing.

"Well! I guess we're all done here," said Marcia, with a cheerfulness that was so phony it was shocking. "Gabe, would you stay for just a moment?"

"Sure," I said.

The others rose and filed out of the office. Kelvin and Sally exchanged looks, Claire hung her head on the way out, and Theresa looked like a zombie. I'd have paid money to hear what they said as they walked down the hall.

Once they left, Marcia said, "What a nice group."

"The best," I said.

"You should remember that what they do reflects on you."

"I do."

"I don't mean the books," she said.

A staring match had begun. I wasn't sure how dangerous a game I was playing, but I was getting tired of watching her run up the score.

"Marcia, I'm usually not a stickler for chain of command, but I think it will be disruptive if you assign things directly to the editors. It'll make more sense if you tell me what needs to be done and let me delegate."

"Really. And why is that?"

Was she toying with me? "Well, let's start with basic management: Claire's an assistant, and all of the editors delegate tasks to her. She can't possibly know how to prioritize everything that's given to her, so I traffic her assignments. That's how editors work."

Marcia snorted. "Well!" she said, throwing up her hands in mock exasperation. "And I suppose there's only one right way to get every job done? What do you *editors* call this little system of yours?"

"There's no system… you just learn this stuff through trial and error. Publishing is a craft with time-proven methods, just like accounting. Or carpentry. Messing with the system is like telling your CPA to do your taxes with a plane."

She looked at me as if I were a child. "A plane? What do pilots have to do with this?"

I blinked. "Never mind. Claire will do the status sheet. But I really think you should check with me before assigning things to the editors."

"Oh, hogwash," she said. "If there's one thing I've learned in *decades* of working as a professional, it's that people are adaptable. In fact, I plan to spread the responsibilities of my departments around quite a bit. When my public relations team gets overworked, our press releases get backlogged and everyone gets upset. I'm sure your editors can handle writing a few press releases, can't they? After all, they're English types."

I gripped the handrests of my chair.

"And," she continued, "I'd like to assign a few books to my P.R. staff, too. They'd love the chance to work on something new."

"I don't think that's a good idea," I said.

"Well," she said, eyeing me down the long bridge of her nose, "you're a new manager. This is an exciting chance for you to learn."

"But... your P.R. people think *editing* means running spell check, and my editors have no training in promotional writing. You can't use the two groups interchangeably."

"They'll do just fine. In time, you'll see that this is the best way to even out the workload when people get too busy."

I checked myself. "Okay. It's your department. I'm not looking for an argument. But while we're on the subject of workloads, I'll need to hire an editor to replace me. Do you want to discuss the wording of the ad, or should I just take care of this myself?"

"Oh, we're not hiring anybody. Charles has noticed that your division's profit margins lag behind the others, and he thinks that the existing staff is... underutilized."

It felt like I'd been slapped. Deep wells of vintage anger, untapped since God knew when, began to simmer. If my silence fazed her, she didn't show it.

"Marcia," I said, enunciating every syllable, "I can't carry all of my books, do Marty's job, and write press releases all at the same time."

"Sure you can," she said, with a cheerfulness that made me want to bite the head off a bunny rabbit. "Efficiency is the key to everything. I have some wonderful books on time management… you can borrow them anytime."

It was one of those moments when the next second—the next spoken word—determines a course of action that has lasting consequences. The temptation to unleash a wiseass comment was incredible. Six or seven of them were on the tip of my tongue. All I had to do was choose.

"Okay," I said, looking at my watch. I had nowhere to go, but I desperately needed to escape and regroup before I murdered Marcia. "I've gotta go now. Can we talk later?"

"Of course," she said, and smiled. It was the smile of victory – she knew it, and so did I.

"We're going to do great work together," she said. "Just you wait and see."

"Right," I said.

In the time it took to slink back to my office, I accomplished four things. First, I made a mental list of all the qualities shared by the great historical leaders I admired. Next, I thought of all the qualities I failed to display that day. Then, right about the time I nearly steamrolled somebody as I was mumbling "This is bullshit" over and over, I realized that the two lists were identical down to the last word. Finally, as I rounded the last turn into my office and slammed the door behind me, I realized that Cathedral had a seven-step program for solving just about any problem in life. But we had no courses, no books, no software, and no Web site for those who worked for people like Marcia.

I collapsed into my chair and looked at the screen. There was no further e-mail from my archangel. I was alone.

Chapter 2

THE LAST DAY OF EDEN

It is better to dwell in the wilderness than with a contentious and angry woman.
—Proverbs 21:19

Tuesday morning brought a wealth of distractions, which was good. I'd thought about Marcia's coup all night long, rolling the covers around me until my wife was marooned on the cold side of the bed. She wasn't happy. Neither was I.

Riding the bus into Manhattan, I tried to distract myself from that New Jersey Transit bus smell—part diesel fumes, part rubber, part stale Ben Gay—by considering ways to comfort the victims of yesterday's debacle. Only one solution held promise: Work as usual. Have one last, normal day, where the old routines continued and no preparations for the new regime were made. If Marcia wanted to scramble my jigsaw puzzle and cram all the wrong pieces together, she could do it tomorrow. Today was mine, and beside every hour in my executive planner I would write the words *carpe diem.*

By the time I reached Cathedral's building, my dread and my optimism had reached a truce. I smiled at the receptionist as I marched into the lobby, zipped through the corridors, and nearly outran the memories of yesterday as they followed me into the editorial area. Reaching my warren of cubicles, I began the morning routine I loved.

"Sound off!" I yelled. "What are the principles by which we toil?"

"To give every author a cheeseball contract," came a sleepy voice from Theresa's cubicle.

Eyes peeped over the dividing wall between Theresa's and Kelvin's cubes. "To bury our beer bills in the budget," said Kelvin.

"To avoid alliteration and assonance always," said Claire.

When I reached the door to my office, we were still one voice short. We were always one voice short.

"Where's Sally?" I said.

The chorus of answers was immediate, as always: "Who gives a shit?"

"Excellent," I said, completing the ritual and entering my office.

Theresa followed me in, sitting down and waiting patiently while I turned my computer on and futzed with the piles of papers on my desk.

"I see *The Spastic's Guide to Yoga* is done," I said, tapping the manuscript on my desk with my finger.

Theresa nodded. "It is. But that's not what I wanted to talk to you about."

"Hold on," I said, fishing a quarter from my pocket. "Heads, I want to hear this. Tails, I don't." I flipped. Tails.

"I'm just hoping that, whatever…" said Theresa.

I pointed at the coin on my desk. "Hold it. I won," I said.

"So?"

I closed my eyes. "Continue."

"As I was saying," said Theresa, with extra bite, "Whatever happens tomorrow, we're all relying on you to stand up for what's right."

"Theresa, she's not that bad."

"This isn't about her. It's about you."

I crossed my arms. "What do you mean by that?"

Of course, I knew exactly what she meant. She stood in the stance of a gunslinger, fingertips twitching. Two people, to date, made Theresa behave this way, and one of them was Kelvin.

Theresa breathed deep. "I can stand having you in charge. I actually respect you, when you aren't screwing up. But that gangly freak you call a friend interferes with your sense of right and wrong."

I sat up in my chair. "Diplomatically put, as usual."

"Kelvin can't help it. He was born a goon. You, on the other hand, should know better, and you're in a position of power now. So I'm hoping you'll act less like Kelvin and more like…"

"You?" I said, smiling.

She didn't smile. "You could do worse."

I looked at the ceiling, but there were no answers written there. "I don't suppose I can ask you to just… have a little faith in me?"

"Keep Marcia at bay," she said, thrusting her jaw forward. "And try to grow some morals. Then we'll talk about faith."

I got up from my chair and looked out the window. It was time.

"Do you have anything else you need to talk about, Theresa?" I said, fixing my eyes on a guy sitting in an office on my level, across the street. He wore a suit. It was dark and projected authority. He wore it often, and for the first time, I found myself liking it.

"No… but I wasn't done talking about this yet."

"Sorry, but… you are. Go back to your cube and do some work, please."

Her eyes squinted. "Excuse me?"

I turned around. For the first time I could remember, she looked hurt. Slightly. It was hard to tell with Theresa… her curly brown hair half-covered her eyes most of the time. But the fun in needling her was gone now, and it dawned on me that I was starting to act like Marcia.

"Look," I said. "I know Kelvin's sense of humor is a little much for you sometimes. And maybe mine is, too. If you really want to know the truth, I feel so comfortable working with you all that clowning around seems… normal. You know?"

"No," she said.

I sighed. "You keep me honest, Theresa. You don't miss a damn thing, and you have strengths as an editor that I don't have. Has it occurred to you that maybe I need you to do that?"

I looked for some reaction in her eyes, but it was like staring at blue tundra.

"You play a role on this team," I said. "And despite anything I've said, and despite anything that Kelvin has done, I like that. I like working with you, and I like working with them. So if Marcia comes storming down here tomorrow and gets in your face, you'd better believe that I'll stick up for you."

One of her eyebrows slowly, glacially, rose.

I've always been there for you and the others, and that won't change now that I'm sitting in Marty's pigpen." I walked around my desk and stood before her, looking down. A little theatrical, maybe, but I needed some of that. "We're still going to yuk it up every day, and I'll have a beer with you guys any time, anywhere. Trust me on that."

Her face didn't betray any emotion at all. She didn't even move.

"Marcia's my problem," I continued. "Not yours. So scram."

Her eyes looked vacant for a moment, and then she stood. Slowly. Then, she nodded — again, slowly.

"Okay," she said. She looked at the door, and then back at me. "I'll hold you to your word, though. Remember that."

She turned and walked out. Settling back into my chair, I wondered if there were job openings at McMurdo Station. Or Guam. Or the International Space Station. Or some other place where the word *synergy* had no meaning. Then, noticing my CathMail icon blinking on my monitor, I clicked on it.

To: Gabriel Marino
From:
Date:
Re:

WATCH THE SKY TONIGHT.

ARCHANGEL

I read the message once, blinked, read it again, and deleted it. Why do power geeks always crave more recognition than anyone is willing to give? This guy would never be satisfied with anonymous messages: I knew the type. He would annoy me with clues and cackle about my reaction with his instant-messaging buddies. So I deleted it, vowing not to say anything to anyone. Maybe then he'd move on to a better target. Like Theresa, maybe.

The sound of someone's knuckles rapping on my door frame snapped me out of my thoughts. I looked up at Claire, who was now leaning against the frame.

"Hey," she said.

"Howdy," I said, fighting the urge to let my eyes do their little dance.

She glanced around the bare walls of my office, as if searching for Marty's pictures, then fixed those dark eyes on me again. "Are we meeting now? Kelvin sent me after you."

I looked at my watch. "Right. Yeah. I'll be right there," I said, and smiled after her as she nodded and left. Sexual harassment wasn't my kind of thing, but something wild in me rattled the bars of its cage when she was around.

Grabbing a pad and pen, I headed for the editors' warren of cubes and parked myself in the empty seat at our Round Table. Next to Claire.

"Sorry guys," I said. "Did you start without me?"

Kelvin rolled his eyes. Theresa looked at me with sad amusement, and her hands made a strangling motion when I stuck my tongue out her.

"Who the hell needs you?" said Sally, feigning a convincing look of confusion. "We're practically done."

It would have been funny if it wasn't true. I knew from Marty's sick days that these people didn't need a boss to have a status meeting. When they talked about work, they weaved it between the petty scandals that drove their day. Missing illustrations and botched TOCs blended with observations of who showed up for work late with the unmistakable hairstyle of the recently reamed. We were young, sarcastic, and bitter about having the privacy of sailors in our little warren. But our tight formation also produced a hive mind that produced better softcover swill than anyone had a right to expect, given what we had to work with. Marty was neither pleasant nor a good department head, but he knew how to build a team.

"Theresa? Any problems? I said.

She shrugged. "Ellie Castleman's bitching about her royalties again, but that's Greenlawn's problem, not ours."

I nodded. "That it?"

"For now, yeah. Tomorrow's a different story."

I caught her sour look and raised my hand before anyone jumped in. "Okay, people, quit complaining about Marcia. Let's try to enjoy our last day of…" I searched for something besides the word I wanted.

"Sanity?" said Sally.

"Knock it off," I said, turning to her. "So how are your books doing?"

"They suck," said Sally.

I smiled. When Sally had a problem to discuss, she said so. When everything was fine, she said it sucked. The habit made her happy, and after considering a mild rebuke, I let it go.

"Kelvin?"

He sighed. "Dude, Legal's on my case about *Parents' Guide to Playing Nice in Little League* again."

"Oh, come on. How many reviews has that been though?"

"Four."

I bit my lip. "What's the problem this time?" I said.

There went the shifty eyes again. "Well," he said. "Two problems. First, they're saying the title says one thing while the manuscript says something totally different."

"Hey Kelvin?" said Theresa, glaring. "Guess what? That's an *editorial* problem, not a legal problem."

"Go pound sand in your ass," said Kelvin.

I raised my hand before Theresa ratcheted up the hostility. Then, turning to Kelvin, I said, "Are they right? Does the manuscript match the proposal?"

Really shifty eyes now. "Well… there's a chapter on how to… you know, bully an umpire. But it's good stuff! You should see the part where…"

Holding up my hand, I said. "Enough. Is there time enough in the schedule to work this out with the author?"

He shrugged. "Barely."

"Good. Talk to him, and if you need me to step in, give me a holler." I was tempted to add *you should know better*, but held my tongue. He was probably right about the chapter being good… Kelvin had an eye for good, salable copy. Focus, however, wasn't his strong suit.

"Hey," said Sally. "It's Tuesday. Are we doing the Tar Bar?"

The mood around the table lightened considerably. The Tar Bar was our name for the roof of our 7-story building. On Tuesday nights in spring, summer, and early fall, our group packed some beers in a cooler and snuck up the ladder on the seventh floor leading to the trap door marked "No Admittance." We had some lawn chairs up there, and a beach umbrella with brown stains and cobwebs on it. We sat atop Manhattan like royalty, getting drunk with a view of the East River and Brooklyn that was partially blocked by two larger buildings. There was also a string of Christmas lights we draped around the umbrella when it got dark. It was undoubtedly against some company or building rule, but since it helped us stay cohesive as a unit, Marty turned a blind eye. Giving him free beer may also have helped. But now the decision was mine.

"Okay," I said. "But let's try not to let Marcia find out we do this. It could lead to problems."

"No shit," muttered Kelvin.

Without further business to discuss, we ended the meeting after that and got back to work. Thankfully, my day progressed exactly as I'd hoped. We worked hard, bantered back and forth, and avoided internal strife entirely save for one unfortunate incident where a fingernail clipping from Kelvin's desk somehow ended up in Theresa's coffee mug. Marcia showed the good sense — I think — to leave us alone for the day… a quick peek into Public Relations revealed that she had other wretches to flog. She didn't see me watching her as she yelled, and I stayed only long enough to hear six or seven words before beating a fast trail back to my safe haven.

Tar Bar time, when it came, provided a sweet ending to the day. I was late getting up there, but when I finally climbed through the trap door the western sky was aglow with a sherbet-colored sunset. The Christmas lights were on and blinking, and everyone was reclining with beers in hand.

"Gabe!" yawped Sally. "You're not gonna believe this. Theresa actually heard somebody use the word *pshaw* on the subway this morning."

"Are you kidding?" I said, grabbing a Harp from the cooler. "I thought only nineteenth-century playwrights used that word."

"Bad nineteenth-century playwrights," said Claire with a giggle. She sat with the orange and purple glory of the western sky behind her, and for once I didn't — I couldn't — come up with a quip to keep the fun going.

"What the hell kind of word is that?" said Kelvin, gesticulating wildly. "I mean, what does it say? What did it ever say?"

Theresa shifted her weight so that she could look at Kelvin with full-bore condescension. "It says that the person using it is old, prudish to a fault, favors natty wool cardigans, and lacks the conviction to use emphatic obscenity."

I shook my head and settled into a chair. "You guys have got to stop hanging around with each other. You're beginning to sound really weird."

"Oh, you should talk," said Theresa, pointing her beer bottle at me. "You used the word *yuk* today, when you were talking to me. As in Y-U-K."

"I did not."

"Did too."

"Did not."

"Fine," she said, shrugging and taking another big sip. "But for the record, I haven't seen the word *yuk* outside that old-fashioned Marmaduke comic strip. Hearing you say it made me want to bathe in iodine."

Claire, Sally, and Kelvin eyed me with looks of suspicion, and I couldn't help laughing. The conversation veered off to stranger topics, and as the setting sun warmed my face, I closed my eyes to enjoy it. I must have nodded off for a moment, because the next thing I heard was "Earth to Gabe?"

"Hmm?" I said, opening my eyes.

"We were just wondering," said Claire with a mischievous grin, "what you were thinking with that big smile on your face."

"Oh," I said, feeling the beginnings of a blush. "Well, you know what? I might as well tell the truth."

I paused, enjoying the silence.

"Spill," said Theresa.

"I was just thinking how lucky I am to be working with you guys," I said, surprising myself with how much I meant it. "Aside from Kelvin's pranks, Sally's foul mouth, Theresa's sanctimony, and Claire's…"

"My what?" said Claire.

Sometimes I hate beer for what it almost makes me say. "Your irritating curiosity, that's what."

And as the laughter and the verbal sparring began anew, I felt sure that tomorrow, when it came, would be better.

Chapter 3

THE SERPENT IN THE GARDEN

And the Lord God said unto the serpent, Because thou hast done this, thou art cursed above all cattle, and above every beast of the field; upon thy belly shalt thou go, and dust shalt thou eat all the days of thy life.
—Genesis 3:14

I didn't want to see the massive circular door at the entrance to Cathedral's office building on Tuesday morning. It had been a sleepness night, and before the tossing and turning even started I'd irritated my wife with an argument about garbage bag ties. We'd already discussed the real cause of my mood, so she knew not to press me too far on Hefty vs. Glad. The discussion took a nasty turn anyway, and after arguing more or less successfully that the drawstring-style ties were superior, it didn't help to have the handle break in my hand, sending the bag tumbling down the stairs to the alley.

No, I didn't want to show up that day, but it was my job. And the first thing on my agenda couldn't wait.

"Hi Jerry," I said, walking straight into Jerry Lanville's office without even looking to see if he was alone. Fortunately he was. I pointed to the door. "May I?"

Jerry looked up. "Gabe. It's good to see you."

I closed the door and sat in one of Jerry's guest chairs. He looked older than he did in our last meeting; his brow was furrowed and his shoulders hunched. He was wearing his best suit, midnight blue and expensive, but the silk that usually projected authority looked rumpled today. Jerry was one of the few Cathedral execs who fit the part without coming across as a poser or a stuffed shirt. He was the real deal, intelligent and charismatic and a great guy to work for.

"So what's on your mind?" he said with a wan smile.

"Jerry, how can this happen? How could they do this to you?"

He shifted in his chair. "I might ask the same of you. How's it going with Marcia?"

"Author, Ken Kesey. Title, *One Flew Over the Cuckoo's Nest.* Character, Nurse Ratched. Any questions?"

"No, I believe that covers it," said Jerry, leaning forward and splicing his fingers together. "Gabe, I want you to know that none of this was my choice."

I nodded.

"There's a lot going on here," he said. "More than meets the eye. And you're probably aware of just a fraction of it."

I thought about that for a moment. Clearly, he'd been outmaneuvered in a power struggle—that would have been clear to a baboon. What else was there?

"So," I began, venturing into territory I'd never explored with Jerry before, "What are we talking about here? Are there going to be more... reorganizations?"

"Perhaps." The defeated look was still on his face.

"What are you in charge of now?"

"My oversight has been transferred to the Core Services Division."

My jaw nearly hit the floor. "Oh, no. The mailroom? Office Administration? The tech geeks?"

Jerry nodded after each of the questions, pretending to find something fascinating about his desk blotter. He was silent after that, and as I leaned back in my chair and contemplated the wreckage of his career at Cathedral, he continued to say nothing. One of Jerry's best traits was also a weakness: He never had anything bad to say about anyone. Some people, like me, respected him for it. Others found ways to whack him in the head with his own niceness, the way Charles and Marcia did yesterday.

"Is anyone going to lose their job?" I said.

He tapped his fingers on the desk. "I don't know," he said. "And even if I did, I couldn't tell you. I just want you to know that you're not being singled out in any way. No one has it in for you."

"Okay," I said. "But what about you?"

The tight-lipped smile returned. "Sorry. I really can't say anything more, except..."

An idea occurred to me: Jerry was in charge of the tech guys now. "Are you... Archangel?" I said.

I watched his face carefully, but he seemed genuinely surprised by the question. "Am I what?"

Feeling that special blush that accompanies only acts of stupidity, I decided to continue. "I got an anonymous e-mail message yesterday. Well, not quite anonymous... it was signed 'Archangel,' and it warned me to be careful. Because I was in danger."

His brows furrowed. "I don't know anything about that. I think perhaps someone is having some fun with you."

"Okay," I said, rising and making for the door. "Sorry to bring it up. And thanks for...well, what you said."

"Of course," he said. Then, just before I made it out the door, he said, "Gabe?"

I turned. "Yeah?"

"Oddly enough, what I was about to say was... the same thing your secret pen pal wrote. As I said, there's a lot going on. And some of it may affect you before long. How that happens will depend on how you perform in the next few weeks. Or so." He suddenly looked annoyed.

"Did you just tell me something you weren't supposed to?" I asked.

The thin smile returned. "Goodbye, Gabe."

Heading back to my office, I mulled over what he'd said. It wasn't like him to speak in riddles. He probably didn't send the message, but something was going on here. Why couldn't he tell me about it?

When I got back to my desk, the CathMail icon was blinking. Double-clicking on it, I looked at the new message's subject line in my inbox.

Blank. I looked for the sender's name.

Also blank.

Feeling a chill run down my spine, I double-clicked on the message.

To: Gabriel Marino
From:
Re:

GO TO THE CAFETERIA AT 4PM TODAY. YOUR CAREER DEPENDS ON IT. AND SO MIGHT THE ENTIRE WORLD.

ARCHANGEL

Smirking, I picked up the phone and punched in four numbers.

"Cathedral. This is Sally."

"Very funny," I said.

A cackle came from the phone receiver. "You saw it?"

"Yes. Ha ha. Does a certain editor have too much free time? Shouldn't you be getting *Physics for Precocious Pipsqueaks* ready for executive review?"

Suddenly the background noise in the phone receiver sounded as if it were coming from a conch shell. I could still hear Sally's voice through the hand covering the receiver. "Hey guys! He found it! HA!"

"So did you do yesterday's message too? Or are you and Kelvin tag-teaming?"

The muted ocean sounds disappeared. "Message? What message?"

"Come on, Sally. Aren't you my fine, winged friend with the halo around her head?"

There was a long pause. "Gabe, for a guy obsessed with language, you're not making sense."

"Wait. What did you think I was talking about?"

Sally giggled. "You mean… you didn't open your desk drawer?"

I pulled it open. Covering my pens and clips was a colorful piece of rubber vomit. "Oh. Charming."

More braying laughter. "Can you see the corn? And the carrots?"

"Yes, it looks delicious. Is the *Pipsqueak* manuscript ready yet, or what?"

A theatrical sigh huffed out of the receiver. "Jesus, Gabe, you take the fun out of everything."

I smiled in spite of myself. "Just get it in here. I want to give it a good run-through before Marcia gets her claws on it."

After hanging the phone up, I pulled the novelty barf from my drawer and looked at it. What Sally could do with mediocre writing was a wonder: She could take an author's jumbled pile of ideas and line them up like Coldstream Guards on review. She also had a poet's ear for rhythm and sound. When it came to details like kerning glitches and enforcing serial commas she ran a distant second to Theresa, but no one I knew was better at shaping B-minus language into something better than it deserved to be. She was a natural. When people like that leave barf in your desk drawer, you don't make an issue of it. You laugh and move on.

Placing it in my drawer, I pulled the math manuscript closer and returned to the business of flagging unsuperscripted exponents. That was all I could do for a book like this. A real math editor was an extravagance we couldn't afford, according to Greenlawn P&L sheets, so quality control was limited to me, Claire, and one of the propellerheads in our math teaching division.

A knock sounded at my door. The knock wasn't really necessary, since the door was already open, but when I saw Marcia standing there, I knew why.

"Knock, knock," she said.

I don't know why, but it always irritates me when people do that. Knocking on a door is normal. Saying, "knock knock" is cute, sort of. Doing both at the same time is worse than redundant... it's wrong, in the same way that what musicians call "the devil's chord" sounds wrong when it's played on the soundtrack of a horror movie. Or maybe it was just that someone who wasn't cute was trying to be.

"Hi Marcia," I said, stopping my frown before it started.

She walked in with a bright smile, waving a piece of paper in each hand. "I had two bright ideas last night, so I created these for you." She placed the first one in front of me, taking great care to make sure the paper's bottom edge was flush with the edge of the desk. "This is an organizational chart, showing the hierarchies of my departments. Have Claire make some copies and distribute it to everyone. The same goes for this other document," she said, waving it with a flourish and placing it next to the chart with equal fussiness. "This is a daily timesheet. Public Relations already uses this to note their arrival times, departure times, and hours spent on each project. I'd like your editors to do the same. What's the matter?"

I felt weary. "Marcia, please don't take this the wrong way, but... these are both bad ideas."

She placed her hands on her hips. "Why?"

"Well, let's start with the organizational chart," I said, picking it up. "This is a management tool. Its purpose is to illustrate the pecking order in a given work area. Used wisely, it helps the person at the top of the chart figure out how to arrange the people in the middle and at the bottom."

"Of course," she said, rolling her eyes. "And your point?"

"My point is waving these charts in the faces of the people who are listed at the bottom makes them feel like puppy poo. It takes their egos, their feelings, and their sense of investment in their work, drops it into a plastic bag, ties the top, and dumps the bag in the trash." I thought again of the stupid argument I'd had with my wife, but it had no bearing here. "It also fosters a competitive atmosphere where people start jockeying for chart positions. We don't need that here."

Her nose wrinkled. "These charts are used by the best companies in the world," she said. "I have a book on management styles in Japan. I'll be happy to loan it to you."

I sighed. "Did you know Japan has one of the highest suicide rates in the world?"

"That was mean."

"No," I said, holding up the chart. "This is mean. You just don't realize it."

She sniffed. "Copy it and distribute it. Now, what's your problem with the timesheets?"

I made a show of crossing my arms. "Are you going to listen to me, or am I going to end up copying and distributing this, too?" It came out snottier than I intended.

"No, no. Go ahead. I'm all for listening to employee input."

I sighed again. "Okay. Let's say everyone fills these out, turns them in, and now you've got a pile of timesheets on your desk. What will you do with them?"

"Read them, of course." Bambi never looked this innocent.

"Right," I said, leaning forward. "Why?"

Bambi blinked back at me. "So I know what everyone is doing. That's a manager's job."

"Marcia, these are editors. Their hours aren't billable. They don't punch a clock. And the sheer volume of work they do should tell you they aren't playing Windows Solitaire all day."

"Well, I see you've become *very* knowledgeable in... how many days has it been? Two, since your promotion?"

Our eyes locked. It was a genuine Pepto-Bismol moment, the kind I've never been good at. Most creatures on earth turn and fight when backed into a corner. I just yell a little before waving the white flag.

Before I could regret not saying anything inflammatory, Sally walked in carrying her manuscript. "Hey guys," she said. "I got *Pipsqueaks*. Want to talk?"

Marcia turned, her glare giving way to puzzlement. "Is that some kind of disease?"

Sally looked at me, then at Marcia. "Uh, no, it's a manuscript. I *was* about to give it to you, though," she said, that dangerous grin appearing once again.

Grateful for the distraction, I beckoned Sally closer and took the heavy pile of papers. Explaining what the book was about, I told Marcia about the executive review process started by Jerry, and that I figured she'd want to at least glance at each manuscript before we sent it to Greenlawn Press.

"Wonderful!" she said, all cheeriness and sunshine again. "Since this is the first book I'm seeing, why don't we all look at it together."

She yanked the rubber band off and began to page through them rapidly. I was amazed. Jerry usually spent at least an hour with a manuscript by himself, holed up in his office. Sometimes he took one home to pore over at night. Often his marks didn't make sense until he explained them, because he was the architect of our book's brand and made sure each book followed his vision of what our Cathedral message was supposed to be. He was thorough in a big-picture way, and watching him dissect a manuscript felt like watching a supercomputer grind through a weather forecast.

Marcia's page turning, on the other hand, was rapid and erratic. Skipping the first 30 pages, she would spent about five seconds scanning one page before skipping another 10 or 20. Watching her eyes flit around each page, I got the impression that she wasn't so much reading the words as inspecting the quality of the paper. In contrast to Jerry and the supercomputer, observing Marcia felt like watching my daughter crank her jack-in-the-box to make the clown spring out. I thought about humming "Pop Goes the Weasel."

While Sally and I exchanged uneasy glances, Kelvin walked in with a cup of coffee. "Hey dudes, what's..." He stopped short, seeing Marcia. "Sorry, didn't mean to interrupt."

Marcia continued to fondle the 20-pound paper.

"No prob, Kelvin," I said. "We're just doing an exec review of *Pipsqueaks*."

"Oh," he said, shifty eyes expressing interest. Stepping closer, he leaned forward to peer at the page Marcia was ogling.

What happened next was one of those unfortunate incidents in life you can't foresee. It was unpreventable, and I truly believe that if our actions are guided by a benevolent higher power, that power was drunk at the time, or maybe doing spinouts in the parking lot of the Almighty K-Mart with the Great Valhalla Death Chariot.

Pausing on a page, Marcia said, "Hmm. Do you have a red pen I can borrow?"

"Sure," I said, but before I could reach for my drawer her hand was already pulling the handle. She reached inside without looking, froze for a moment, and then looked at what her hand had touched—the rubber vomit. With an audible sucking in of her breath, Marcia snapped straight from her bent-over position. I was watching the horrified look on her face, and didn't immediately see her collide with his coffee cup. Jerking away to avoid the hot waterfall of coffee, Kelvin whacked the back of his head into the face of Sally, who'd moved behind him in an effort to see what Marcia would write on the manuscript. Droplets of coffee splashed onto Marcia's pants.

"Ow!" said Sally.

"My slacks!" said Marcia.

"It's not real vomit!" I said.

"Ow! Ow! My EYE!" shrieked Sally.

"Dammit, these are CASHMERE!" wailed Marcia.

My eyes shifted from Sally's convulsing to Marcia's pants. Dark blobs were spreading across the gray material. Looking back at Sally, I saw she was holding both hands over her right eye. Kelvin stood between them, watching like an unhappy tennis spectator.

"Oh God, this hurts!" said Sally, backing away from Kelvin as if he might attack again.

Marcia bent over to fan the blobs with her hands, then looked up at Sally with a puzzled expression. "Sally? Are you all right?"

"My eye!" wailed Sally. Her hands remained on her face.

I moved towards her and raised my palms in the international gesture of harmlessness. "Let me take a look," I said.

She flinched as my hands touched hers, but she allowed me to slowly draw them away. The skin around her eye looked flushed, but thankfully there was no blood. Her eye was a little bloodshot but definitely not injured. There'd be a bruise tonight, of course, and by tomorrow she'd look like she went 12 rounds with Muhammad Ali. That, in turn, forecast bad things for Kelvin tomorrow... things that were forbidden by the *Policies and Procedures Manual.*

"How's it look?" she asked, her voice trembling a little.

"It's fine," I said. "You're okay. Kelvin, could you get some ice from the cafeteria? Kelvin?"

"Ah, sure. Sorry, Sally," said Kelvin, snapping out of his trance and slinking out the door.

Marcia gave her pants one last baleful look, then turned to Sally. "Are you all right?"

"Oh, I'm just peachy," said Sally. "This is nothing compared to what I get in the mosh pits."

"Good," Marcia said. "Gabe, why would you keep something like that in your desk?"

My mind whizzed through all the possible answers. "It's a stress toy. You'd be amazed at how relaxing it is... or, um, maybe you wouldn't."

That earned me a withering look, but she said nothing more.

"I see. Well, getting back to this manuscript, I want to know why you would allow something like this." Her arm stretched out and pointed to a piece of art in the book.

I leaned closer. It was an artist's rendering of a snake, with some anthropomorphic touches to make it appear happy and childlike. It peeked out from a patch of green grass, and a thought bubble over its head read, "My name is Newton. Let me tell you all about gravity!" The snake was brown, had big, slightly crossed eyes, and looked like something from a Disney cartoon.

Sally leaned over to look at the page. "What? It's a snake."

Marcia crossed her arms as her face assumed a who-are-you-kidding expression. "It's not a snake," she said. "Look at it."

We did.

"I don't believe this," Marcia snapped. Pointing to Newton again, she said, "Can't you see? It's a phallus!" Her voice dropped to a hiss for the last word.

We looked again. And again.

"Marcia..." I began, but was interrupted by Sally's braying laughter.

"That?" said Sally, now pointing herself. "You can't be serious."

Marcia's eyes took on a flinty look. "You don't see it? The bulbous head? The shape of the body? The grass? The... the color?"

Sally hooted again. "So what are you saying? Do black men have green pubic hair?"

"I'm saying," said Marcia, hands balling into fists, "That this illustration has no place in a children's book. I want it removed."

Sally stopped laughing. "Marcia," she said, "It doesn't look anything like a penis." She turned to me and placed her hands on her hips. "Gabe, would you please show Marcia what a dick looks like?"

"You're not helping the situation," I said, scowling.

Marcia looked back in horror. "I see no reason to be vulgar," she said.

Sally grinned. "What's vulgar? The word *dick*?"

"Of course it's vulgar!" said Marcia through gritted teeth.

"Sally..." I said.

Sally didn't look at me. That look of evil amusement returned. "Well, maybe Gabe's is vulgar. I wouldn't know, myself, although frankly I wouldn't be surprised. Who knows what he does with it in his free time."

Kelvin appeared in the doorway again, carrying some ice cubes in a plastic baggie. "Hey, I've got the ice."

Sally turned to Kelvin. "Better give it to Miss Prude here," she said, hooking a thumb at Marcia. "She'll need it to clean her cashmere."

Kelvin stopped, visibly sensing danger, then took a step back into the hallway. "I can come back if you guys want."

I looked at Marcia. The calm look on her face was chillingly familiar. In the schoolyards of my youth, a bully wore that expression right before he threw the first punch. On the subway, I saw it right before an argument over a seat became a shoving match. And now, to my disbelief, I was witnessing the preamble of a hair-pulling match between Marcia and Sally over Newton the Big Black Phallus.

What happened next was worse. Leveling that look of violence on me, Marcia said, "I want her gone within one hour."

"Marcia!" I said, struggling for words but finding none. I looked at Sally. Her arms slowly lowered to her sides, and her jaw dropped open. I'd never seen her speechless before.

Looking as if she was summoning her last reserves of dignity, Marcia walked past me, Sally, and Kelvin. From the hallway, she turned back one more time.

"I also want the vomit gone. Then I want the illustration removed. Or replaced. I don't care. And then I want to see you in my office," she said, and disappeared down the hall.

Chapter 4

PHARISEES IN SUITS

And if a kingdom be divided against itself, that kingdom cannot stand. And if a house be divided against itself, that house cannot stand.
—Mark 3: 24-25

For the next two seconds, my office was quiet enough for me to hear my heartbeat.

"How DARE she!" said Sally, stamping her foot.

I looked at her, then at Kelvin. "Ah, Kelvin?"

"Hmm?"

"You wanna give us a minute here?"

The shocked look gave way to embarrassment. "Okay. Um, I'm sorry about your eye, Sally. And for..." he trailed off, looking at his shoes.

"It's okay, Kelvin," said Sally.

"Get out, please, Kelvin," I said.

Fortunately, he closed the door behind him. I say fortunately, because if the rest of Cathedral heard the next 20 minutes of invective from Sally, all work would have stopped. The colors she wove into her verbal tapestry were profane and awe-inspiring. Marcia's business acumen, ethics, morality, and education were brutalized. Adding extra interest were speculations about Marcia's parentage and her sexual appetite for farm animals. She paused to catch her breath after that, and for a moment I thought the worst was over. Then she blasted into realms I'd never explored with her before, and for the first time I felt uncomfortable about working in close quarters with Sally for the past two years. But the rage faded soon after that, giving way to bewildered projections about her rent and student loans. Then she was quiet, slumping into a chair and wiping her eyes on her sleeve.

I didn't know what to say. "Sally?"

"Yeah?" she said, the anger in her eyes now mixed with hurt.

"I'll be happy to write you a recommen—"

"Dammit, Gabe!" she said, banging her fist against the arm of the chair. "Why won't you fight for us?"

The lump that had been rising in my throat creeped up another half-inch. "There's only so much I can do. Not everyone appreciates your sense of humor, you know."

"No," she said, crossing her arms. "I don't believe that. Marty would never tolerate this shit."

"Marty never worked for Marcia."

She looked at me sadly, and some dim part of me recognized that her departure from Cathedral wasn't all she was mourning. This wasn't a time for arguing, though, so I segued into the prescripted Cathedral dismissal speech with as much grace as I could. I tried to maintain a blank expression, but I don't think I succeeded. Fortunately, my voice remained steady even though it cracked twice in midsentence. By the time I wrapped it up with the bit about seeing the Human Resources director, I sounded as if I was reciting a grocery list.

"Well, that's it. Any questions?" I asked, praying she didn't have any.

Sally had been sitting quietly while I spoke, looking down at her hands crossed in her lap. She said nothing for a moment, then slowly rose to her feet. Her mouth opened as if to speak, then closed into a frown. Turning towards the door, she shuffled towards it with shoulders slumped and head down. Please, I thought, say something. Anything. My heartbeat echoed in my ears as she passed through my doorway.

She didn't say a word. She just left.

I stared at the door and wondered where, in the multitude of generations that existed between me and the first people to bear my family name, the weak link was. If some distant foremother in Rome had only married a centurion in Caesar's legions instead of some shepherd, this would never have happened. I could have been strong enough to rein in Sally's sense of humor. Had my foremother mated with Julius Caesar himself, I may even have been able to stand up to Marcia. But it just didn't happen that way, and so my career limped on.

I rushed out the door and turned left, away from where Sally had gone. I wasn't sure where I was going, but I if I sat in my office any longer, the next visitor would find me counting my toes and drooling. Careening through the hallways was becoming my favorite hobby, and as I marched past Accounting I wondered who I'd steamroll next. Then I spotted the double doors to the company cafeteria ahead, and stopped. A memory sparked, then fizzled. I was supposed to be here for something... the message from Archangel said so. But at what time? Four? I looked at my watch. It was 4:05.

In front of me, the solid oak doors to the cafeteria were closed. They were usually open at all times, since people used this space to hold meetings outside lunch hour. A handwritten sign taped above the doorhandle read:

CAFFETERIA CLOSED 4 "FLOOR WAX"

I smirked, in spite of my foul mood. Like many editors, I have a hard time with signs, especially those handwritten in haste. Seeing a misspelled word on a sign feels like biting on tinfoil—a pain we can't relieve with a red pen because the sign is already a finished product. I can't change it. The same goes for the use of numbers as a lazy shorthand for words and the use of quotes to add emphasis. A special irritation in this case was the unintentional use of *wax* as a noun, which meant that the cafeteria was closed not because its floors were *being* waxed, but because the wax somehow asked for it to be closed.

I stared at the sign. Had the meeting, or whatever it was, been canceled? Or relocated? Stepping closer to the doors, I thought I heard voices inside. I couldn't tell whose. Perhaps the meeting was still on, despite the sign? If so, I'd look foolish for not knowing the agenda. I looked up and down the hall and saw no one coming. Then, leaning against the door, I pressed my ear to the wood and listened.

"Hey!" said a voice behind me.

Busted. A thousand obscenities howled through my mind, followed by a number of lame explanations for why I was snooping on a janitor waxing floors. I stiffened, then turned. Claire stood in front of me, her face no more than six inches from mine. She must have snuck up behind me before speaking, and now she wore a big grin. I could feel my cheeks redden.

"Hi," I said. Her body was close enough for me to feel heat. My ability to think straight, already compromised by my embarrassment, took a further pounding by her failure to step back. "There's, um, something going on in there," I said, pointing my thumb towards the door and wishing I'd said something witty or clever.

"Really?" she said, and now there was mischief in those dark eyes. "What?"

"I don't know," I said. "But I'm going to find out." She turned to look up the hall, and as she did my eyes did a quick slalom around her body. The blue sweater she wore pulled tight against her breasts; the khakis below the sweater were loose, but since I was well versed in the shape of her legs, the baggy shape didn't matter. The legs were there. That was all I really noticed.

Satisfied that no one else had seen us, she turned back to me. If she caught me ogling, she didn't let on. "Okay. Can I see, too?"

I blinked, then stifled a mad laugh. "Okay," I said, turning back to the door. Yanking it open, I walked in, hearing Claire's footsteps behind me.

The cafeteria contained several circular tables, all of them empty save for the one in the far corner. Around that table were an odd collection of very powerful people at Cathedral. Standing and addressing the rest was Howard Brannon, our chief operating officer, dressed in his usual pinstripes. Brannon was always impeccably dressed, and whenever he stood next to Charles Ting (who favored more casual clothes) he looked less like Charles's right hand man than his butler. The age difference between the two didn't help: Brannon was iron-haired and wore his facial wrinkles like war paint, while Ting looked like Brannon's younger cousin from the more slobby provinces.

Seated at the table were Jerry Lanville, my department's old VP; Louise Dreyfoos, second-in-command of Cathedral's legal eagles; Bobby Ortiz, Chief Financial Officer and trumpet player at our Grand Ordinations; and a youngish guy in a fine gray suit that outclassed even Howard's duds. I mean, the material looked less stitched than sculpted. Everyone's eyes were on Howard, and no one had noticed my entrance.

"Mr. Barney here has read our proposal," said Howard, gesturing towards the guy in gray. "And, save for a few reservations which I hope we can clear up in this meeting..."

The cafeteria door thunked shut behind me. The look of shock when Howard turned his head didn't bode well for what was about to happen. In the brief silence that followed, I watched the others turn to stare at Claire and me. Louise hunched quickly over the table, apparently in an effort to conceal the papers in front of her—as if I could read them from 20 paces away. Mister Gray Suit eyed me coolly, crossing his arms and looking suddenly like a blowhard formulating his next tirade. The surprise on Jerry's face gave way to distress, and as Howard spoke his next words, Jerry rose to his feet.

"May I ask what you're doing here?" said Howard, looking over his gold-rimmed glasses.

I swallowed. No explanation seemed adequate. "We," I said, gesturing to Claire, "were invited. Sort of."

Gray Suit glared at Howard. "What the fuck is this, Howard? You said this was secret." His deep, coarse voice was a kind not often heard at Cathedral; it advertised neither sophistication nor any patience with manners.

"It is," said Howard, fiddling with his tie knot. "This is just an interruption. Pay it no mind."

Jerry rose to his feet. "It's all right, Mr. Barney. Gabriel here is one of my most trusted staff. Although frankly, I'm not sure why he's here."

Gray Suit's eyes never left Howard's. "Simple question, Howard. Can you keep order in your own house, or can't you?"

I wasn't sure who was sweating more at this point, Howard or me. I never saw Gray Suit before, but I'd seen his type many times: Something happens to people on a rich diet of money and stress. At best, it's a form of selective amnesia where traits like civility, empathy, and nonoffensive breath are lost. They aren't taught any of this lilywhite stuff in business school, and they certainly don't pick any up from *The Art of War*. They wear the stress that comes with their titles like a medallion, unaware that a sphincter is engraved right smack in the middle.

"I think," said Howard, "that perhaps Jerry has a few things to explain later. But I assure you that, ah, our plans are not endangered in any way." He turned to Jerry and gestured towards Claire and me. "Would you take care of this, so we can proceed?"

"Sure," said Jerry, pushing his chair aside. "Excuse me for a moment, everyone."

No one said anything else until Jerry had escorted us out of the cafeteria. When the doors thunked closed again, he placed a hand on each of our shoulders.

"Gabe, Claire, I have to ask you for a favor."

I looked at Claire. "Okay," she said. She looked frightened, and I felt an insane urge to hug her and lead her away.

"What did you hear just now?" he asked.

"Nothing," I said, "besides that jerk ordering us out."

"Good. Under no circumstances can you talk about any of this. There will be very serious consequences if certain people find out."

I cleared my throat. "Consequences for whom?"

He frowned. "I can't answer that."

"Is this part of the secret goings-on you were telling me about?"

"I can't answer that, either."

"Of course you can't," I said, rolling my eyes. "I'm not wearing my Spy Club pin. Jerry, if you didn't want me to find you here, why did you send me an invitation?"

"I didn't," he said.

"The message, Jerry! The Archangel thing. Who else could have sent it?"

He looked from me, to Claire, to me again, and his expression was so grave that I believed him when he said, "I'm not hiding anything from you this time, Gabe. In fact, I'd like to find out who that person is, too. He or she could undo everything I'm trying to accomplish here. And that would be bad for everyone."

I thought back to Archangel's message and smirked. "Yeah. For the whole world, I imagine."

Jerry's eyes bugged out. "Did your e-mail friend tell you that?"

"Yeah. Why? I thought it was a goof."

Jerry's expression took on a hard edge. "This is far more serious than I thought. It must be dealt with... but not now. Again, don't tell anyone anything about this."

He turned and walked back to the cafeteria door. As his hand reached out for the handle, Claire spoke.

"Jerry?"

He turned, and to my surprise I saw fear in his expression. "Yes?"

Claire looked at me, then looked back at Jerry. "I guess whatever you're doing in there is important, and it's none of my business, but... I'm just wondering how good it can be if it involves that nasty guy. The one in the silk suit."

I felt a smile creep onto my face. Bright as she was, Claire was also quiet and reserved. It couldn't have been easy for her to ask that question. I don't know which was more telling: Her asking or Jerry's refusal to answer. He fretted for a moment, then opened the door and disappeared into the cafeteria.

I looked at the door for what felt like a long time before I felt a tugging at my sleeve. Claire stared at me with a solemn look I'd never seen her wear before.

"Hey," she said. "There's some kind of struggle going on, isn't there?"

"I think so," I said. "And it's not over yet."

She looked up and down the hallway again. We were still alone. "Are you sure you know who the good guys are?"

"I thought I did, until now."

"Do you know who the *bad* guys are?"

I smiled. "Some of them. I'm not sure where you stand, though."

She scowled and punch-tapped me in the shoulder. We walked slowly back towards the editors' area, nodding to the few people we passed. When we reached an intersection of hallways with no one else in sight, Claire said, "Gabe?"

I was preoccupied with the possibilities of Jerry's secret tea party, so I hadn't noticed she stopped walking until I was a couple of paces beyond her. I turned, and saw that the unsettled look on her face had given way to her usual amusement.

"Hmm?" I said.

"Do you wanna... maybe go out for a drink after work? Or something?

I stopped breathing for a moment. It was an innocent request, made between two coworkers. Wasn't it? It involved a platonic semi-friendship between two people who were… platonic. Didn't it? Claire leaned against the wall of the hallway, waiting for my answer as if she'd just asked where the toner cartridges for the copy machine were. Her weight was shifted on one leg, with the other leg bent so that the heel of her right sneaker beat a slow drumbeat on the carpet. The loose khakis were pulled against the athletic curve of her thigh as her foot rose, then became baggy again as her foot fell. It was time to start breathing again… wasn't it?

"Um, sure," I said, trying for nonchalance.

"Okay," she said, and the near-whisper of her voice told me she'd been holding her breath. She turned and walked away down the side hallway, leaving me alone with the cyclone raging between my ears.

I made a beeline for my office, nearly slamming into two people emerging from their cubes before finally making full body contact with a mailroom guy who rounded a corner with an armful of packages. He was okay, more or less, but the boxes tumbled down the hallway and one of them made a tinkling sound when I sheepishly handed it back.

Slowing down, I pondered the situation. I was married. There was nothing going on here. Claire and I had exchanged nothing more than pleasantries, professional chatter, and the occasional wisecrack since we first met. Five hundred more important problems vied for my attention, and even if this proposed get-together — no, it was more of a hangout session — qualified as a problem, it ranked dead last on my to-do list. Claire's suggestion was a perfectly acceptable thing to do. So was my agreeing to it. This junior-high-school behavior, then, was inappropriate.

Wasn't it?

Chapter 5

A TASTE OF EVE'S APPLE

Again, if two lie together, then they have heat: but how can one be warm alone?

—Ecclesiastes 4:11

The rest of the afternoon took on a dreamy quality, but it was the dream of a fever and not dancing sugarplums. I futzed with the math manuscript for a while, then called up a spreadsheet to decorate my screen while I considered this weird thing with Claire. What was I afraid of? True, I had just a touch of an adolescent crush on her, but that was no reason to act like a teenager. There were hundreds of ways we could get together without… getting together. In fact, one reasonable idea came to mind. Clicking on CathMail, I selected Claire's name from the address book and typed, "Tar Bar at six o'clock? I'll bring the refreshments?"

I sighed as I sent the message. The Tar Bar was on Cathedral premises, and therefore disqualified my occasion with Claire as a date. Sort of.

The last thing I did that workday was hold a meeting to explain the Sally situation. Kelvin was upset, and Theresa looked the way a postal clerk might before shotgunning her coworkers, but thankfully there was little unpleasantness. They knew my speech was coming because Sally said goodbye to them before leaving, and what I said seemed to depress them more. The past few days had extinguished the fire of righteousness in us all, to the point where a cartoon of a snake seemed like passable, if not logical, grounds for termination. After some halfhearted complaining and expressions of anxiety, they filed out of my office and went home to recover.

All, that is, except for the dark-eyed woman who smiled at me from her lawn chair when I clambered through the trap door on the roof, holding a six-pack of Anchor Steams I'd filched from Accounting's cafeteria fridge.

"Hey," she said.

"Hey yourself," I grunted, nearly losing my balance as I stepped onto the tar roof and pretended to bobble the thermos over the open trap door.

She chuckled, then pointed at the door. "Better close that," she said. "We don't want any unwanted attention."

True, I thought, as I did what she suggested. We certainly don't. Another lawn chair sat arm-to-arm with hers beneath the umbrella, and after I'd popped open a bottle and held it out to her, she patted its seat.

"Siddown," she said, wriggling in her seat so that she could face me better. "You've had a very interesting day."

I opened my bottle and took a long swallow of cold, clean beer. "God, that's good," I said, settling into my chair and turning to look at her. "One more interesting day, Claire, and I'm jumping off this roof. One scream, one splat, and Marcia gets a new whipping boy."

"Oh, come on," she said, taking another sip and giving me a thoughtful look. "It can't be that bad. You're our fearless leader." She spoke the last sentence as if it were the trump card that proved her point.

I made a show of taking my next long gulp. "No I'm not," I said. "I'm the walking embodiment of the Peter Principle."

She giggled. "You're the head doggie in our wolf pack. We look up to you."

Shaking my head, I couldn't help but smile. "I'm a squid. And quit with the animal metaphors, will you? The last thing we need here is more of that author crap."

"True," she said. "That guy who wrote the golf book I'm proofreading really sucks. By the way, what is it with guys and sports analogies? Don't you get tired of touchdowns, play-by-plays, and slam dunks?"

I put my beer down and crossed my hands in a T. "Okay, time out. Fifteen-yard penalty for the blanket statement, and another ten for the personal foul."

She smiled and took another sip of Anchor Steam. I looked out over the truncated patch of river to the west, towards the haze that enshrouded Queens, trying to remember the last time my wife had looked at me like Claire did. Or at least, the way I thought she was looking at me.

"Gabe, did you recognize that guy in the cafeteria before? The one in the expensive suit?"

"No. Should I have? Did you?"

"Oliver Barney."

I nearly dropped my bottle. "No way."

"My brother's going for his MBA at Stern. He actually has Barney's picture tacked to his mirror. That was him."

Once again, my thoughts had been dumped into the proverbial Cuisinart, given a rip-roaring spin, and poured out as so much mental goo. Barney had the kind of wealth most people couldn't even fantasize about. His usual habitats were the board rooms at investment houses, the front page of *The Wall Street Journal*, the high rankings on various *Fortune* lists, and (once) the cover of *Time* for a tobacco company's high-profile acquisition of a fast-food chain. Apparently they couldn't kill enough people with smoke, so he helped them stuff cholesterol down people's throats. There was an article in *People* last year that said he'd been tapped to star in *The Apprentice* before Trump got the call, but Barney had turned them down. What was a guy like that doing, sneaking around where Cathedral's rank and file bitched about their jobs over chicken salad?

"Well, well," I said. "Our little mystery isn't so little."

Claire sat up straight in her chair. "You think we're gonna buy some other company?"

I thought again about the motley collection of characters in the room with Barney and shook my head. "No. I think Charles would have been in the meeting if we were. There's no way something this big would be delegated. And Linda's only the second-in-command in Legal. Or maybe she's the third. Who can tell with lawyers?"

She took a big sip from her beer, and as I admired the graceful curve from her chin down her neck, renegade thoughts popped up again. I finished off my beer, hoping it would sluice them away.

Reaching into the cooler for another, a new thought came to mind. "Maybe we're going under, and need a cash infusion to pep things up," I said.

"Could be," she said. "I don't know much about this stuff."

"Neither do I," I said.

The stars were beginning to emerge in the west. Beyond the visible strip of the East River, smog mixed with the blue of twilight. A few clouds were lit by the waning glow behind us, and some of the windows in the surrounding office towers still reflected a dull orange. The city seemed to be breathing a sigh of relief after a hard workday. Seven million people's worries were ending for the day, while mine were just getting started.

"What are you thinking about?" said Claire.

I got up from my chair and reached for the chain of Christmas bulbs. "I think it's time we plugged this in."

Slipping the plug into the weatherproof socket, I watched as the gloom was chased away by the cheesy sparkle of the Christmas lights. All we needed to complete the picture was a waitress asking if we wanted to order burritos or some Cuervo.

Settling back into my lawn chair, I took a big sip of my beer and looked at Claire. Her eyes, always dark in the fluorescent light of Cathedral's offices, now reflected... I don't know what. I had a nice buzz going, and to celebrate the occasion, my id granted my eyes permission to rove.

"Can I ask you a personal question?" said Claire, a faint smile rising on her face.

"Sure," I said. Something that felt like a hiccup bubbled out of my esophagus. I fought it back with some success.

"Was anything going on between you and Sally before she got fired?"

The question felt like a slap, and as the beery reverie between my ears fizzled, the hiccup seized the opportunity to burst out as a full-fledged burp.

"What?" I asked, grateful that the shadows probably hid my blush.

She looked down at her lap. "I dunno," she said. "There just... seemed to be chemistry between you two."

I was shaking my head before she finished. "It might have looked that way, but what you saw was..." What? Sometimes the unpredictable work dynamic between men and women defies analysis, and I couldn't deny the rapport I enjoyed with Sally made me wonder on occasion. But the closeness I felt was based mostly on my appreciation of her reliability—and my admiration of a talent that exceeded my own. She was indispensable even before I became her boss, and our personal compatibility only made the work we did easier and better. There was nothing scandalous about the bond between us... not like the warmth I was beginning to feel now.

"It wasn't like that," I finished. "Even if it looked that way."

"Oh," she said. "Okay. I was just curious. I mean…"

"What?" I asked, sitting bolt upright. "Are people talking?"

The look of happy mischief returned to those eyes.

"Relax," she said. "I was just curious. I mean, you don't keep a picture of your wife or daughter in your office, and you never seem to call your wife while you're here. At least, nobody has heard you, anyway. You don't even talk about her."

More beer was a poor defense, but I fortified my castle walls with Anchor Steam nonetheless. Claire was looking at me with a smile and one eyebrow cocked, and I wondered if she knew where she was treading. There were reasons why I didn't talk to my wife during the day; not good ones, but certainly big ones. I wasn't about to detail these for Claire, nor was I inclined to squelch the pleasure of this night by describing how slowly—and how terribly quietly—a marriage could unravel.

"I failed her," I said. "Sally, that is. Not my wife. Lately, I can't understand why you and Theresa and Kelvin don't stage a coup and stick my head in a guillotine." Looking up at the stars, I wondered if it was wise to press on. Could any good come of this? "I meant what I said before, Claire. I suck at being anyone's boss. Not that it matters... Marcia's such a control freak that I'll never decide anything for myself, except what color paper to copy her goddamn timesheets onto."

Claire looked at me thoughtfully, then put down her beer and pulled her lawn chair closer to mine until the arms touched. Leaning towards me, she placed her hand on my forearm, inciting a small riot in my central nervous system.

"Listen," she said. "You don't suck at this." And if everything else she said was starting to swim in a cheerful haze of beer, the word *suck* came through clear and sweet. "And believe me, I should know. Marty had a bad temper. He was such a jerk when he did my last performance review, and not once... once!" She thumped my forearm with her fist, "...did he ever show he cared about us."

I smiled. The description was pretty accurate.

"You're not like that," she continued, caressing my forearm with her fingertips. "You make us laugh, and you look after us, and you protect us from a lot of the crap that comes out of Marcia's mouth."

I looked into Claire's eyes, and saw that she was serious. Reflected in the soft reds and golds of the Christmas lights, her face hovered in the shadows, closer to mine than it ever had been.

"Claire?" I said, unable to raise the volume of my voice to something conversational.

"Hmm?" she said, and now her eyes were all I saw as I neared a great crossroads once again. I had maybe half a second to consider the hundreds of ways in which I and several other people could get hurt. Half a second, before I did something really stupid. I knew better than this. Really, I did. Half a second...

Then that time was gone. Lips touched, then pressed, then slid, and finally opened. The fever began to rise, and as my hands brushed her sides and then her back, I fought against my half-drowned superego still fighting the booze and lust:

Hey, this isn't how our kisses usually feel...

I felt a hand caress my neck, and another wrapping around me as we pulled at each other over the arms of the lawn chairs.

Um, Gabe? Superego here. We just made tongue contact, and all hell's breaking loose between the legs. Who is *this we're touching?*

Soft friction against my belly as my shirt was pulled up, and the sensation of fingers on skin told me a whole lot of other wonderful things. And still, Superego wouldn't quit.

Something's wrong something's wrong it's too fast too hot it's not HER*!*

I had pulled Claire mostly out of her chair onto me, and as the wriggling and groping started in earnest I pulled back and said, "Wait." We both gasped for breath. Her eyes were glazed, and for a moment I nearly dove right back into the madness.

"What's wrong?" she said.

As if in answer, the trap door in front of our chairs swung open and clanged against the tar roof. Feeling Claire tense up, I watched helplessly as a bottle of Heineken, held by a hand, rose into view, followed by a forearm, followed by a head.

Theresa's head. In profile.

"It's a nice night," she said, and climbed another step up so that most of her upper torso was in view. Then she turned to look at us, and froze. "Hey guys! Oh my God," she said.

"What?" said Kelvin, from somewhere beneath her.

Suddenly Claire's weight felt like a truck on me. "Um, hi Theresa," I said, feeling the blood run from my face. "We were…"

"Arm wrestling," said Claire.

Theresa's jaw dropped open, then slowly closed. "I suppose this isn't what it looks like?" she asked, raising one eyebrow.

"No," I said, looking at Claire. "It's a pretty funny story, actually. We..."

"Hey, is that Gabe up there?" yelled Kelvin.

Claire scrambled back into her lawn chair, leaving my shirt up and my belly exposed to the night. "Theresa," she began, "Please don't tell anyone. Anyone." She gave Theresa a pleading look, and as Theresa's eyes shifted back to me I drew two fingers along my lips.

"All right," she said quietly.

"All right?" said Kelvin. "What's all right? What's going on up there?"

"Shut up, Kelvin," said Theresa. "Get off the ladder. I'm coming back down."

"No you're not!" said Kelvin. "Let me up!"

Everyone remained motionless for a moment. Then Theresa said, "Give me 10 minutes to get Kelvin out of here. I'll do my best not to tell him. After that, I really think you guys should leave."

Her face had a look I hadn't seen since high-school detention. Then, after a sour exchange with Kelvin that may have involved a few kicks, she slowly disappeared from sight. The trap door banged closed behind her, leaving Claire and me alone in the terrible quiet.

Chapter 6

THE PUSHCART THEORY

Because I have called, and ye refused; I have stretched out my hand, and no man regarded; But ye have set at nought all my counsel, and would none of my reproof: I also will laugh at your calamity; I will mock when your destruction cometh as a whirlwind.

—*Proverbs 1:24-26*

The apprehension I felt the next morning was a relief, coming after a night of guilt. Fortunately, I got home late enough so that a few cursory exchanges of boredom with my wife, followed by a kiss on my daughter's sleeping forehead, were all that happened before the beginning of my seven-hour stare into the darkness. Tucking my daughter in was the hardest... I was bound by love to protect her from the google-eyed monsters in the closet. I hoped she would never know the boogeyman was standing watch over her that night.

The office was quiet when I entered the next morning, practically tiptoeing on the industrial carpet. I was looking forward to a moment's peace, the kind of mental supercharging I needed for a day of unknown horrors. No sooner had I collapsed into my chair and turned on my computer than a knock sounded at my office door.

"Yeah?" I said. It was the most welcoming statement I could manage.

The door opened.

"Hey!" said Kelvin, bursting in and closing the door behind him. "I was hoping you'd be in early. Theresa wouldn't tell me—"

I held up my hand. "Don't go there."

He paused, squinted at me with shifty eyes, and continued, "Okay, I know you were up there last night. I heard you, man. And I know something weird was going on because Theresa got all shellshocked. What gives?"

"Nothing," I said, toying with a pen.

"Come on!" he said. "What, were you choking the chicken up there?"

"Cute."

He sat down in the chair across from my desk and crossed his arms. "I'm not leaving until I find out."

I sighed.

"Come on, man! I got kicked in the face three times last night, and then Little Miss Prim threw a hissyfit and chased me out of the building with a stapler. I think I'm entitled to an explanation."

That made me grin, but I was quick to stifle it.

Kelvin uncrossed his arms and leaned forward. "Okay, here's the deal. Either you spill now, or—"

Another knock sounded at the door.

"What?" I said, with even less cheer than before.

The door opened, and Theresa's head poked into view. She looked at us, then stepped into the office.

"We have to talk," she said.

"Hooray!" said Kelvin, beaming.

She turned to him. "Not with you here."

"Yeah," I said, avoiding Kelvin's eyes again. "Could you give us a minute, please?" I hated treating a friend like this, but the subject was too raw for me to risk feeding the Cathedral grapevine. So Kelvin rose to his feet, pulled his shirt down in a mock display of regaining dignity, and headed for the door.

"Fine," he said. "Be that way." He raised a finger to Theresa. "But I've got issues with you, sister. There's gonna be payback for that stapler business. And the kicking."

"Bring it on, sportsboy," said Theresa, turning her back on him and giving me a rare, one-sided grin.

"Yo mama," said Kelvin, trudging out the door and closing it.

I waited a moment before breaking the silence. "You enjoyed that, didn't you?" I said.

Her lopsided grin disappeared. "He's a savant. Someone taught him to edit—sort of—but he's more ape than human."

I smiled. "He's also my friend, so please don't hurt him."

"Suit yourself," she said with a shrug. "You want to talk about last night?"

I held up my hand. "Don't go there."

"I was just curious about something. Are you deliberately sabotaging our peaceful, small-group dynamic, or are you just thinking with the small head instead of the big head?"

I buried my face in my hands. "Theresa," I said. "Please. Don't. Go. There."

"Because," she continued, "this whole thing with Marcia and Sally's firing has everybody pissed off. We're a step away from utter chaos."

I dawdled with my pen some more. "Ever notice that the word *utter* always precedes *chaos*?" I said, in the tone I'd use to ask about the weather. "It's either that, or *sheer*. As if *chaos* isn't chaotic enough."

"I'm serious!"

"Well, who died and made you morale officer?" I said. I was surprised at the volume of my voice, and Theresa's shocked expression made me regret it.

"Someone ought to be thinking about these things," she said, quietly. "I just thought it should be you."

"I made a little mistake. Let me deal with it."

"Little?" she said, bringing the problem of volume back to the discussion. "She was on you like whipped cream on a sundae! I couldn't tell whose tongue was whose!"

I started to roll my eyes, then noticed the upper corner of my office door, which wasn't open before, moving behind Theresa's shoulder.

"Oh my," came the sound of Marcia's voice. "Am I interrupting a little spat?"

Theresa whirled around. I froze, horrified, and then felt anger surge. Marcia stood in the doorway, ramrod straight, with her arms crossed. The navy pantsuit she wore looked starched and immaculate, the garment of a ranking corporate royal. It was at odds with the tight-lipped grin on her face.

"Marcia," I said, "it's common courtesy to knock before entering."

"Oh, pshaw," she said. "I'm your supervisor. You should have nothing to hide from me."

Theresa and I exchanged glances, allies once more. I wanted to snap at Marcia, but I also wanted to laugh. In a rare show of good judgment, I did neither. Theresa followed suit.

"I just dropped by to make sure you were coming to the marketing meeting," said Marcia.

I blinked. "Marketing meeting?"

"Of course," she said, now backing out the door again. "In three minutes. We're in conference room four."

I watched, amazed, as Marcia disappeared into the hallway again. No one had told me about this.

Theresa watched her, too, then turned to me, crossing her arms. "I suppose we should discuss this later?"

I sighed. "We're not discussing this at all. It's none of your business."

"Fine," she said, and stomped out.

Leaning back in my chair, I studied the doorway and wondered at Theresa's world of black-and-white distinctions. My world was now one big gray area, yet I got the impression that Theresa would do a Torquemada on me for my sins if she had the time. In her work, she was judge, jury, and executioner for all breaches of grammar and diction... yet I wondered if she was aware that the same approach to life didn't work. But then again, who was I to offer lessons on life's problems?

I noticed my CathMail icon was blinking. Clicking on my inbox, I saw one new message.

To: Gabriel Marino
From:
Re:

GO TO THE ROOFTOP AGAIN TOMORROW NIGHT.

ARCHANGEL

"I don't believe this," I said.

"Excuse me?" said a voice from the doorway. I looked up.

"Hey," said Claire.

"Hey," I replied.

She pointed to the door and tilted her head slightly. I shook my head.

"I just thought we should talk about... well, you know," she said.

I held up my hand. "*Really* not going there," I said.

"No," she said, stepping forward. "I just wanted to—"

"Please," I said. "Let's not do this now. I just found out I'm supposed to be at a meeting, and I'm not prepared. If I go in there thinking about… that kiss, I won't be able to concentrate on anything."

Her eyes went wide. I had no intention of saying that. I suddenly felt an urgent need to be on another continent.

"You're my Archangel, aren't you?" I asked, realizing too late that the question sounded a lot sappier than what I meant. She gave me a bemused look. "I gotta go," I said, picking up a legal pad and pen from my desk and hurrying past her out the door.

"Let's talk later, okay?" she said from behind me.

"Okay," I said.

The distance from my office to conference room four was about 90 feet, but it felt like a hike to Patagonia. All things considered, I'd have forgone my promotion if it meant avoiding the typhoon of guano raining down on me since the Grand Ordination. Of course, some of that guano was of my own making, so I couldn't blame everything on the promotion. But still. Perhaps it's a good thing we can't see our future choices coming, because if we could, the khaki-clad carcasses of Madison Avenue window-jumpers would have to be bulldozed away.

I paused at the doorway of conference room four to assess the situation. Seated at the table's head was Mitch Mitchell, one of the guys from Marketing. Mitch was about my age, dressed exactly like the mannequins at The Gap, and would probably have been a friend of mine if we spoke the same dialect of English. But alas, there was no saving me from the clarity and brevity of my college writing classes. I hated buzzwords. Mitch hated the truth. He was perched somewhere around the director level on Cathedral's master organizational chart. I felt some relief in seeing him today, since his presence meant the meeting would probably be a farce. As a marketing professional he was cheery enough to work with, but he seemed oblivious to many important things. Among these, apparently, was the poor marketing decision made by his parents in choosing his first name. Among the editors, he was known as Mitch-Mitch or—perhaps worse—Dumbass.

Seated at Mitch's right was his assistant, Jenna, a recent college grad who smiled so often, and sometimes so inappropriately, that her code name among the editors was Big Grin. Watching her chat sunnily with Mitch, I remembered that Sally liked to do a killer imitation of something Jenna said in her first meeting with us: Right after Mitch introduced her, she chirped, "I'm just so totally psyched to be in marketing!" It said a lot about her, and the fact that we giggled at Sally's imitation said a lot about us, I guess.

Marcia occupied the third chair, and the fourth sat waiting for me.

"Ah, there you are," said Mitch. Big Grin turned, gave me a little wave, and... grinned.

"Sorry I'm late," I said, plopping my pad onto the table and sitting down. "I only found out about this meeting just now."

Marcia shot me a look of disapproval. "Don't you read your e-mail?"

"What e-mail?" I asked.

"The one I sent about this week's timesheets."

I stared. There was a message from Marcia a few days ago, addressed to all of the editors, asking them to turn in timesheets promptly on Friday. My interest had plummeted when I read the subject line, "Timesheets," and my finger— as if it was sentient—had pressed the delete key before I could reach the second sentence. It was only later, while talking to Theresa, that I learned what the message said.

"Lemme get this straight, I said. "You wrote an invitation to a marketing meeting, for me alone, at the end of a message addressed to all of the editors about something as trivial as timesheets?"

Marcia's frown turned into a scowl. "There's nothing trivial about them. And if you can't be bothered to read your e-mail, perhaps we should find a position with less responsibility for you."

What was up with this? Had she set me up to miss the meeting? No, that couldn't be... she dropped by my office to make sure I was coming. Was her intention to make sure I showed up unprepared? Or was the important and the unimportant all the same to our new Grand Lizard? I looked at Mitch and Big Grin, hoping to find sympathy, but Mitch looked puzzled while Big Grin continued to look... well, like we'd been telling knock-knock jokes. She could have been watching a tennis match, or grass growing, or albino dwarves hopping on pogo sticks.

I thought about lecturing Marcia about subject lines in e-mail, but merely said, "I apologize to everyone. Please, let's continue with the business at hand."

Mitch shrugged, glanced at his notes, then looked at us. "Okay," he said. "Jenna and I called this meeting to propose a new marketing direction for Cathedral's books. As we all know—and, uh, this is no reflection on you, Gabe—our sales figures have gradually dropped from okay to crummy in the past two quarters. To address this, Jenna and I have just completed a study, and we're confident that we can both identify the reason why *and* propose the perfect solution. Right, Jenna?"

Big Grin's smile widened into a vaguely disturbing likeless of the Cheshire Cat. "Totally! This is gonna be awesome!"

I sat up straight. This was interesting. Our dive-bombing sales were no secret, and neither was the true cause. Cathedral did not buy manuscripts from agents or authors with real qualifications because to do so would cost money. We did not spend; therefore, we did not make. We paid the paralegal who wrote our guide to the LSAT exam less than the fee charged to actually take that exam, and to this day, I'm not sure that my old boss Marty was lying when he said the "specialist" who sold us our book on Caribbean medical schools was given a bag of cannabis and a steel drum for his trouble.

Of course, higher management at Cathedral read the damning reviews we got in trade publications, and threw all the appropriate tantrums. Likewise, they were dimly aware of the literary jihad against us in Amazon.com's customer comments section: Police assistance was once sought after one disgruntled reader threatened to rent a Sherman tank, park it outside our corporate headquarters, and roll over us one by one as we exited the building. But on the whole, nobody on staff complained too much about our mediocre books, because we weren't losing money.

It was also no secret that Greenlawn's distribution system was half competent, at best. They did a fair job of feeding the big chains on the East Coast—Barnes & Noble, Borders—but they ignored other venues like college bookstores, Wal-Marts, and department stores. And the near-total absence of sales west of the Mississippi was a confounding mystery to us for years, until one day—in a beery Tar Bar epiphany—Sally, Kelvin, and I came up with the Greenlawn Pushcart Theory. We noticed that, of all the western states represented on the monthly sales reports, only one state would report sales in any given month... and when it did, only one or two books were sold, tops. Then, the next month, there would be no sales at all in that state... but some other state bordering it would then report sales of one or two books. And so it would go, in a different contiguous state each month, with no explanation given by Greenlawn. We finally decided that Greenlawn Press's entire distribution system for the central and western portions of the country consisted of some guy with a pushcart wheeling up and down the interstates, peddling Cathedral books, roadside snacks, and bumper stickers that read, "Honk if You're Horny." He probably played the accordion and had a monkey waving a tin cup.

All of this meant that Mitch's next comment would be fascinating. If he suggested that we improve our books' content, he'd be tacitly confessing that he had no new ideas beyond those we had thrashed to death in previous meetings. In which case, I would disembowel him with my Bic pen. On the other hand, if he suggested that the $1.95 we made as profit last year was Greenlawn's fault, that accusation would touch off an amusing but fruitless bickering war between Cathedral and Greenlawn. The pattern was legendary: We'd complain about the low sales, then they'd call us dilettantes who knew nothing about publishing, and then we'd shut up. Because in the end, some bigwig at Cathedral—maybe it was Charles—seemed to value the partnership more than the profit it was supposed to produce. And so the Pushcart Man wobbled on down the interstate, a walking emblem of synergy pursued for its own sake.

"So," said Mitch, "in the interest of identifying the problem without bias and fixing it as quickly as possible, let's not pull any punches here. I'm just going to say it." He looked at us with anticipation.

"All right," said Marcia.

"Go for it," I said, holding my Bic like a dagger.

Mitch looked to Jenna, as if for moral support, then cleared his throat. "The problem," he said, cueing Big Grin, "is the color of our book covers."

At this, Big Grin held up a blowup of the front and back cover of *The Lazy Athlete's Guide to Winning at Lacrosse.* It was one of Kelvin's favorites, and pictured a dumpy-looking guy in a lacrosse uniform, leaning on his stick with one arm and holding a can of beer in the other, against a dark purple background.

"Take this one, for example," said Mitch. "The cover art's pretty good, showing a nice action shot. Sort of."

Big Grin pointed to the schlump with the stick and beamed.

"But the purple color dampens the effect. It's plain, it's washed out, and it doesn't bring energy to the visual palette," said Mitch.

I wasn't sure what he meant by this, but Mitch stepped on my question before I could ask it—a favorite technique of our marketing types.

"It's time for a change. And change is always good. So our recommendation for all future Cathedral covers is..."

Big Grin held up another blowup. It was the same book cover, only now the cover photo was backed by the color—

"Pink!" ejaculated Mitch, with a quick gesture of his hands that was meant to appear grandiose but ended up looking spastic.

"Pink!" said Big Grin, dropping the cover blowup so that she could applaud. She looked at Marcia and me expectantly while she clapped, but when we didn't follow suit, she stopped and held up the cover again. The smile never wavered.

"Pink?" I asked.

"I know it's unconventional," said Mitch, looking pleased that I'd asked a question, "but our market research has shown that people who buy our books are... well, anxious. They're uncertain how to get a job, or do well on a test, or otherwise improve themselves. People are afraid of the unknown. They want to be reassured. And now, with this new pink color, the message our books will convey is, 'Relax. Buy me, and everything will be okay.'"

I looked at Marcia, who was squinting at the cover as if it was a calculus problem she couldn't quite solve. Somebody had to say something. I was leery of further antagonizing Marcia, since I couldn't tell how she was receiving this new suggestion, but my feelings about the cover were stronger. I decided to plunge ahead.

"Mitch," I said, "If memory serves, you guys suggested the purple covers two years ago."

Mitch nodded. "That's correct. But we were acting on old information at the time. This is new information," he said.

"You say we did market research on this... color?" I asked.

"That's correct," said Mitch.

"Did we do any last time, when we chose the purple covers?"

"Certainly."

I smiled. "What did *that* research tell us?"

"Old information."

Ah, yes. The venerable times-have-changed tactic. It was a Cathedral favorite, by which any crappy idea enacted more than a week ago could never be used against the moron who first proposed it. If the idea failed, you could always blame unforeseen circumstances. Or old data. Or the devil whispering in your ear, saying you should pursue a career in marketing.

"Mitch," I said. "If you don't mind my asking, who did this latest research?"

Mitch smiled and looked at Big Grin. "We did."

"Uh-huh. And where'd we get the sample groups?"

Marcia cleared her throat. "Gabe, I'm not sure we need to question Marketing's methodology here..."

"No, it's okay," said Mitch. "We know most of our readership is young people, twentysomethings. So we chose a sample of college students and recent college grads."

I sat back in my chair. That explained it. If Marketing worked with the same sorry level of resources that we did, this "market research" consisted of Big Grin calling up her sorority sisters and asking for their favorite color.

Turning to Marcia, I said, "This is nonsense."

The frown on Marcia's face told me I had no ally here. "And why is that?" she said.

A vision of my career sploshing down the tubes flashed before my eyes. As usual, I ignored it. Whacking my forehead and squinting my eyes in a pantomime of anguished thought, I said, "Ooh! There's a tough one! Let's see here. We can put a pink cover on, say, a guide to raising little girls. Or maybe a book on growing carnations. Hell, I can see pinking up a cover showing Richard Simmons in a tutu. But this?" I pointed to the cover that Big Grin still held up. "*This* color, for the entire Cathedral imprint? All 90-something books, on all different kinds of subject matter?" I made a show of looking under my chair, and then the table, as if searching for something. "I mean, who's hiding the bong here? Because I could use a hit, too."

I looked from one face to another. Mitch looked hurt, Big Grin looked the way she usually did, and Marcia wore an expression that would burn a hole in sheet metal.

"I think the color is fine," said Marcia. "I applaud your good work, Mitch. And while it appears that Gabe and I need to discuss this a little further," she glared as if I'd brought up a family secret at an inappropriate time, "I'd like to forward your proposal to Greenlawn for final approval."

"Oh, God," I said, looking down at my lap. Greenlawn's marketing people were loonier than ours. The entire profession seemed devoid of empirical thought.

Marcia bared clenched teeth. "Excuse me, do you have something more to add?"

"Well, yeah, if I may." I leaned forward and rested my hands on the table before me, meshing my fingers together and trying to appear as if I was about to say the most heartfelt thing they'd ever heard. "If we could add a last-minute addendum to this proposal, I'd like to suggest that we change the typeface of all the new pink books to Zapf Chancery, to add a little... oh, I don't know, frilly ambience to the mix. And let's make it 50-point Zapf Chancery while we're at it. A nice, big, fancy font to attract that lucrative senior-citizen market that won't buy anything besides the *Reader's Digest* large-type edition. And wow! You guys are gonna love this. Instead of going to all the cost and trouble of having different cover photos for each book, why don't we use the same piece of art for all the covers! Like maybe," I raised my hand to my mouth and squinted. "Yes! A big smiley face! A big, *yellow* smiley face with a pink background. How's that for a cheery, relaxing image that's sure to attract any and all comers?"

They stared. Big Grin looked nearly convinced.

"Have no fear!" I yelled. "CATHEDRAL IS HERE!" I leaped to my feet and raised my arms in the air, like a referee signalling a touchdown. "Woohoo!"

With that, I grabbed my pad and pen and did an exaggerated jog to the conference room door. Pumping a fist in the air, I yelled, "Buy our books! Everything's going to be okay!"

Marcia and Mitch looked back at me with slack jaws and blank eyes. Big Grin, on the other hand, aware that this moment somehow required her participation, applauded and said a quiet "Yay!"

I smiled and pointed to her. "You sing it, sister," I said, giving her a wink before I ditty-bopped out the door.

Chapter 7

THE PILLAR OF FLAMES

And the LORD went before them by day in a pillar of a cloud, to lead them the way; and by night in a pillar of fire, to give them light....
—*Exodus 13:21*

I spent the rest of that afternoon holed up in my office. I was looking for peace. Silly me.

Number one on my agenda was a letter to an author who was clueless enough to send a manuscript with no page numbers. This is a trifle to people in other professions, but it means everything to editors who keep too many heaps of paper on their desks and who—like me—occasionally drop some of these heaps onto the floor. As a result, my only copy of the manuscript entitled *The Secret Semiotics of Standardized Testing Grids*, by J. Pennington Stubbs, now formed an 800-page carpet that would never be reassembled in the proper order.

Some editors hate writing letters like the one I was writing to Mr. Stubbs. I drool at the opportunity. Thanking him for considering us as potential publisher, I expressed Cathedral's gratitude for his research efforts, noting on how fascinating it must have been to spend hours analyzing the geometric patterns of black ovals on SAT answer sheets. It was therefore a shame—a tragedy, really—that an office mishap caused the pages to be shuffled beyond our ability to repaginate them properly without page numbers. We were therefore returning his opus to him for proper reassembly. If it was any consolation, we felt that the scrambling of pages actually improved the book's readability in some places—perhaps he might consider one more revision? And while we were discussing improvements, I remarked that his printing the entire manuscript on purple onionskin stock with a dot-matrix printer was a remarkable achievement, but added—reluctantly—that few people appreciated such skills, and that I wasn't one of them. Ditto for what looked like chocolate stains on the first several pages. In conclusion, I thanked him again for sharing this work and hoped therapy was going well.

As I wrote my signature, I noticed that my CathMail icon was blinking. I ignored it for five more minutes. Then my curiosity kicked in... the message waiting for me might have something to do with the meeting I'd just ruined.

I clicked on the icon. I was not disappointed.

To: Gabriel Marino
cc: Mitchell Mitchell, Jenna Davies
From: Marcia Gold
Subject: Marketing Meeting

Your behavior during this afternoon's marketing meeting was disgraceful. Marketing put a lot of time and effort into that prezentation. I'm sure they didn't apreciate your disrespect. Please apologize ASAP.

mg

It was unfortunate that I read this after writing a snarky author letter. People should never e-mail me when I get like this.

To: Marcia Gold
cc: Mitchell Mitchell, Jenna Davies
From: Gabriel Marino
Subject: Re: Marketing Meeting

Marcia,

I'll confess to a show of disrespect, but mine was not the first in that meeting. Their presentation was poorly thought out and, I suspect, based less on research and hard facts than on personal whim. The only thing I found more unbelievable than their presentation was your support for it.

Please note: I ridiculed the idea, not the people. I think Mitch and Jenna know this is business... not personal. We need to reconsider this color.

Gabe

P.S. There is no Z in *presentation*, and *appreciate* is spelled with two P's.

To: Gabriel Marino
cc: Mitchell Mitchell, Jenna Davies
From: Marcia Gold
Subject: Re: Re: Marketing Meeting

Nothing personal??? Your wisecrack about the dong wasn't personal? Your questionning of Marketing's expertise isn't personal? Your challenging my judgment and correcting my spelling, in front of them isn't personal? Apologize, Gabe.

mg

To: Marcia Gold
cc: Mitchell Mitchell, Jenna Davies
From: Gabriel Marino
Subject: Re: Re: Re: Marketing Meeting

Marcia,

You are correct, for once. None of the items you mention in your last bird splat of a message was meant to be personal. However, your kicking me around in front of other departments because you can't spell *is* personal. I await your apology.

Gabe

P.S. There's a big difference between a *bong*, which is what I spoke of, and a *dong*. I can draw you some pictures.

P.P.S. Let's play "Find the extra letter in *questionning*," shall we? You go first. No, really… I don't mind.

P.P.P.S. What in the world made you put that comma after *spelling*? Did you hiccup while you were typing?

To: Marcia Gold, Gabriel Marino
cc: Mitchell Mitchell
From: Jenna Davies
Subject: Re: Re: Re: Re: Marketing Meeting

Hi everybody! :-)

I just wanted to say that I thought we had a GREAT meeting! I'm not mad.
As Chaucer once said, "Amor vincit omnia."
Have a nice day,

Jenna :-)

To: Jenna Davies
cc: Mitchell Mitchell, Marcia Gold
From: Gabriel Marino
Subject: Re: Re: Re: Re: Marketing Meeting

Ah, Jenna, the voice of sweet reason. I feel like I'm clubbing a puppy for writing this, but... have you actually read the Prioress's Tale? Or did the Cliffs Notes only cover Chaucer's prologue? If you read between the lines, you'll see that the Prioress isn't what she seems to be. In fact, she's a lot like Marcia.

Gabe

To: Gabriel Marino
cc: Mitchell Mitchell, Jenna Davies
From: Marcia Gold
Subject: Re: Re: Re: Re: Re: Marketing Meeting

What the hell do you mean by that?

I don't know why your being so unreasonable. You and your group resist me at every opportunity. And now your being spiteful. I will not tolerate this.

I have tried to be reasonable with you. And believe me, it has not been easy. I think I've been very patient. And still you won't take direction. And you go out of your way to embarass me in front of our collegues. You seem to think that everything should be run your way. I especially resent your mean-spirited attitude. It's not fair. To be honest, I think you're punishing me because you, Marty, and Jerry can't have your little good old boys' club anymore. Well, too bad, I say. If you don't like it, you've given me more than enough grounds for termination.

Apologize, Gabe. Do it now, or clean out your desk.

Mg

To: Marcia Gold, Gabriel Marino, Jenna Davies
From: Mitchell Mitchell
Subject: Re: Re: Re: Re: Re: Re: Marketing Meeting

Everyone,

Please! I think we're all being a little hasty. We're very flexible here in Marketing, and maybe we can find a color that makes everyone happy. For example, if we bump the Pantone number down a little, we get a pink with some violet overtones. Or maybe we could try adding a little orange to the pink? That would add a little youthful excitement to the relaxation inspired by the pink. A little citrus on the strawberry, if you will. How's that for a paradigm shift?

What do you think? Jenna and I would be happy to meet again so we can build some consensus.

Mitch

To: Mitchell Mitchell
cc: Marcia Gold, Jenna Davies
From: Gabriel Marino
Subject: Re: Re: Re: Re: Re: Re: Re: Marketing Meeting

Mitchie baby,

Understand that I mean this in the nicest possible way: It's not about whether you see strawberry, boysenberry, or fuckleberry in this pink color. If you don't like the purple covers we've been using, then maybe—I'm going out on a limb here—you shouldn't have suggested that color two years ago.

Still, you're a stand-up kind of guy, and I want to offer you and Jenna my sincere apologies. But not for dissing your proposal and questioning your judgment... oh, no. That I meant. C'est la vie.

What I'm sorry for, Mitch, is the position my boss has put you in. It can't be easy for you to sit through message after message of this drivel. She can't spell, which is a shame, and she can't reason, which is a lot worse. Poor guy; if I were in your position, I'd blow my own brains out just to avoid the misused homonyms.

So I'll tell you what: I'll stop copying you in on this pointless debate. That'll give you and Jenna time to smoke some more oregano and come up with a better color.

With every last milligram of due respect,

Gabe

To: Marcia Gold
bcc: Theresa Bowerman, Kelvin James, Claire Morrissey
From: Gabriel Marino
Subject: Re: Re: Re: Re: Re: Re: Re: Re: Marketing Meeting

Marcia. What a message that was! I've never seen the like. Watching your train of thought run helter-skelter from false conceits to competence to implied sexism to threats, I was reminded of those automatic vacuum cleaners that roll across the bottoms of swimming pools, bumping into walls and careening off in random directions, never quite cleaning the entire pool because one spot is always missed. It must be hard, bouncing through life with a mind like that.

Your point—if I understand it—is not well taken. I don't know where you got the idea that I resent working for a woman. Some of the people I admire most are women... in fact, you fired one of them last week. If you keep this up, the only noseprints on Cathedral's glass ceiling will be yours.
And when, may I ask, did you show this patience you speak of? You haven't listened to a word I've said since I started working for you. Sure, you allow me to speak in turn... but when I'm done, the vacuum powers up and trundles on its blind way once again.

Truth be told, I don't expect everything to go my way. This is no temper tantrum. But I do expect the decisions in my department to be made with a nod to logic and common sense. I've been looking for those as I've gauged your performance. Did you know that subordinates do this? Would you like to know how I rate *your* performance so far? Quite simply: It sucks. It sucks all the way across the pool, bangs into the far wall, and sucks all the way back.

So go on, wreck this department if that's what you're trying to do. Watch the sales figures plummet while everyone under you quits or gets canned. No one can stop you: I don't have the power, and Charles apparently doesn't have the good sense. But I have one more thing to say, and if you've never listened to anything I've said to date, please take this one thing to heart:

Your decisions have consequences. Not only on projects and profits, but also on careers and lives. Think about that, the next time you fire somebody over a cartoon. Or, come to think of it, over pink book covers.

Gabe

P.S. CathMail has a spell-check function. Look up *embarrass* sometime. Will wonders never cease?

To: Gabriel Marino
cc: Theresa Bowerman, Claire Morrissey
From: Kelvin James

Subject: Nice one

Power to the people, dude! WOOOOOOOOOOOOOOHOO!

To: Gabriel Marino
cc: Kelvin James, Claire Morrissey
From: Theresa Bowerman
Subject: You Idiot

Oh, no. What is WRONG with you?

To: Gabriel Marino
cc: Kelvin James, Theresa Bowerman
From: Claire Morrissey
Subject: Oh my god

Gabe? Are you okay?

To: Marcia Gold, Gabriel Marino
cc: Mitchell Mitchell
From: Jenna Davies
Subject: Re: Re: Re: Re: Re: Re: Re: Marketing Meeting

Hi!

I'm confused. Are we going with the pink?

Jenna :-)

To: Gabriel Marino
From: Marcia Gold
Subject: Re: Re: Re: Re: Re: Re: Re: Re: Re: Marketing Meeting

Clean out your desk. You are terminated.

mg

Chapter 8

BY THE LIGHT OF THE MOON

Now I urge you, brethren, keep your eye on those who cause dissensions and hindrances contrary to the teaching which you learned, and turn away from them. For such men are slaves, not of our Lord Christ but of their own appetites; and by their smooth and flattering speech they deceive the hearts of the unsuspecting.
—Romans 16:17-18

Peace reigned for all of two minutes after Marcia's message. I sat back, put my feet up on my desk, and marvelled at what I'd just done. Bravado doesn't come naturally to me unless it's on paper. Had Marcia known that written challenges send editors into rooster mode, she probably wouldn't have baited me. But she had, and now I felt ashamed. And, I should add, a little fearful. Had recent events not been so bewildering, I would have shown the patience I show my daughter when she beats on my knees and demands another ride on Gabe's Shoulder Airlines. But it didn't go that way. Now, after piledriving Marcia in an e-mail smackdown and dancing the mashed potato on her carcass, I felt like the bigger moron had won.

As I waited for her to burst sputtering through my closed door, it occurred to me that she couldn't fire me. At least, not yet. I'd have to explain it to her, of course, and that didn't sound fun, but at least it made the knot in my stomach unclench a little.

Two minutes of reflection was all I got, and in the last ten seconds I decided that the true sound of hell breaking loose is silence. The din that follows—if it comes—is just effect. In this case, the effect began when Marcia huffed into my office and slammed the door behind her.

"Get out!" she shrieked. "Get out now!" Her fists were clenched, and she was panting so hard it sounded like wheezing.

I had leaned back and placed my feet on the desk, and her red face was now framed in the V made by my shoes. She now looked like a talking, poisonous flower. The Venus Deathtrap, maybe.

"Could we talk this over?" I said, stretching and bringing my hands to rest behind my head. "Because you can't fire me, and the only one who cares about all these dramatics is you." This was a dangerous move, but remaining calm seemed like the only way to defuse this before it got even uglier.

"Excuse me?" she said.

"It's simple. You can't fire me," I said. "Not without committing professional suicide. It would be like pulling the pin on a grenade and handing it me."

She brought her hands to her hips. "And how do you figure that?"

"Again, It's simple," I said. "Now that Sally's gone, we're all overworked. We're also behind schedule. If you terminate me, your problem goes from bad to impossible."

Marcia snorted. "I can hire another editor. You're not so special."

That one hurt. "Maybe not," I said, "but your problems don't stop there. We have 21 books to crank out in the next quarter, which means that Theresa and Kelvin have no time to train newbies. And you'll be no help, because you have sixth-grade editing skills, at best. That leaves you with two choices. First, you could start missing bound book dates, in which case your partnership with Greenlawn Press goes bye-bye.

"Or, if you prefer, you could crash production on everything and get all books done on time. But if you do, the reviewers will eat you alive. People won't pay $25 for a shoddy book. Well, okay, they will if the book has vampires in it. But we don't sell fiction. And when our sales take a nosedive, your partnership with Greenlawn Press will go down with it. Any of these options sound good so far?"

She glared, then pouted, then looked thoughtful.

"Marcia," I said, "I know what I'm doing. And I know that you're good at..." I paused to reach for something positive, but came up dry.

"...whatever it is you do in Public Relations. If you don't respect me, fine. But you can't ditch me without trashing your own future. At least, not now."

Marcia's eyes were fixed on a point somewhere over my shoulder. Her head was tilted like a cocker spaniel's when it hears an unfamiliar noise.

"You know," I said, removing my feet from the desk and leaning forward, "This is the most you've ever let me say in one stretch."

I thought I saw a nod.

"I'm not fighting for my job here," I said. "And I'm not fighting for your job, since I'd rather be sucked through a leaf mulcher than do P.R. for a living."

Whoops. There's nothing like tapdancing through a minefield to get the blood pressure going.

"I just don't want to see a few bad decisions make everything we've worked so hard to build crash and burn."

Her eyes reestablished contact with mine, signifying that I had only seconds left to finish.

"And most importantly," I said, "I don't want to see our people burdened with chaos and failure. I don't want to see them get laid off and take lousy jobs elsewhere. They're a good team, and I care about them. You can question my attitude if you want: I admit that it sucks lately. I guess I'm just thrown by everything that's happened. But if you question my dedication, then you don't understand anything about me."

Quiet settled again, with neither of us looking at the other. My torrent of honesty had the same effect as loud flatulence. I didn't want to say it, she didn't want to hear it, there was great embarrassment all around, and we both wanted to be anywhere but my office right then.

Marcia's jaw thrust forward, and her hands returned to her hips. "Don't think you've won anything here," she said. "I'll keep you on until I can find a suitable replacement. And until that day comes, I'll be watching everything you do."

She turned, and as she walked towards the door I heard something that sounded like exhaling from the hallway. She stopped when she reached the door, her glance snapping from right to left. "What are you doing here? Are you eavesdropping?"

More exhaling and shuffling from the hallway, and then Kelvin's voice saying, "Uh, sorry." The sound of a small herd of buffalo stampeding down the hallway brought a smile to my face, and Marcia's scowl as she set off in pursuit made the moment even better.

I looked at my screen. The CathMail icon was blinking.

To: Gabriel Marino
From:
Subject:

GO TO THE ROOFTOP NOW!

ARCHANGEL

Ah, yes. I'd forgotten about my invitation to the Tar Bar. The day was over, I was tired, and now Claire was getting antsy. A few sacriligious Archangel images came to mind, and I forced myself to think of my wife and daughter as I rose and headed for the rendezvous. All we were going to do was talk. Really.

When I reached the ladder, I looked up and saw moonlight shining through the square where the trap door usually was. Climbing the steps, I remembered the feel of Claire's kisses and tried to picture that memory being forced into a safe and locked inside. Reaching the top step, I peeked out onto the rooftop and saw five people standing at the far edge of the roof, facing out towards the East River. They were aligned in a row, and I could tell from the bulging shape of the man on the far left that he was Bobby Ortiz. Three of the others were men in suits, and the one on the far right looked like a woman. Someone was speaking.

"...have been made. Everything is now in place, except maybe you, Jerry. And frankly, I find that disturbing."

I froze. The voice was Howard Brannon's. He was the suit next to the woman I now recognized as Louise Dreyfoos. The Gang of Six I had seen in Cathedral's cafeteria was meeting again, only now they were on the roof. What was it with these people and strange meeting places? I looked closer, wondering where Jerry was.

"There's a lot that's disturbing about this," said Jerry, apparently from somewhere in front of the line of figures.

"I don't understand this," said Howard. "I thought a man of your education would appreciate what we're trying to accomplish."

Jerry Lanville's head appeared between Howard's and the one belonging to the man on Howard's left, whom I couldn't identify. Jerry looked nervous in the moonlight. "I only asked for a discussion," he said. "I think Oliver's being honest when it comes to the future of Cathedral. I just thought we should get his intentions on paper. Before we make our move."

There was a low chuckle, and I saw Howard turn to the man on his left. Gray Suit. Oliver Barney.

"Jerry, I'm a simple man," said Gray Suit. "I don't have your fancy-pants education, so I don't get confused by ideas. Everything's either a good decision or a bad one. Black or white. So if I give you my word that I'm in this for the long run, then I mean it. If you doubt my word, we've got a problem."

Jerry's gaze shifted from Gray Suit to Howard and back again. "Did you give your word to Federal Airlines? Or the West Coast Food Group? Am I the only one here who reads *The Wall Street Journal*?"

Howard shifted his weight to the other foot and crossed his arms. "Mr. Barney's reputation has no bearing on this. We're already profitable. You've seen Bobby's P&Ls. We just need an infusion of capital to reach the next level, and Mr. Barney sees long-term profit in becoming our partner. Our agendas are compatible."

"So you're also *compatible* with running me off a rooftop, just for wanting documentation?" asked Jerry. "For Christ's sake, Howard, I feel like I'm in a DeNiro movie here. Is this how we'll do business in the future?"

I looked around the rooftop, but no one else was up there to see this. The pain in my fingers made me realize that I was gripping the ladder hard. Then something tapped my left foot three times, and before I could stop myself, I yelped.

Looking down, I saw Kelvin staring up at me with a shifty-eyed grin. "Man, what is it with you and the roof?" he said.

"Who's there?" barked someone on the roof.

For a split second I thought I would soil myself. Then the second was gone, I was scrambing back down the ladder, and Kelvin was yowling from my shoe's accidental contact with his head.

"Ow! Ya know, I'm getting sick of this!" said Kelvin as I hit the ground and looked for an escape route.

I clasped his arm and yanked him into motion as I started running down the hallway. "Shut up and follow me," I said. "And don't say my name again."

Somebody else was coming down the ladder now, a man's black shoes and black suit trousers. Kelvin and I bolted through the cube farm in Accounting, where everyone had left work for the day. The empty chairs looked spooky.

"Hey, pardner," said Kelvin from behind me, voice wavering as he ran. "Am I Butch or Sundance?"

"Shut up!" I hissed. "You'll lead them right to us!"

When we reached an intersection of hallways, I stopped short. Which way to run?

Kelvin plowed into my back with a loud "Oof!" He was breathing hard. "It's drugs, isn't it?" he said, tongue lolling like a dog's. "Are you buying or dealing?" Thumps on the carpet far behind him told us that someone was coming after us.

"I don't have time to explain," I said, and resumed my sprint down the same hallway towards the editorial section. This was a bad time to risk yet another hallway collision, but fortunately, no one was around. Kelvin followed close behind.

The editorial cubes were abandoned too, save for one. Claire sat with her back to us, typing, and as we hustled towards her she turned around.

"Hey," she said, her eyes growing wide at my expression. "What's going on?"

My eyes scanned the room for a fast exit. Running here had been a dumb idea, since there was no easy exit besides the way from which we just came. Making my way towards her, I brought my finger to my lips and pointed behind me. "I don't know," I hissed. "Just hide. Now."

"Hide?" said Kelvin. "What are we running from?"

"There's no time to argue," I hissed, and as if to prove my point, we heard rapid footsteps becoming louder in a big hurry. Whoever was chasing us was fast. And worse, he was here. Reacting on instinct, I lunged forward, grabbed Claire by her shoulders, and pulled her down with me under her desk. I kept one arm around her as we made a soft impact with the floor and stayed there, silent. I leaned my head forward until my lips touched her earlobe.

"Don't make a sound," I whispered. "Please."

We stayed that way as the footsteps slowed and halted a few desks away. In my terror I had pulled Claire's body tight against mine, and as I listened to our pursuer's breathing, my id danced a foxtrot with my superego. For once, my id was not leading. Along the length of my body, I felt Claire shudder slightly. Terror and eroticism don't go very well together, but the sensation wasn't lost on me. Involuntarily, I shuddered back. She couldn't help but feel it, and I wondered what was going through her mind.

"Okay, knucklehead. Where'd ya go?" said a male voice, one desk over. I didn't recognize him. The accent was old-style Brooklyn, the kind no one speaks anymore, if they ever did. He walked right down our row, passing our desk. Shiny black shoes, black trousers... and that was all I could see from below the desk. That, and what looked like the last two inches of a handgun making a clicking noise against our desk as it passed by. Claire stiffened at the sight of the gun. So did I.

We listened to the man's clothes rustle as he turned the corner, and then there was a new sound. It was a slight scraping, almost unnoticeable, and then it was gone. I swallowed hard. The man was standing right where I had last seen Kelvin.

I braced for a scream, or a gunshot, and heard... the rustling of paper. Then silence. Then some more rustling. And then, to my horror.... a deep chuckle.

"Herkel!" The yell was Oliver Barney's, distant and enraged.

More chuckling, and more page rustling. The guy's shoes, polished black leather but cheap looking, shifted in front of my face, as if he was planning on standing there awhile comfortably.

"Herkel!"

Another rustle. "What?" boomed our pursuer, his voice deep.

"Do you have him?"

"No!" The word crackled with annoyance.

A moment of silence followed, and then Barney's voice, a little closer: "What the hell are you doing, then?"

"I'm readin' somethin'."

Another set of footsteps pounded through the room. "What have you got there?" said Barney, and a tearing sound told me a book was being mistreated. "*Golf for Blue-Collar Blowhards*? This is what I'm paying you to do?"

"I dunno where they are." said Herkel. "Fast little knuckleheads. I'm all outta breath."

There was a pause.

"Hey, you should keep that," said Herkel. "Maybe you'll quit killin' gophers on the fairway."

Another pause followed, followed by the clatter of a book being thrown across the room.

"Fuck!" said Barney, his footsteps resuming and growing faint. When they were gone, Herkel's black shoes walked past our desk again. I was just about ready to emerge from beneath the desk when I heard his clothes rustling back, and the shoes strode into view once again. He walked back to Kelvin's desk, and I heard the sound of a book hitting the desktop.

"Shoulda kept it, ya stuffed shirt," mumbled Herkel, now walking in the direction where Barney went. "Swings a driver like a friggin' ballerina."

Silence reigned again. I held Claire and thought about life. By law of averages, a run of bad luck ends after a day or so, tops, for most people. I mean, sure, everyone has bad stretches from time to time, and I wasn't unique in having a crappy day or even a week. But this Bataan Death March of Neverending Suckage that started with my promotion and ended—so far—in a quick golf lesson for Knucklehead the Henchman was too much. I was a skeptic when it came to karma, but the idea that I piloted the Enola Gay or diddled the Dalai Lama in a past life now seemed possible.

"Gabe?" said Claire.

"Yeah?" I said.

"I think they're gone now."

I listened. "Yeah."

"So... I guess you can let me go."

"Um, right," I said, pulling my arm back and feeling the coolness along my front as she wriggled away.

"Hey Kelvin?" I said, flinching at the volume of my voice.

From somewhere across the room came a shuffle. "Yo."

I smiled. "You okay?"

"He liked my book!" said Kelvin.

I sighed, rolling out into the aisle and rising to my feet next to Claire. "Congratulations. Now let's get the hell out of here."

We dusted ourselves off and stood still for a few seconds, listening for any sign of Barney's return. Apparently he was gone, which was fine by me. Still, not trusting our ears, we bypassed the elevator for the stairs, blew out the front door, and sprinted for a block or so before slowing to a halt near a subway entrance. A breeze blew from the west, drying the sweat from my face.

"So who was that? Are we gonna call the cops?" said Kelvin as we stopped for a traffic light.

"I don't think so," I said, looking at Claire. "It might make things even worse."

Claire gave me a quizzical look. "Worse than what? Why was Oliver Barney chasing you?"

"Who's that?" said Kelvin.

I sighed. "This is going to take some explaining."

"You bet your ass," said Kelvin. "And we're still gonna have words about the face kicking. Does this have something to do with you choking your chicken on the roof?"

The shock of the question was bad enough, but the sideways kick to my ankle that Claire delivered was worse. Pain, sharp and exquisite, reminded me that discretion would be a good thing right now. It wasn't enough to break my stride, and Kelvin didn't notice a thing, but the message was delivered.

"Ah, sort of," I said, wincing. We were coming up on the Blarney Stone, a filthy dive that was never cleaner for all the steam we blew off there. "Why don't we get a beer before we head home, and I'll explain everything."

A split second elapsed, and I realized that another kick might be imminent. "Everything I *can* explain, that is."

Chapter 9

...IN LOVE AND WAR

But draw near hither, ye sons of the sorceress, the seed of the adulterer and the whore. Against whom do ye sport yourselves?
—Isaiah 57:3

The next morning, I approached the doors of Cathedral's building with a loathing that was beginning to feel normal. I wondered what had happened to Jerry after my dash through the office. I also thought about the beer-soaked hour I spent with Claire and Kelvin last night, proposing and rejecting wild conspiracy theories. We wondered whether Jerry was still alive. I didn't mention that Claire was with me when I discovered the Gang of Six, as we now called them. She seemed grateful for that, but I caught a few sidelong glances and it seemed like our Big Talk was imminent. Thus, I stayed only until I saw Kelvin yawn for the first time. The possibility of his leaving Claire and me alone with pitchers of booze was too dangerous to risk. So I bailed, feigning a headache.

Now, squinting before Cathedral's building in the horrible morning sunlight, I noticed a line of buses at the curb. Cathedral people were milling around on the sidewalk, gathering in clusters and looking confused. All of them wore red T-shirts with our company logo on them. There was a weird polarity in their expressions: Some looked delighted, while others were pissed off. Oh God, I thought. Jerry was dead.

Reaching the building, I pulled the sleeve of the first person I recognized: Rajput, my favorite techie. He turned around and beamed at me.

"Gabie baby!" he said.

"Hi Raj," I said, gesturing to the crowd. "What's all this about?"

He smiled. "All this about. It's a corporate retreat! Charles is taking us to nature!"

"A retreat?" I asked. "Today? Where? I can't go today... I have work."

"Work," said Raj, smiling wider. "No work. Charles said so."

"That's right," said a voice behind me, and I spun on my heels to face our president, Charles Ting. He wore a red T-shirt like the others, and he was smiling too as he pulled a shirt from the pile draped over his forearm. "It's a surprise. Just put this on and board the bus."

"But Charles," I said, momentarily distracted by sight of our CEO in casual duds. "I have meetings scheduled for today. This wasn't announced... was it?"

"No," said Charles. "It wasn't. And that's one of the reasons why today's staff retreat will be so effective in boosting morale and teamwork at Cathedral. The element of surprise, Gabe. The element of surprise!" He smiled, then turned to pass out T-shirts to other latecomers.

Like many CEOs, Charles enjoyed talking in riddles and cliches. Sometimes there was a kernel of truth beneath the bluster and fluff, but most of the time he sounded like a politician with mild dementia. He was infamous among the editors for spouting non-sequiturs and using analogies to make the obvious seem profound. He was a man of vision, our Charles Ting, and like most of that breed, he made sure everybody in Cathedral marched to the beat of his drum. The fact that this drummer had the rhythm of a toddler banging on a pot with a wooden spoon meant only that we staggered, skipped, and lurched in unison... as best we could.

I rushed up to my office, replaced my Oxford shirt with the T-shirt, and returned to the buses. Most of the seats were taken by the time I boarded, and as I rose up the steps and faced the aisle I saw only two empty seats. One was next to Marcia, up in front, and the other was next to Bobby Ortiz. None of my group were on this bus, probably because they'd hung back and waited for Marcia to pick a bus, then boarded another. Good for them.

"Hey, Bobby," I called out, as if were old war buddies. "How's it going?" I walked past Marcia without looking at her.

"Okay," said Bobby, scrunching his flabby body over to the window seat . His trumpet rested on his lap, where he cradled it in his hands.

"Did Charles make you bring that?" I asked, sitting down next to him.

"Yeah," said Bobby, looking out the window at the cars going by. "Crazy."

That was the extent of our conversation – or at least, his half – for the first 20 minutes of the trip. His silence unnerved me for a while, making me wonder if he caught a glimpse of me on the rooftop when he stood there among the Gang of Six. He couldn't have, though, since my head was down during my spat with Kelvin. He might have held some kind of grudge against me for my cafeteria intrusion, but then again, Bobby was always pretty quiet. A chill went down my spine. Was Jerry dead? And if so, could this quiet, tubby trumpet player really have helped kill him?

Most of the people on the bus were surprised by the unexpectedness of this trip, and the chattering ranged in tone from the delight of the rank and file to the growling of middle managers. And so, when Charles stood up in front and waved his arms, it took a while for them to shut up and listen.

"Okay, everybody!" said Charles, with a giddiness that made me wonder if he'd been hitting the sauce for breakfast. "Today's retreat is designed to foster team building and personal interaction. So without further ado, I'd like to introduce the corporate communications consultant we've hired to make this day truly hyperproductive. Let's have a nice round of applause for Mr. Stuart Flowers!"

The short, balding man sitting next to Charles then stood up and waved to the four or so clapping people. Tufts of red hair sprouted from his head like wings, and he wore a white T-shirt printed with the words BIG STU in red.

"Okay, how ya doing, people? My name is Stu Flowers but today I want to be like your big brother. So from now on, I want everyone to call me Big Stu. Okay? On the count of three, I want you all to say 'Hi Big Stu!' Ready? Okay, one, two, three!" He raised his hands like an orchestra conductor, and his head tipped in preperation for a thunderous response.

"Hi, Beef Stew!" yelled Kelvin from the back of the bus. There was no other sound, save for some snickering.

Our new corporate consultant crossed his arms and pouted. "Not loud enough, people! Show me some of that Cathedral spirit! And it's Big Stu, people, not beef stew." He waggled his finger at us, as if we were a kindergarten class being scolded. "Okay? Now again, on the count of three! One, two, three!"

"Hi, Beef Stew," I said, joining about a dozen others in the same bored tone.

He looked worried for a moment, then smiled. "Okay, people, that's good! I can take a joke. You're showing teamwork. Working together! I've got the perfect activity to start off our day of team-building. So tell me, by show of cheers... who's up for a singalong?"

"Yay!" shrieked Jenna Davies, clapping and bouncing in her seat. Everyone else said nothing.

Beef Stew sighed. "Okay, I can see we're a little bashful. It's perfectly normal. Once we start singing, I'm sure you'll be roaring like lions. Now, on the count of three, I want everyone to sing 'Michael, Row the Boat Ashore'. Now, I understand we have an accomplished jazz trumpet player with us today?"

Bobby's hand shot up, whacking my arm.

"Excellent!" said Stew, raising his fist in a salute. "This is gonna be great, people. Now, on the count of three, I want everybody singing along with Mr. Trumpet Player over there. Okay? One, two, three!" He raised his hands like a conductor again.

The voices of Jenna, Mitch, Marcia, and Charles blended to sing while Bobby's trumpet bleated in my ear like a tortured goat. From behind me, almost as loud as Bobby's trumpet, Kelvin sang "If I Said You Had a Beautiful Body, Would You Hold It Against Me?" off key. Everyone else continued their chattering. I turned around to see Jenna and Mitch swaying to the music, which fizzled out halfway through the song. Bobby's trumpet burped on for a few more seconds, then that, too, surrendered to the silence with a last mournful note.

In the front of the bus, Beef Stew clenched his fists. For a moment it looked like a temper tantrum was imminent, and then his shoulders sagged, and he said, "Fine. I can see we're not in the right spirit yet. Do what you want." And with that, he slumped back into his seat. I was close enough to hear him mutter, "Fucking *people*" before the talking around me resumed.

And so our bus made its sullen way to what I soon learned was Darlington Park in Mahwah, New Jersey. Disembarking from the bus, we breathed in the fresh air and beheld lawns, lakes, woods, and picnic tables. It was a beautiful place, and as I looked around I wondered if our presence would contaminate it somehow.

Beef Stew led our group over to a wide lawn where several volleyball nets were set up. With his cheer returned, he explained that that volleyball was the best corporate team-building sport because it required cooperation to succeed. "Bump, set, and over!" he crowed, waving his hands. "It's as easy as that. And no spiking, please... we don't want to get too competitive."

We were to play department versus department. This was Beef Stew's first mistake. Our publications team was herded over to a court in the center of the meadow, and Beef Stew chose Accounting as the team we would play. This was his second mistake. Finally, after appointing referees for the other games, Beef Stew walked back to our court and announced that he would officiate for our game. This was his last, and worst, mistake.

Our group's relationship with Accounting was best compared to the low-level warfare that usually exists between Israel and its neighbors. For reasons we never understood, every third or fourth request we submitted—an expense reimbursement, or a check for a vendor—went unheeded. It just vanished. And every time we complained, Accounting blamed it on our shoddy paperwork. This always led to accusations that Accounting threw away forms without notifying the senders that they were filling them out improperly. In turn, Accounting would call the editors prima donnas, expecting the world to bow when we banged our gongs.

And so it was a surprise to no one—except maybe Beef Stew—that our frolic in the sunshine became a raging hatefest almost immediately. It was ugly even by our standards. Beef Stew's no-spiking rule was a casualty in the first 10 seconds of the game. We slammed the ball at each other over the net, under it, and around it, dancing jigs each time time an opponent was knocked on his ass. Beef Stew whined and gesticulated for the first 10 minutes of the carnage, then gave up and sat down, pouting on the grass. It was terrible. And God, was it fun.

Then, with the score tied 10-10, Theresa belted a screaming serve over the net. Fearing for their lives, the bean counters in the front row ducked. As the ball neared the ground, someone in their back row dived at it. This was Mort Bingerton, a senior financial analyst in his 40s who was the most pugnacious of the group and a favorite target of our complaints. With both arms locked together, Mort clubbed the ball in the only direction his desperate leap allowed—sideways.

Beef Stew had been sniffing dandelions on the grass, but for the past few points he had shown extreme interest in the fit of Claire's T-shirt. He was in the middle of a full-blown leer when Mort deflected Theresa's serve, and only at the last possible moment did he sense that something was amiss. This was unfortunate. Had he been watching the game, the ball might not have thwacked him upside the head with a sickening *foomp* and sent him backwards in a tumblesault.

"Ug," said Beef Stew, staring at the sun with glazed eyes. Grass stuck to his shirt, and the puffs of red hair over his ears now pointed at odd angles.

"Uh oh," said Theresa.

"Ha!" said Kelvin.

"Are you okay, Beef Stew?" said Mort, all aggression gone as he rushed to the fallen referee's aid.

Beef Stew drew a hand across the bottom of his nose, where blood had trickled onto his white T-shirt. "By dame ith Thtu, goddabbit. Thtu Fwowerth."

I walked over to take a look. The nosebleed wasn't bad, although a few drops had fallen on his shirt to form a scarlet apostrophe between the T and U in BIG STU. The message now looked oddly foreign. When his eyes uncrossed, he looked from Mort to me with the stare of a wide-eyed child.

"You have a vewy agwethive compady," he said, pulling himself to his feet. "That bakes teebwork harder. And cautheth all kideth of pwobwemth."

"Yeah, we know," I said. "Sorry."

His nose wasn't broken, but he declined to referee the rest of our game. Accounting eventually won, guaranteeing ill will between our departments for at least the next 10 years.

After volleyball, everyone descended on two picnic tables loaded with burgers and hot dogs barbecued by Charles and Howard. I wolfed down a dog while commiserating with a couple of mailroom guys who had been routed by our lawyers and admin assistants. I then looked around for my group, but everyone had spread out over a wide area and they were nowhere to be found. I did, however, see Claire.

She was standing alone in a small playground by the shore of the lake, spinning a small merry-go-round with her hand. As I approached her, she moved on to a large slide that was designed to propel its riders into the shallows of the water. She grabbed hold of one of the metal steps, then hesitated. When I was close enough to be heard, she turned to face me.

"Go ahead," I said, smiling. "Everyone needs a thrill once in a while."

She looked down, the beginnings of a blush on her face. "Yeah," she said. "But sometimes thrills can be dangerous."

I looked at the slide, and then up at the few clouds drifting across the sky.

"It's a nice day for a lakeside walk," I said. "Care to join me?"

She smiled. "Sure."

We followed the shoreline away from the red-shirted horde. A cool breeze blew in off the lake, turning the sweat of the volleyball game into a distant memory. I looked at Claire a little longer than I should have.

"I guess you've been wondering about that night on the roof," I said.

"Funny, I was about to say the same thing," said Claire.

"Uh-huh," I said. Something clever would have been preferable. "The thing is," I said, "I have no alcohol tolerance at all."

"Me neither," she said.

"No," I said. "We can't be talking about the same thing here. I once wore a bear costume to a college lacrosse game and waggled my naked butt for about 500 other students, their parents, and their younger siblings. I did it on two beers and a dare. Imagine what I'd do after some shots."

She laughed. "I kinda figured." Her dark eyes were locked on mine, and I felt the same thrill—or maybe it was danger—I felt on the rooftop that night. "You know," she said, "I don't think you realize how irresistable you can be. At least, to a certain type of girl."

Klaxons wailed in my mind. This was what I was hoping to prevent by taking this walk. It was also what I most wanted to hear.

"Claire," I croaked, trying to slow the triphammer in my chest, "I made a vow to a certain woman years ago that I never intended to break."

"I know," she said.

"I also have a daughter. And some major career issues. And... well, I think I'm going through some kind of pre-midlife crisis. Or something. I don't have that part figured out yet."

Claire said nothing, looking down at the sand beneath our feet.

I sighed. "If you're looking for a dreamboat, what you have here is a trash barge with a broken rudder."

She chuckled. "Aren't you making a lot of assumptions?"

"Such as?"

She looked out at the lake again, then back at me. "Well, just because you've got a few things to smooth over doesn't mean that your life's all messed up. And just because I kissed you doesn't mean I'm a homewrecker."

I looked behind us to make sure no Cathedral people had snuck up to within earshot, then turned back to her. "So you kissed me because you just... wanted to know what it felt like?"

Her eyes found mine again. "No," she said. "I kissed you because I never want to know what it feels like, never to have kissed you."

I stopped. I couldn't have been more stunned if she'd whacked me with a two-by-four and demanded my wallet.

She shrugged and gave me a mischievous smile. "That's all," she said.

I was looking at her when she said that, and although the words lit up my bloodstream like endorphins, making me feel like a little kid watching his first Fourth of July starburst high above the rest of the mundane world, something was amiss. This was no time to look for dishonesty, but sometimes a certain inflection of voice, or a raising of the eyes, can reveal a lie... whether you want it to be there or not. I didn't see anything like that in Claire. She stood next to me and looked right at me, her smile giving way to an expression of desire that looked very, deliciously, real. I know I returned it. This was bad.

"Let's go, people!" squawked Beef Stew from somewhere behind us. "We've got a schedule to keep."

We turned away from each other. He was standing at a point halfway between the barbecue tables and us, waving and looking peeved. A few yards behind him, a couple of the mailroom guys pantomimed his actions. Even from where I stood, I could see them muffling their laughter.

"It's time for trust-building exercises!" yelled Beef Stew. He put his hands on his hips. "Don't make me chase you all over this park!"

I looked at Claire, and we both laughed as we turned and walked back towards the mass of red-shirts near the trees. Feeling like a killjoy, I wondered if I was inventing this "dishonesty" out of guilt. I tried to remember an instance where my conscience acted this way before, but came up with nothing. There were no explanations for any of this... just the lingering euphoria of a man who'd nearly been kissed... again.

As we rejoined the red-shirted horde, I kept to the fringe of the group and followed them away, lost in thought. Everyone, at one time or another, senses that everything isn't what it seems to be. Maybe that paranoia is hard-wired into us. We can't help it.

I looked at Claire, walking a few yards ahead of me. Her hair was blown back by a breeze, looking so much like my wife's used to before she cut it short.

Yeah, I thought. That was probably it.

Chapter 10

A LEAP OF FAITH

O daughter of Babylon, who art to be destroyed; happy shall he be, that rewardeth thee as thou hast served us. Happy shall he be, that taketh and dasheth thy little ones against the stones.
—Psalm 137: 8-9

The next scheme hatched by Beef Stew looked ominous. Leading us over to another grassy lawn, he pointed to about a dozen aluminum stepladders aligned in a row, so that they faced our red-shirted mob like a metallic firing squad. The fear of heights is one of the least appreciated traits I inherited from my parents.

"This is where we separate the big dogs from the puppies," Beef Stew shouted, pointing to the stepladders and trying to look as macho as he could with his shirt bloodied and his hair messed up. "You volleyball guys think you're tough? Well, just wait 'til you try this!"

From behind me somebody mimicked Beef Stew's last six words in a lilt. Beef Stew couldn't hear this, but the cackling that followed caught his attention and his look of manly triumph faded into a pout again.

"Okay, people, I want all department heads standing on these stepladders! Come on, don't be shy! Step forward!" he said, looking tired. The department heads moved forward, shooting wary glances at each other.

As the department heads mounted the stepladders, he added, "Everybody else should stand in a group on the grass behind their department head. That's right," he said, pointing to the cluster of people gathered in front of Mitch Mitchell like disciples. "They've got the idea." He looked at the rest of us. "Well, *move*, people! We haven't got all day!"

Slowly, the editors walked towards a nervous-looking Marcia on a creaky-looking stepladder. The P.R. people also converged towards her, but since the editors were already closer, Beef Stew waved them over to Howard Brannon, who had gamely mounted a stepladder even though he'd risen above the level of department head years before. The lawn now looked like a red-shirted zealots' convention, gathered around 12 speakers like the judges in a "Who's the Messiah?" contest. Somebody let loose with a loud belch, provoking giggles that squelched Beef Stew's next instructions.

"Could you repeat that?" said someone a few stepladders away from me.

Beef Stew sighed and placed his hands on his hips. "Are you people deaf or something? I said that, on the count of three, every person on a stepladder should put their arms out to their sides and fall backwards off the stepladder. Just fall, and allow yourselves to be caught by the rest of your group. Don't be afraid. This exercise builds trust. You need that."

A wave of excited murmuring rolled across the lawn, and the editors looked from Marcia to each other with looks of concern, then amusement... and then cheerful malevolence.

"Don't even think about it," I said, watching as my voice checked the grins on Theresa's and Kelvin's faces. Claire was not smiling, but was looking at Marcia the way a Doberman eyes a pork chop.

"Ah, Stuart?" said Charles from somewhere on my left. "I'm not sure this is the best selection of activity..."

Our president now commanded everyone's full attention, getting looks of gratitude from the people on the stepladders and glares from everyone else.

Beef Stew's eyes darted around the crowd, looking for the speaker. "Is somebody questioning my judgment?" he cried, his voice breaking on the first word. He balled his fists and marched towards us. "Who said that?"

"I did, Stuart," said Charles. "The guy who's paying you for all this."

Beef Stew's face softened a little at that, but his jaw remained thrust forward. "This is a trust-building exercise. If you want your company to function as a cohesive unit, then you'll have to learn to trust each other. I've been doing this for fifteen years, so you people should goddamn well trust me on this!"

Even Charles remained silent as we watched this outburst. Beef Stew was trembling with emotion.

"Ooh," came the low voice of one of the mailroom thugs off to my right. "A rough, tough, creampuff." Some nasal squawking followed, but otherwise no one challenged Beef Stew further.

"Now is everybody ready?" bellowed Beef Stew.

"Go Beef Stew!" yelled Kelvin.

Beef Stew's hands went to his hips again. "Stop calling me that. Now on the count of three, I want the ladder people to fall!"

I looked up at Marcia. There was something both regal and ridiculous in this scene: On the one hand, she looked like a prophet up there with her arms outstretched, the wind ruffling her T-shirt and knee-length black skirt. On the other hand, the stepladder she stood on was rickety and creaked under her weight. Her mouth opened as if to speak, and for one bizarre moment I expected her to start yelling The Ten Commandments.

"You'd better catch me, you... you..." she said.

"Topple, bitch," muttered Theresa under her breath. "Make my day."

"One!" yelled Beef Stew.

"Knock it off, Theresa," I said in a near-whisper.

"Two!"

We looked up at Marcia, who was now staring straight up at the sky in an uncanny resemblance of Jesus on the cross. She was breathing hard. My knees felt weak.

"Three!" shrieked Beef Stew, raising his hands in the air like a football referee calling a touchdown.

Marcia leaned back ever so slightly, and it happened so slowly that for a moment I thought she'd rock forwards again. But she hung there, fingers splayed out and wiggling. Then, ever so gradually, Marcia began to fall to the ground. She did not do so with grace, or dignity, or silence. Instead, she twitched and jerked in mid-air while emitting a sound that could only be compared to a ululating parrot. Her legs, no longer supporting her weight, began to kick the air. And then, so help me God, her body was horizontal in front of us.

My arms shot up from my sides, and as Marcia's body swooped before me I saw that Claire, who was standing opposite from me, had already done the same. We caught her around her knees, her weight pushing our arms down a bit. But Kelvin and Theresa, who faced each other where the rest of Marcia's body was now passing, had not moved. Now, to my horror, Marcia's feet rose again as my arms formed the fulcrum of a human lever. She had become a human see-saw in a corporate physics experiment. And she was still squawking.

Right before Marcia's head hit the turf, Kelvin and Theresa made a last-minute attempt at stopping her fall. Grabbing her by the shoulders, they slowed her descent enough so that her head touched the ground with only a mild thump. Instinctively—as if to compensate for Kelvin and Theresa's failure—Claire and I raised Marcia's legs higher in the air. As a result, when Marcia began to scream for real, we held her body upside down while her feet flailed. Paralyzed by indecision and fear, we didn't know what else to do.

It was then that Beef Stew, attracted by the ruckus, marched over to see what was going on. "What's wrong?" he whined, elbowing his way through the gathering crowd. Marcia had begun to scissor her legs open and closed, and her knee-length skirt had ridden way up. As a result, when Beef Stew emerged from the circle of gawkers, he was greeted with a commanding view of Marcia's nethers before her feet boxed his ears with a one-two punch. That finally snapped Claire and me out of our shock, and Marcia's legs hit the ground at about the same time Beef Stew's entire body did.

"AAAAAGH!" yelled Marcia, face-down into the grass.

"Oof," said Beef Stew, lying on his side.

Marcia sat up first, smoothing her skirt down and snarling at everyone who dared look back. Beef Stew slowly picked himself up to his knees, then wobbled. Blood was trickling from his nose again.

"You people awe... awe of you... yaw... tewwible!" he said, his eyes focusing on a point three miles behind us.

"That's it!" shrieked Marcia. "I've had it! I'm gonna fire you ALL!"

"I've bid doing dith activity for yeeath," said Beef Stew, wiping his nose and looking at the blood. "Doeboddy does dith. Doeboddy!"

"You dropped me!" wailed Marcia.

"You're nathty!" said Beef Stew.

"I can't believe you just let me fall!" said Marcia.

"Thith compady thuckth!" said Beef Stew.

"We're sorry," said Claire, extending a hand to help Marcia up.

"Thuckth!" said Beef Stew, rising to a crouch. "I can't help you! Doeboddy cad help you!"

By the time Charles had bullied his way to the center of the mob, Beef Stew and Marcia both stood, eyeing each other warily.

"What's going on here?" said Charles. "Stuart! You're all bloody!"

"I quit," said Beef Stew. "Your thtaff are a bunch of thyckopaths. I can't work with theeth people." He turned and weaved a slow zig zag back towards the buses, clutching his head with one hand and gesturing to nobody with the other.

"But Stuart," said Charles, pursuing Beef Stew. "What about the rest of the retreat? What about the permanent position we discussed?"

Beef Stew stopped but did not turn to face Charles. "Shove it up your ath," he said. And with that, he stumbled back to the bus, his tufts of hair waving goodbye in the breeze.

Charles marched back to the center of the group and faced Marcia. "I can't believe you, Marcia," he said. "What did you do to him?"

Marcia glared back at him, then one lip puckered and she turned to stomp away without saying anything.

Charles gaped. "Could someone please tell me what happened here?"

"It's... sort of our fault," I said. And then, as if I was confessing sins to a priest in a Catholic confession, the floodgates opened. I told Charles tales of giant lizards and purple snakes. I told him stories of pink book covers and salesmen pushing carts across the Continental Divide. I drew imaginary timesheets in the air with my finger. I beat my fist into my palm when I mentioned Sally's termination. The rant took about five minutes, and at the end I had traced a causal relationship between Marcia's first day as our boss and impending global doom. All the while, Charles listened and nodded sagely in all the right places. When I reached the end of my tale, he rubbed his chin for a moment.

"Gabe, I'd like a word with you, please."

"Okay." What the hell, he was buying the hot dogs. He could say whatever he pleased.

Charles placed a hand on my shoulder and steered me away from the crowd. When we were out of earshot, he said, "Your department's problem, as I see it, is a lack of strategic vision."

I nodded. I had no idea if we were talking about the same problem, but if Charles had a problem with my area's higher management, that was okie-dokie by me.

Charles sighed. "I'd hoped that Stuart Flowers would be the remedy for situations like this. I wanted him on as a permanent corporate consultant, but… well, it seems he lacks the drive."

I bit my tongue. This was like saying the Titanic had a glop of ketchup on its deck.

"Anyhow," continued Charles, "I want to ask you something, now that you've told me that… remarkable story. How would you assess Marcia's overall performance? Is she screwing up?"

Had I not turned my head at his first question, Charles would have seen my eyes do something rarely seen outside of Bugs Bunny cartoons. I hesitated and stammered while my shock gradually morphed into euphoria. What a chance this was! I could dance the electric boogaloo all over Marcia's career, and she'd never know it. My entire group would know peace. And I would bring justice. Oh, rapture.

Watching my face with amusement, Charles said, "I see you're having trouble with this. Let me simplify the question. Do you think that Marcia, as a woman, can do that job as well as a man could? Or have we been seeing the manifestations of… how can I describe it? Certain feminine limitations?"

At once, the marching bands in my brain stopped playing. I looked at Charles, and he smiled back at me with one eyebrow raised, in that you-know-what-I'm-talking-about look. What could I say? Could this incoherent but polished executive really be this sexist? Once again, Marcia came to mind. The things she said were awful. The things she did were worse. But now, listening to Charles allude to ideas that had no place in fair management, I began to understand something about Marcia that I didn't know before.

"Gabe? Are you all right?" said Charles.

"I'm fine," I said, with all the enthusiasm of a wind-up talking doll. "And so is Marcia."

"Hmm. That's not what I'd infer from the story you just told."

I breathed deep and exhaled. It was goodbye to salvation, and hello to more days of being crapped on by lizards.

"I don't know what the point of my story is, Charles," I said. "Lately, it seems like the more I know, the less I understand." Of everything I'd said in the past few days, this was probably the most true.

He shrugged. "All right, then. My door's always open if you ever want to… exchange ideas." With that, he walked away.

I watched him go and wondered what, if anything, I would tell the editors about this conversation. Theresa would probably slap me upside the head for missing the chance to frag Marcia… politically correct principles be damned. Or would she? Kelvin might have done what I'd done, if only out of fear that Marcia would find out and kick his ass. Or would he? I thought for a while, but found no answers. Hearing a disturbance somewhere behind me, I turned around to see the red-shirted horde split into two big groups, each yelling at the other. I couldn't make out what they were saying, but it was looking like an amateur reenactment of Pickett's Charge. Curious, I abandoned my problems and walked back to join whatever battle was to be fought.

After all, what did I know? I just worked there.

Chapter 11

JUDGMENT DAY

...the priest and the prophet have erred through strong drink, they are swallowed up of wine... they err in vision, they stumble in judgment.
—Isaiah 28:7

To: All Cathedral Employees and Associates
From: Charles Ting
Re: Nuremberg at Cathedral

I have never written a memo like this. It never occurred to me that anyone, anywhere, would need to say these words.

Yesterday's staff retreat had several purposes. First and foremost, it was intended to foster a sense of collective spirit... an eagerness to cooperate in surmounting any obstacle we might face in the future. It was intended to raise morale. It was intended to solidify our various departments as teams and minimize the petty differences that might separate us as working groups. It was intended to do all of this, yet somehow it turned into something else.

Another objective was to hire Mr. Stuart Flowers as a permanent Corporate Communications Consultant. His expertise would have been invaluable in shaping our future as a company, but he declined my offer after yesterday's events. This is not his loss, everyone. It is ours.

I am saddened by this debacle. And so, in the spirit of justice, I have scheduled a tribunal for 3:00 this afternoon to identify and remedy the causes. It is time for a reckoning. I expect all department heads to attend.

Charles

This was the first thing to grace my monitor screen the next morning. I read it with astonishment. Charles's pompous metaphors were entertaining at best and annoying at their worst, but this was offensive. True, we had turned his tea party into a mosh pit, but... *Nuremberg?* What was it about warfare that fascinated executives? Cathedral existed for the sole purpose of making a buck. Comparing us to Nazis for bloodying some wimp's nose and hiking Marcia's skirt up was almost as stupid as holding a company-wide blamestorming meeting.

A knock at the door interrupted my fuming. Marcia stood in my doorway, arms crossed. I felt a whole range of feelings well up. Guilt was foremost among them, and—surprisingly—sympathy, too.

"Hi Marcia," I said.

"Don't give me that 'Hi Marcia' crap," she said. "You *will* be attending this afternoon's tribunal, won't you?"

I sighed. "Marcia, I've already said I'm sorry about what happened to you yesterday."

She stared at me with beady eyes.

"I'm not sure why it happened," I continued, "But I really wish it hadn't."

The reptilian look didn't waver. "It's a little late for that, don't you think?" she said.

"This has nothing to do with the tribunal," I said. "I'm not afraid of Charles, or whatever ridiculous 'charge' he might bring against me. I'm not even afraid of getting canned." I hesitated. Was that really true? Would I have said that if my family was here? "I've been doing some thinking since yesterday, and I don't think anyone understands anyone else around here."

Her head cocked to the side.

"I mean, we're supposed to play roles in the workplace. We have to, so things get done. But this wacko culture we work in makes people take it to the extreme, I think." I shrugged. "I don't know where the real Kelvin was yesterday, or the real Theresa, or even the real Claire. I do know that they didn't mean to hurt you. And I'm pretty sure I haven't met the real Marcia, even though I talk to you every day."

Marcia looked at me as if I were offering the deed to the Brooklyn Bridge. I could feel sweat on my brow. It was time for decisive action... of some kind. Otherwise, nothing would ever change, and some people would be on the unemployment line very soon. The words needed to be spoken. It was time I ate my spinach.

"Marcia, would you like to have lunch with me today?"

There. It was out. The impact of a thousand invisible feet against my ass followed, and I wondered what was going through her mind. Not so long ago, I would rather have spent an hour cleaning tiger cages at the zoo than have lunch with Marcia. But I guess we all know what they say about desperate times.

Marcia looked at the floor and made a few weird motions with her jaw, as if she had a gobstopper she couldn't quite position right. Her hands rose to her hips, then fell, then rose again as she gave a loud sigh. "Fine. Call me at twelve-thirty." And with that, she stomped out.

Mirabile!

The dread was really beginning to set in when I noticed my CathMail icon blinking.

To: Gabriel Marino
From:
Re:

Jerry needs you. Be ready to help.

Archangel

I recoiled into the back of my chair. Jerry! In all the ruckus yesterday, I'd forgotten about the Gang of Six and my former boss. What had happened? And what was my Archangel friend up to now?

Arriving at no answers, I puttered around my office with busywork until my appointed hour for vittles with Marcia. I looked at my watch, feeling my jaw clench. Part of me didn't want to go through with it. But this was not the part of me that would get promoted, or keep the Rice-a-Roni on my daughter's dinner plate. So I walked down to her office and, fighting off one last urge to slink back to my phone and feign a schedule conflict, presented myself in her doorway.

"Good afternoon," I said.

She looked up from something she'd been reading. "Oh. Hello, Gabriel."

"So," I said, leaning against the door frame, "Are you hungry for anything in particular?"

With some surprise, I noticed that she looked uncertain. It was an expression I didn't see often. "Oh, um... we should stay close to the office. I have a busy afternoon. But otherwise... you decide."

"Okay," I said, and although the smile creeping on my face reflected pleasure at having a conversation with Marcia without baring fangs, it also reflected some mischievous anticipation. If the choice was mine, I was going to have some fun with it.

And so both of us wore exactly the same expressions as we walked through the doors of Jalapeño Paco's Mexicali Shack. This was a favorite haunt of mine... the portions were big, the prices were not, and the cheesiness of the decor had a charm that few people from Connecticut's Gold Coast ever saw. She looked at the life-sized cartoon statue of Jalapeño Paco—a six-foot rat wearing a sombrero and holding a taco like the Statue of Liberty's torch—and for one delicious second I thought she would bolt. But she saw me smirking, and her poker face returned.

"How delightful," she said, without a smile. "I walk past here every day, but I never realized this place was here."

"Yeah, I kinda guessed that," I said, pointing to the dining room. "Booth or table?"

She looked around. "Isn't there a maître' d'?"

"He's, ah, probably out sick today. Let's take a booth over there... it's farther from the kitchen, so there are fewer roaches."

She stiffened, but followed me to a booth and sat down. I tried to make her more comfortable with some small talk about the weather, but as we talked her eyes flicked down to the floor every 10 seconds or so. At first I thought it was a tic I'd never noticed before. Then it occurred to me.

"I was kidding about the roaches."

"Of course," she said. "I knew that." She smiled, spread her napkin on her lap, and shot another glance at the floor.

"Well," I said, "I thought we'd have lunch together today because... I think my whole relationship with you has been one misunderstanding after another." I watched her face carefully, but saw no reaction. "I didn't mean a lot of the things I said to you in the past, and I think—I hope—that maybe you might be going through the same thing."

Her eyes rolled to the right for a moment, then found mine again. "No," she said. "I meant everything I said to you. I always do. I consider myself a very honest person."

I held up my hands, "Wait, that's not what I meant. It's happening again. I'm trying to say that..."

"Hola!" barked the waiter, a skinny guy with slicked-back hair. He'd snuck up behind me without warning. I knew this guy from previous visits... he looked and sounded about as Mexican as Al Gore, and always walked a line between boredom and hostility towards the customers. "You gonna order?"

He directed the question at Marcia, and the sullen look on his face disappeared when she glared back at him.

"I beg your pardon," she said. "But if you can't address me with respect, I want to see your manager."

"Ah," squawked the waiter, looking to me for backup but finding none, "I apologize, señora. What, ah, would you like to have this fine, fine…" He looked at me again, this time with reproach. "Day?"

Marcia glowered for a moment longer, then looked down at her menu for the first time. Anger turned to concentration, then uncertainty, then bewilderment. I was about to offer some explanations when she fixed her glare at him again.

"I'll have what he's having," she said.

"Okay," said the waiter, turning to me. "You?"

I smiled. "Can I have the El Macho Grande Beef Burrito special? And give me some extra guacamole on the side for the nachos. A big dollop should do me fine."

I looked at Marcia. She looked like a trapped animal.

"You got it," said the waiter, scribbling on a pad. "And to drink?"

"Hmm," I said, scanning the list of sodas. Looking at Marcia, I said, "Why don't we make this a true business lunch?" Then, turning to the waiter, I said, "Two Coronas, please."

The waiter slouched off, leaving Marcia and me to our politeness. Several times I tried to steer the topic to current events, or to changing fashions, or to something funny the mayor said the other day. But each time, she yanked the conversation back to work... the status of my projects, somebody's late timesheet, the excessive volume of the Metallica songs blaring from Kelvin's desk radio. It was a sad substitute for the meeting of minds I'd hoped for. Then our beers came, with two solid thunks on the table and another grimace for Marcia from the waiter before he snuck back to the kitchen.

Marcia looked at the bottle in front of her. "No glasses?" she asked.

I picked my Corona up, clinked it against the one sitting on the table before her, then brought it to my lips. "Salud," I said, taking a welcome first sip.

The food, when it came, posed a similar problem. The burritos at Paco's were delicious, but Paco wasn't big on presentation: a burrito was a burrito, and if you had a problem with that... well, don't let the big rat bite you on the way out. When the waiter left, Marcia peered at hers. A lovely stream of bean curd and cheese oozed from a fissure in the side of her entrée, making my mouth water.

"How does one... eat this?" she said, her eyes never leaving the burrito.

I picked up my fork and knife. "Just rip into it with these, and whatever falls out, you scarf up before I snag it off your plate."

She poked at the burrito until some beef and rice crumbled off, then sampled the beef only.

"Not bad, I suppose, but a little dry," she said.

I smiled. "That's what the Corona's for," I said.

And so we dined, with me ravaging my lunch and Marcia prodding her burrito as if she expected it to explode. She liked the beer much better, after the initial shock of placing her lips on a bottle faded. And, in time, that allowed her to enjoy the food and the conversation... or at least, as far as I could tell. I ordered another round of beer when we'd drained our bottles, and by the time she was lunging at her burrito with gusto, it was time for a third round.

"You know," she said, "this is actually quite good."

"I thought you might like it," I said, handing her another Corona.

Then she began to talk, and great googly moogly, did the floodgates open. I got the lowdown on the history of her Mayflower family, and her daughter's grades at Bryn Mawr, and the outrageous property taxes she and her husband paid for their estate in Greenwich, and a whole slew of ultraconservative political opinions. Her husband, a Marine colonel, worked in military intelligence—a fact that brought a glow of pride to her face as she picked rice from her teeth. The Corona was dancing the light fantastic in my head by then, and as she chattered, I had visions of what her daughter's life must have been like, raised by a spook and a lizard.

"So tell me," said Marcia, chewing with her mouth open, "What's your favorite daddy moment with your daughter?" Before I could answer, she continued, "My favorite mommy moment was the day my daughter got her B.S. *summa cum laude*," she said, treating the phrase like a magical incantation.

I shrugged. "Easy. I was playing airplane with my daughter one day, hoisting her over my head like this," I said, raising my arms. "She had her arms stretched out like wings, and I ran around the room with her, again and again."

Marcia stopped chewing. "Goodness!" she said, eyes like two cue balls.

"No," I said. "She loved it. Not every kid would, I guess, but... well, that's my daughter. She was laughing and shrieking. And then, after a few minutes of that, I lowered her down like this." I brought my hands to my chest. "And she kissed me on the cheek."

"Aww," said Marcia.

"Then she barfed on my shoes," I said, smiling.

She stopped chewing again. "That's disgusting! Why would you tell me something like that?"

A look that was all too familiar returned to her eyes.

"Well, kids *are* disgusting, Marcia. Sometimes, that is. It's part of the charm."

Her lips drew into a pucker I knew too well. "But why would you say something like that, while... while I'm eating?"

I saw the hardness in her eyes again, and knew our sojourn into cameraderie was over. For the first time since I'd known her, we almost connected. It was what I'd been hoping for... what the beer and the burritos and the check was supposed to accomplish. Yet somehow, I screwed it up again. We missed each other somewhere, and now the only contact that seemed likely was the palm of her hand upside my face.

"I'm sorry," I said, looking down at my plate.

She looked up at the ceiling fan with that give-me-strength expression that pissed me off every time, then fixed her gaze on me again. "It's not the story, Gabriel. That was almost cute. I just don't understand how you... *are* sometimes. You don't respect authority, you betray my trust, almost injure me during the corporate retreat, and now you made me nauseous with that... that scatological word."

"Ah, Marcia... *scatological* actually means…"

"I don't give a shit!" she barked, banging the table.

I shifted uneasily. "…that."

"Stop correcting me!" she said. "That's another thing you and those animals in Editorial do."

"Marcia—"

"I've had enough," she said, wiping her face with the napkin. "You only brought me here to embarrass me, didn't you?"

I shook my head. "Pull you out of your element, yes. Embarrass you, no."

She scowled, then left.

As I ate the rest of my burrito, I imagined all the different paths my conversation with Marcia could have taken. We could have discussed the weather. Books. Cookie recipes. The topic would never matter, I now realized, because we were good for about 10 minutes of civility before someone came out swinging. Granted, she usually struck first, but... was I really as innocent as I thought? Or did I unconsciously wave from my side of the DMZ, with a peace flag in one hand and the middle finger extended on the other?

I had no answer as I returned to Cathedral, and my dread of our next encounter was soon compounded by the realization that it was about 3:00. The long lunch was over. It was tribunal time now.

Most of Cathedral was assembled in the big foyer where the Grand Ordinations were held, seated in rows facing a scarlet dais. Charles and the executives sat behind the table, note pads and glasses of water in front of them. Jerry was not among them. One chair was placed before the dais, and to my surprise I saw Marcia seated there. She was talking. I slipped into an empty seat in the last row, hoping my late entrance wasn't noticed.

"So I raised my arms like that cute little Mr. Flowers said, and I floooooooooated back! Like a sparrow in the air! Whee!" said Marcia, flapping her arms up and down.

People around me were whispering and giggling. The executives wore grim expressions... except for Charles, who was smiling slightly.

"And then! Then!" Marcia turned and pointed a finger at the assembled crowd. "Those ungrateful people in my group just... DROPPED me!" She looked perplexed for a moment, and then seemed to realize that she was pointing directly at Bobby Ortiz from Accounting. "Bobby!" she said, breaking into a smile.

I couldn't see Bobby's face from where I sat, but his chubby body shrank noticeably in his chair at this.

"Bobby!" she said again. "I love that tie, you big, strong, bull you. If I wasn't married..."

Muffled whoops of laughter erupted as Bobby covered his eyes with his hand. Everyone was talking now, with expressions of shock and amusement. Raising his hand, Charles yelled, "Silence! Please! No talking in this tribunal!"

Everyone shut up.

"Marcia," said Charles, his smile gone. "Are you drunk?"

Marcia turned in her seat again to face forward. "Me?" she said. Something like a hiccup followed, and then she said, "Never. My mind is clear, and my hands are steady."

Charles cleared his throat again, and the smile returned. Watching him, I now understood why he'd been smiling. This was bad... real bad. "Marcia, it's the determination of this tribunal that you are intoxicated. For the record, this is evidenced by your wild gestures, your lack of voice control, your referring to Stuart Flowers as 'that little doodiehead,' and by your inappropriate... ah, admiration for Robert Ortiz."

I looked around. If anyone was breathing, I couldn't tell.

"You were brought before this tribunal to help identify the people who ruined our retreat yesterday," said Charles, rising to his feet. "But now I think we've identified a larger problem. This disgraceful behavior casts doubt on your credibility... to say nothing of your competence."

"But Chuckie!" said Marcia. "He *was* a little doodiehead!"

Something needed to be done. I swallowed hard, then found the strength to rise.

"Charles?" I said.

All faces turned to me.

"Gabriel?" said Charles. "Do you have something to add?"

"Well, yes. I just wanted to say that I'm mostly responsible for Marcia's... um, exuberance. We had lunch together, and I insisted that she have some drinks with me."

Charles's expression of triumph faded as the murmuring started again. "Oh?"

"Yes," I said, looking at Marcia. "We were having a great conversation, exchanging lots of ideas for improving the market share of Cathedral's books. It was very productive, and we were very enthusiastic, and... well, in the spirit of this, I guess we had one too many."

Marcia gawked at me, her mouth open.

"Are you sure you want to say this?" said Charles. "A record is being kept, you know."

I raised my hand in the air. "Permission to, um, approach the bench?" I didn't know what hokey rules of order prevailed here, because I'd never been to a tribunal before. It sounded about right, though.

"Get over here," said Charles, crossing his arms.

Silence reigned again as I walked to the dais. I could feel Marcia's eyes on me as I passed her chair, but she said nothing. Then I stood directly in front of Charles, out of earshot to everyone but him and the executives flanking him behind the dais.

"You said that if I ever wanted to talk..." I said in a low voice.

Charles glared, but kept his voice low. "What are you trying to do here, Gabe?"

"Not here," I said. "In your office. Like you said."

He looked at me for what felt like 10 years, then motioned me to step aside so that everyone could see him again.

"This tribunal is suspended," he said. "Everyone should go back to their offices now. We will reconvene at a later date if necessary."

And that was that. With a rush of mystified babbling, everyone rose and clumped together in groups as they departed from the foyer.

"My office," said Charles, after everyone had gone. "Now."

Chapter 12

TAKE THESE BROKEN WINGS

And Zacharias said unto the angel, Whereby shall I know this? for I am an old man, and my wife well stricken in years. And the angel answering said unto him, I am Gabriel, who stands in the presence of God; and am sent to speak unto thee, and to show thee these glad tidings.

—Luke 1:18-19

The inside of Charles's office was a showcase for pomposity, a dumbass American imagining of an English baron's office. Lemon-scented Pledge oozed from all the mahogany and oak, and the overstuffed leather chairs groaned with a rich flatulence as we settled into them for our chat. Charles's great slab of a desk had nothing on it—save for a bejeweled clock that ticked too loudly and a bust of some guy wearing a laurel wreath—and as Charles gazed at me across the sea of wood, I marveled at how the finest desks are always purchased by people like Charles. The veneer would never know an errant pen stroke. The wood would never be seasoned by hand oils. Once, in college, I wrote a love sonnet using a box of Fruity Tooties on my lap as my working surface. But the only things that touched this desk were the elbows of Charles's suits and (it was rumored) the bare butt of his secretary.

"This must be quite a moment for you," said Charles, leaning on that lovely oak.

"You have no idea," I said.

He smiled—I think—and pushed the bridge of his glasses up his nose. "I've been hoping for this, you know. And I'm happy that you're here so soon."

"Why?" I said. "You don't know what I'm going to say."

"Oh, I think we're on the same page. Your dissatisfaction is no secret, Gabe. Had you spoken up sooner, you could have saved many people some… unpleasantness."

"Including you?" I said.

The sharklike smile, which I'd first seen in the tribunal and noticed again here, faded. "My opinion on the subject doesn't matter. Until, that is, I hear from competent professionals like yourself that one of our company's leaders isn't leading. Then my opinion matters a great deal," he said.

"Okay," I said. "But shouldn't I be talking to someone in H.R. right now? Or, come to think of it, shouldn't I be complaining to my supervisor first, before breaking the chain of command?"

Charles crossed his arms. "Perhaps you don't understand," he said. "I'm giving you an opportunity here."

"No, I get that part," I said. "What I don't follow is why you're looking to fire someone you promoted only a few weeks ago. You called Marcia a rising star then."

"Why are you defending her? You *are* the same Gabriel Marino who got Marcia drunk before today's tribunal, are you not?"

"I got her lunch, Charles. She got herself drunk. And no, I wasn't trying to pick a fight today. I was trying to avoid one." Sweat broke out on my brow. Some peacekeeper I was.

Charles leaned forward again. "So why are you here?"

He stared at me, and—even though it made my stomach churn—I stared back. It was a twist on the art of business: We were here to make a deal. His agenda was on the table, whether he acknowledged it or not. Mine had not yet been revealed. It was the only way I could think of to make him uncomfortable. Time to make my move.

"I want you to leave her alone," I said.

"Pardon?"

"Marcia. Don't fire her, and don't go snooping around my department looking for dirt. Just let her be."

That cocky look returned to his face. "Are you familiar with the battle of Gettysburg, Gabe?"

Oh, crap. More war metaphors.

"I think I remember a thing or two from my school days, yes."

Charles got up, walked over to a small oak cabinet near the window, and flipped up the top. This was intriguing—the hinges were hidden well. Reaching inside, he pulled out two glasses and a bottle of what looked like brandy. He poured a glass for himself, then one for me. Raising the bottle up to stop the flow, he miscalculated the timing a little and sent a few drops raining down to the carpet.

"Damn," he said.

"Oopsie," I said, smirking.

"Anyway," he said, "the most important lesson from that battle is the value of good ground." He walked back towards me, holding the glasses. "Seize the good ground, and you can defend yourself from anyone. If you get to the top of the hill before your adversary does, you get to fire down at him. And win."

He handed me a glass. "You're not standing on good ground, son," he said.

"Maybe not," I said, taking a sip and trying not to grimace. It was the cheap stuff. "But I have something you want."

"Oh really?" he said, sitting back down in his chair. "And what would that be?"

I thought for a moment. "Well, there's probably an analogy for it in the Boer War somewhere, but who really gives a shit about history?" I said.

The smile disappeared from his face. God, that felt good.

"Don't ask me how I know this," I continued, "because it's a long story. You might not even believe it if I told you, but here's the gist of it." I paused for effect, and sipped my brandy. "Yuck, where did you buy this stuff? A bodega in Washington Heights?"

He said nothing, but the look he gave me was icy.

"Anyway, here's the thing," I said. "Six of your other rising stars are plotting against you, behind your back. They're being helped by at least two other men from outside. One's a big, doofy-looking guy who carries a gun and uses the word *knucklehead* a lot. Don't ask. The other one's his boss, I think. I don't even know how to describe this guy... he's worth more than most major corporations.He knows that money is power, and he knows how to use it." I stopped there, expecting Charles to bust out laughing. The whole story was pretty thin, but now that I'd put it into words, it sounded—

"Interesting," said Charles. "Do these people have names?"

"Yes," I said.

"But you don't want to tell me."

"Not unless you promise to leave Marcia alone," I said. "No firing. No harassment, sexual or otherwise. And no digging around for excuses to fire her, either. You do your job, she does hers, I do mine, and everybody's happy." My bravado wavered as I realized two things. First, at this moment—and perhaps only for this moment—I had more power than anyone at Cathedral. And second, this moment was about to end.

Charles studied me without expression, then said, "If you're trying to impress me, you've succeeded."

I sighed. "Honestly, Charles? I don't care what you think of me."

"Perhaps, but the stunt you just pulled would impress Nietzsche. I respect that," he said.

"So, do we have a deal?"

"Yes," he said. "I will do as you ask. Now tell me, who are these people, and what are they up to?"

I nodded, then began my story. It didn't take long. I left out the parts about kissing Claire and getting chased around the office by Knucklehead, but I was pretty thorough in explaining everything else. When I was done, Charles looked thoughtful as he swirled the brandy in his glass. I expected anger, or at least surprise, but he belied no feeling as he mulled my tale over.

"You're sure about this?" he finally asked.

"Positive," I said.

"A hostile takeover? You heard Oliver Barney say that?"

"No," I said, "But it seems logical, given the circumstances."

He stood up. "Very well," he said. "I'll take it from here." He extended his hand. "Thanks for stopping by, Gabe. This has been very... productive."

I shook his hand. "You'll stick to our agreement, right?"

He smiled again. "As long as this meeting remains our secret, yes. I'll be watching you, Gabe."

He said nothing more, so I walked out of his office and headed back towards mine. I wasn't sure whether he meant that last remark as a threat or as an unspoken promise of rewards to come. I hoped it was the latter. A tiny voice in my head reminded me that I'd passed up an opportunity to remove the 800-pound gorilla from my back: Marcia was going nowhere, and I couldn't even tell her about my good deed, since Charles put a gag order on me. Thinking back to the Archangel's last message, I wondered if I helped Jerry somehow by cutting my deal with Charles. Too many questions, and not enough answers. It was time for an appeal to a higher power.

The workday was ending as I made my way back, and I saw Claire and Kelvin laughing together as they headed away from me towards the door. Turning into my office, I sat at my desk and called up CathMail. I didn't know how to address the message, since the recipient didn't have an e-mail address. Then an idea hit me, and when I called up the Archangel's last message, I hit the reply button. Presto! The usual message form popped up... something that never happened if the address line was left blank.

To:
From: Gabriel Marino
Subject: A Little Help?

My Fine Winged Friend,

Hi there. Frankly, I'm at a loss for words, since the last time I directly addressed a divine being was in grade school. The circumstances are the same this time: I need some assistance—or at least some good advice. And I'm putting it in writing this time, since I'm no longer 9 years old and afraid of going to hell for flinging dog poop at my sister.

Still, I'm troubled. I've tried to do the right thing in the past few weeks, and I admit that in a few cases I could have tried harder. My friend Jerry is in trouble, if he's still alive at all. And I... well, I was about to itemize my recent failings for you, but you probably know all about it. Could you...

Oh, screw it. This message is only going to bounce, right? Do they have a dead letter office in heaven? And if so, do all prayers end up there? Is the postmaster asleep on the job? Or is he dead? And what was he thinking when he created the platypus?

Theologically,

Gabe

Smirking, I hit the send button and was surprised by an onrush of despair. I'd just survived a pissing match with my CEO, and now I was thumbing my nose at my creator. Recent events had me convinced I was slipping into a mild depression, but now it was looking more like a metaphysical death wish.

Suddenly, almost instantaneously, Cathmail dinged over the computer speakers and the icon blinked. Nah, I thought, as I clicked on the icon. It can't be. It had been only seconds.

To: Gabriel Marino
From:
Subject: Re: A Little Help?

Don't forget that your role in the world is constant. You are Fortitudo Dei. You are one of the Four. You are the messenger; the gift of hope must come from you.

Archangel

I felt the feet of a thousand little angels dancing down my spine as I read this. How could anyone have the time to read my message and respond so quickly? And more importantly, what the hell was he talking about? Before I knew what I was doing, I clicked on the reply button and started again.

To:
From: Gabriel Marino
Subject: Re: Re: A Little Help?

Yo Archie,

Love the cryptic Latin stuff, though *fortitudo* seems kinda questionable. "Strength of God" I most certainly am not. You're writing to a guy who fires innocent editors. Who drops his boss on her butt. And who—when he's sure everyone else in the house is asleep—watches that cable channel where ugly people have angry sex. I mean, sure, my name's Gabriel, and it's not like I didn't hear that where's-your-halo joke a thousand times in Catholic high school, har dee har har. But you've gotta trust me on this. The being of light who appeared to St. Joseph and the shepherds looks very pretty on the Christmas manger, but he ain't me.

Besides... if I really have an army of angel-soldiers at my back, you've gotta admit that I suck as an overseer. How am I supposed to instill hope in anybody when my career, my marriage, and my LIFE are going to pieces? I'm just trying to do my job down here. Now I have to do yours, too? Speak, o feathered one. Act. Do I have to get down on my knees and beg?

Gabe

P.S. Don't answer that last question.

P.P.S. How did you send that message so quickly?

My finger depressed the send button again, and although I half-expected an immediate reply, I still flinched when my computer dinged and the icon started blinking again. There was another sound as well... a brief sputter from somewhere within the CPU's frame. As I started reading, I thought I smelled burning plastic.

To: Gabriel Marino
From:

Subject: Re: Re: Re: A Little Help?

When we crossed descension, we lost our light but not our truths. Why do you ask what you already know?

I stared. If I wasn't mistaken, my archangel was getting a little testy. I shook my head in wonder. Apparently my talent for pissing people off extended beyond the mortal world. Why was all this stuff happening at the same time? The acrid smell from the computer was growing stronger, and now I thought I saw my screen flicker a little. I reached for the phone, dialed the techies' number, and stared at the message on my screen.

"What do you want?" The voice on the other end sounded male, slightly foreign, and annoyed.

I haven't said a word yet, I thought. *Is the whole world mad at me now?*

"Raj?" I said.

"Yes."

"This is Gabe. I think you better get down here. I've got smoke coming out of my CPU."

"Smoke. Okay. I'll be right there."

I smiled as I hung up the phone. *That* changed his tone pretty quick. It's hard to get a techie's attention most of the time because hanging around users makes them feel unclean. But if you tell them your machine's on fire, they leave skid marks on the carpet getting down to your office. I looked at my flickering computer and sighed. If the techies didn't have a spare box in that dimly lit cave of horrors they worked in, they'd have to order another one for me. They'd want to know if I budgeted for any spare machines this year, and when I told them I didn't, they'd pout and gnash their teeth. This would lead to an impassioned but ever-so-slow exchange of e-mails between their VP and mine, with each trying halfheartedly to force the other to pay for my machine. It would be the corporate equivalent of watching turtles fight. In the meantime, my projects would pile up while the deadlines marched towards the brink of today.

"Hello," said Raj, standing in my doorway with a fire extinguisher in one hand and a bottle of spring water in the other. "Is there fire?"

I pointed to the machine. "No, but I think something burned out in there." I could feel a headache coming on, probably from the smoke.

Raj set his firefighting equipment down, looked at the screen, and then sniffed around the back of the machine.

"Power supply," he said. "Is burned out."

I slouched in my chair, feeling defeated. "Does that mean the whole thing's trashed?"

He looked at the machine, bringing his hand to his mouth. He chewed on his thumbnail for a moment. "Maybe. We'll see," he said.

He disconnected the CPU from the monitor and the wall and picked it up, leaving my monitor on the desk. I watched his hands as he did this, noting how gently he handled the components. He now held my CPU in his hands, and I nearly cracked up because he cradled it like a baby. I half expected him to start rocking it, but he only looked down at it with an expression of concern. Man, these tech guys develop weird relationships with their machines.

"I'm sorry about this," he said.

I grinned, rubbing my temple. "It's okay, Raj. It's not your fault I got a machine made by K-Mart."

I expected him to smile back, but he didn't.

"No," he said. "I lost my temper when I sent that message."

I looked at Raj, and he looked back at me. As I wondered what he meant, my hand went to my temple and rubbed it. The headache was getting worse, but that wasn't the strangest part. Raj, too, was looking green around the gills all of a sudden. I could feel something—the rude beginnings of an idea—being formed in my mind, but it wasn't forming easily. It was something akin to the burning frustration I felt back in high school, staring at some bizarre problem on the board in chemistry class. Now an idea was growing, and it took the form of words, and I found myself saying those words without really knowing why.

"You were never angry with me before," I said. The sentence came from nowhere, and I spoke it with a hurt as profound as it was uncalled for.

Raj looked back at me with an expression that looked divided between puzzlement and regret. "It caught me by surprise, too," he said. "You never asked me a question that stupid."

Somewhere in the back of my mind, the underpinnings of reality as I knew it were buckling and straining. I remember a film clip I saw on the Discovery channel once, showing the Tacoma Narrows Bridge—that marvel of bad engineering—undulating in the winds of a storm like a child's crepe paper streamer. It's a fascinating thing to see, because ordinarily your mind just doesn't go there. Bridges don't have waves that toss cars around like toys. It seemed to defy the laws of physics... and yet, there it was. I looked hard at Raj now, and he looked the way he always did. His English had improved suddenly, which was odd, but the Pakistani accent was still there. Yet somehow this wasn't Raj I was addressing. No, this was very different.

"What are we talking about, Raj?" I asked.

He smiled. "You."

I felt nauseous all of a sudden.

"I gotta go," I said. "I think I'm going to be sick."

Raj shifted the bulk of the CPU's weight from one arm to the other, but stayed in the doorway. "Sick," he said. "No, you're all right. Why don't you come out for a beer after work?" He looked at me with amusement. "I think it's time we talked."

"Okay," I said. Again, the word was just... there.

"Meet me by the front door," he said, and walked away down the hall with my computer.

I just sat there, stunned. Then, pulling my trash can over to my chair, I did what any man would do if he thought he was in the presence of his maker... or at least, an agent of his maker: I barfed. Hard. And wondered how this, too, was going to affect my career.

Chapter 13

WHEN ANGELS DRINK

Yet Michael the archangel, when contending with the devil he disputed about the body of Moses, durst not bring him a railing accusation, but said, The Lord rebuke thee.

—Daniel 1:9

Raj and I walked out of Cathedral into the night. A steady breeze cooled the sweat on my forehead as we headed towards the Blarney Stone, but I still felt feverish. I wasn't sure why. The awe I felt in my office was gone now: I was just taking a stroll to the Blarney Stone to have a beer with Raj the techie geek. And while he was brilliant when it came to computers, my Pakistani pal did *not* have wings—his English was sputtery, and he made occasional mistakes on the job that were legendary. Show me a guy who was almost fired for redirecting Cathedral's web hits to "Goliath Gary's WankCam," and I will not show you a divine being on Earth.

As we neared the bar, I slowed and waited for Raj to turn and match my pace. Someone had parked a Harley Davidson on the sidewalk, right in front of the door. Its chrome shone with a pugnacity I've rarely seen in a vehicle, and spraypainted on one side of its black gas tank were the words, "Judgment Cometh." My curiosity got the better of me, and as Raj gawked at the bike I walked around to the other side, where the tank read, "So Get Your Shit Together."

"Raj?" I said.

"Yes?"

"I don't want you to get the wrong idea here, because I'm married and I'm pretty happy with my hetero ways. But I'm wondering about that feeling I got when we were talking." I looked around to make sure no one was listening to this.

Raj grinned. "And what feeling would that be?"

"Well, that's the thing. I don't know what it is. I got a headache, and then I felt this... this overwhelming joy, and love, and then... I threw up."

He laughed, then turned to open the door to the bar. "Threw up. If you think that something, you're in for big surprise," he said. gesturing me inside.

We entered the smoky dive and looked around at today's crowd. The Blarney Stone wasn't the kind of place where they swept the eyeballs up after last call, but you wouldn't want to order a spritzer or a sloe comfortable screw with a twist here, either. The usual assortment of scavengers slouched at the bar, and a few Izod-clad college kids were slumming in a booth against the wall. The ones who caught my attention, however, were two people seated at a table in the middle: a man and a woman. There was nothing remarkable about them, really, but for some reason they seemed like Technicolor people seated in a black-and-white world. And they were looking right at me, from the moment we entered the bar.

"Raj?" I said, leaning against the jukebox by the door for support. "I'm not feeling so well, all of a sudden."

"It will pass," he said, taking hold of my arm. "Go to that table. I want you to meet friends."

I didn't want to, but I allowed Raj to steer me to where his two pals sat. Fortunately, he was right about the queasiness... it was fading slowly, and as we approached the table I noticed that Raj's two friends were wearing grim expressions as well. The closer I got to the man, the more I realized how huge he was... broad shoulders with a potbelly and halfway between six and seven feet tall. He wore a leather motorcycle jacket and sported a beard that made him look like Lenin. As Raj and I reached the table, he rose to his feet and grinned.

"Gabie baby!" he boomed, offering me his meaty hand.

I took it and felt instant regret, for he nearly shook my shoulder out of its socket. His big grin continued to widen as I looked into his eyes and felt that trippy feeling come over me again. Gone was the gloom of the Blarney Stone, vanished were the woes of the world. Suddenly I was five again, on Christmas eve, with a stack of Christmas presents taller than me under the tree, and all the time from now to forever to open them.

"Mikey?" I said, only it was more like the child speaking now.

"Haya doin', buddy! Damn, it's good to see you!" he said.

At this, the woman seated next to him rose and thwacked his bicep with her hand. She was conservatively dressed, blue blazer over a crisp white blouse and her black hair tied in a severe bun. The hairstyle made her look old, but there were no crow's feet or wrinkles. As she fixed Michael with a stare of disapproval, I marvelled at how the features of her face could seem so friendly and open, yet convey a strength that I somehow never wanted to test. The big man she glared at didn't respond to the look, but he did look cowed.

"Gabe, this is Muriel," said Raj.

"Pleased to meet you, Gabe," she said.

I took her hand, looked at each of them in turn, and shook my head.

"Okay, guys," I said. "I like a joke as much as anybody, but isn't this a little heavyhanded? I mean, I'm Gabriel, and you're Michael, and you're Muriel—although if I remember my Sunday school correctly, that M in your name doesn't belong—and... Raj?"

My voice seemed to startle Raj out of a daydream. "Huh?" His eyes shifted from Muriel to me.

"Call me crazy, but I don't remember any Pakistanis in the Old Testament."

He nodded, as if he'd been expecting the question. "I'm not an angel."

"Nor am I," said Muriel with a kindly smile.

Michael laughed and took a gulp of his beer. "Ain't no wings on me, man." This earned him another thwack on the arm from Muriel.

I stared for a moment, then realized my error. "Okay, I meant *archangel*."

The three of them looked at each other. No one spoke.

"Well?" I said, making a show of looking at my wristwatch. "I'm just trying to play along with the joke, guys. The least you could do is show a little wit."

Muriel looked down. "It's not a joke, Gabe. We're people, just like you. And those are the names our parents gave us. Please be patient. The answers to your questions aren't easy to explain."

"So I'm not an archangel," I said. "And neither are you."

"Nope," said Michael.

Something about this didn't seem right. I remembered the nauseous feeling that nearly overpowered me when I first sat down. It was gone now.

"Are you guys in some kind of weird cult?"

They looked at each other again. It wasn't a good look. In fact, it was the kind of look I'd wear if I had to teach a 7-year-old how to do my income taxes. At this point, the waitress came over and said, "Hey. Can I get you guys anything?"

I looked at my three tablemates, but no answer was forthcoming. Turning to the waitress, I said, "Yeah. Can I get the strongest drink in the house, please? I don't care what's in it, as long as it's nasty."

She blinked back at me. "You sure?"

"Yeah," I said, shifting my gaze to my tablemates. "In fact, give me two of them. I need it to deal with the Significant Look Society here."

"It's your funeral," she said, marking her pad. She looked at Muriel. "You?"

"Could you tell me if you have any blush wines, please?"

The waitress scrunched her lips into a pucker and appeared to think hard about this. "Yep," she finally said.

"Wonderful," said Muriel. "Is there a list I could see? Do you recommend a particular vineyard?"

"We got pink," said the waitress.

"Lovely," said Muriel. I looked for sarcasm on her face, but found only gratitude.

The waitress sighed, noted Muriel's order, then turned to Michael, who had been mentally relieving her of her tight black jeans and snug-fitting T-shirt for some time now. "You?" she said.

Michael grinned. "I've been looking for a reason to avoid utter despair at the pointless, nihilistic tendencies of humanity. Your ass does that for me." He looked around expectantly, but no one reacted except Muriel, who cracked him on the arm with—it seemed—more than her usual vigor.

"What?" said Michael.

The waitress sighed and crossed her arms.

"For someone who provides such a valuable service to the world," said Michael, "you're no fun. I'll have a pint of Yuengling."

Muriel tensed for another strike, then lowered her hand. Michael only grinned, shaking a little with malevolent good cheer.

I looked at Raj, who'd been watching all this with disappointment.

"He doesn't remember," said Raj. "I thought I bring him here, it might..."

"Jog his memory?" said Muriel. "Of course not. You saw how he fell."

I crossed my hands in a T. "Okay, time out, everyone. First, let's stop talking about me in the third person. It's annoying. Second, I want somebody to tell me who I am, or was, or will be, without looking at everyone else first."

Silence followed this. I could almost feel them not glancing at other, but their eyes never left mine. Finally, Michael spoke.

"Well, let's just say we thought we'd find you working in a mailroom somewhere. Or doing phone sales," he said. "Maybe anchoring a local news broadcast."

"You are Fortitudo Dei," said Muriel.

"You are Gabriel, who stands before God," said Raj.

"All righty then," I said, as deadpan as I could manage. "Now, what do you people think that means, exactly? And don't tell me I'm an angel or archangel or whatever. I'll pour this beer over all your heads. I mean it."

"It's not a question of what you *are*," said Muriel, "We're trying to tell you—and we apologize for doing it so badly—is what you *were*."

"I need to get hammered before I hear any more of this," I said. As if on cue, the waitress reappeared, setting down our drinks. I looked for a moment at mine—two vile-looking shot glasses filled with something purple—and bolted them down, one after the other. My eyes crossed from the scorching in my throat, but otherwise the shots weren't acting nearly as fast as I wished.

"Slow down, man," said Michael. "You're gonna need every synapse. We've got some heavy metaphysical shit to lay on you."

I swallowed the firewater, then plunked the glasses down on the bar. "All right, I'll play the straight man. Assuming I'm going along with this—and I'm not, okay?—and that I'm Gabriel, and you're Michael, and you're Uriel, and you're... Vishnu the Pakistani Destroyer of Computers?"

"I am Raphael," said Raj, glaring at Michael, who was stifling an outburst of laughter.

"Okay, so we've got that settled," I said. "What I want to know is, how come you guys know all this and I don't?"

They looked at each other.

"Stop that!" I said.

Muriel took a deep breath. "It's because you were the first one to cross descension," she said. "It's hard to make this clear for you. This language is so limited."

"*That's* why!" said Michael, banging the table with his fist. He looked overjoyed. "I thought I was stupid, or somethin'."

Muriel smiled at him and said, "Well, in your case, a certain hormonal imbalance gets in the way of effective communication. But then again, you never needed to be very bright."

Michael beamed. It sounded like an insult, but if he took it that way, I couldn't tell.

Muriel continued, "You crossed first, and we followed... but not before watching you complete the fall, we'd never done it before. As it turned out, we were wise to hesitate because the fall was, shall we say, hard to predict. Raj, for example, ended up on the other side of the planet. And you..."

"What about me?" I said, still not sure I was believing any of this.

"Well," she said, "what happened can't be described in the words you use now."

I sighed. "Try. Please?"

She looked thoughtful for a moment, then nodded. "You fell on your head."

Another amused snort came from Michael, and now even Raj was pretending to wipe beer from his chin with a napkin.

"And this is why I don't remember anything you're telling me?" I said.

"Right." She cast her eyes down, and once again I was struck by the regal beauty that was half-hidden there.

I motioned to the waitress for another drink. Emphatically.

Raj shook his head. "It was horrible. I wanted so badly to help you, but I couldn't."

Muriel smiled. "Poor Raj," she said, patting his arm. "Always the healer."

"I thought it was awesome," said Michael, shrugging. "I mean, a celestial fuckup of that magnitude doesn't happen every day. BA-BOOM!" he yelled, raising his hands into the air for emphasis. Some of the night creatures at the bar glanced our way. "Like a mushroom cloud, only way cooler," he said, smiling. He caught sight of the nosy boozers at the bar. "The fuck you lookin' at!" he roared, causing several heads to spin back around.

"You'll have to forgive Michael," said Muriel. "He's still a little judgmental these days, only his judgment isn't what it once was."

"Look guys," I said as the waitress placed another little glass of sulfuric acid in front of me, "This started out as a pretty far-fetched story, but now you're piling it high and deep. My head is fine. Yours, on the other hand, I don't know about. Maybe some lithium would help." I slammed my drink down and wiped my lips. My tablemates hung their heads. "Besides," I said, smiling and offering my palms, "If you were angels in heaven, playing your little angel games all day, why would you leave that to come here?"

More silence. Someone had cranked up the old jukebox while I was talking, and the first few fiddle notes of "Devil Went Down to Georgia" were playing. Raj and Muriel didn't seem to notice, but Michael's eyes met mine and we both chuckled.

"Well," said Raj, "We left because we were following you."

I rolled my eyes. "Guys, if you want me to buy this crap you're peddling, it won't help to blame the whole thing on me."

Muriel leaned forward. "Gabe, we don't know why you left, but you did. It wasn't like you to do something like this unannounced. You were always so… verbal. It was clear that you were looking for something, or someone, but you never explained it. You just went."

I smirked. "Well, why didn't you ask God why I did it? He's supposed to know everything."

They did the annoying look-at-each-other thing again, and now Michael looked angry.

"Because we don't snitch, you ungrateful ass. You know what would've happened if he saw you? I mean, fuck, he struck Onan dead for playing with himself. Can you imagine what he'd do to you?"

Raj looked thoughtful. "He never said we no come back. Other places, it was no problem."

Muriel sighed. "It's not the destination that matters. We're not supposed to be *people*. I doubt he's happy about this."

It was hard to keep from bursting out laughing. Pretending to look around conspiratorially, I raised my hand to my mouth and mock-whispered, "You think he knows we're here?"

They all nodded. No one smiled. I could feel my spirits sink as I realized that, although these people were kooks, they weren't much fun to play with.

"Did you ever find it?" said Raj.

"Find what?" I said.

"What you were looking for," said Muriel. "Do you know what it was? An object? A person?"

Despite the torrents of alcoholic fun in my bloodstream, I was tiring of this game. My eyes had wandered over Muriel's shoulder towards the door, and as she spoke I began to invent excuses for leaving. But now the door opened, and in walked Kelvin, Claire, and Theresa. Claire was laughing at something Kelvin said as the three of them walked towards the bar. Theresa looked serious, as usual. I wondered how I would introduce my new friends when they spotted us. The truth probably wouldn't go over so well.

"Gabe?" said Muriel.

"Huh?" I said, still looking at Claire. I hadn't realized how incredible she looked today.

"Have you found it? Or her?"

Before I could answer, I saw Michael's entire body twitch. He'd followed my gaze to the bar, and was now glaring in that direction.

"Son of a bitch!" he said, leaping to his feet. Before any of us could react, he grabbed the bottle of Budweiser he'd been drinking by the neck and, with a flourish, smashed it on the edge of the table. I recoiled, trying to protect my face from the glass shards and beer flying everywhere.

"Michael!" shrieked Muriel.

Holding the broken bottle in one hand, Michael picked up the chair he was sitting on and thrust it before him like a shield. The effect was striking, given the sheer size of him. It wasn't the first time I'd seen an angry biker cut loose in a dive, but the size of this one—and the lunacy of our conversation—gave his anger a scary edge.

"Long time no see, dirtbag!" bellowed Michael, walking over to the bar with his weapons. To my dismay, he was walking straight towards my three coworkers. This was going to be hard to explain at the water cooler tomorrow, if anyone survived at all.

Theresa looked back at Michael in horror, and Kelvin screamed. Michael's body blocked my view of Claire, but since Michael had paused in front of them and faced directly forward, I assumed he was talking to her. I rose to my feet.

"Wh-who are you?" said Claire, in a voice wavering with terror.

"Kicked your ass clear around the lake of fire, and you don't remember me?"

"Michael," said Theresa, her voice carrying far more conviction than her face. "You're mistaking her for someone else."

"Hey, buddy, ease up, will you?" said the bartender. I wondered if he'd have one of those buttons on the floor that he could press with his foot to summon the cops, the way banks do. Probably not.

"Stay out of this," said Michael. "You don't know what this... *thing* is." He pointed at Claire with the bottle, eliciting gasps from Theresa and Kelvin.

"Michael," I said.

"Just you and me now, asshole."

"Michael!" I yelled, walking towards them. I had no idea what I could do to stop him if he decided to maul Claire—he outweighed me by at least 80 pounds—but I had to do something.

"Let's finish what we started!" As Michael said this, the hand holding the jagged bottle also rose.

"Gladium Dei!" I yelled. I have no idea where that came from... it was out of my mouth like a hiccup.

He stopped and turned to glare at me. "Are you going to help me here, or what?"

"Stop it," I said. "Put the bottle down, and the chair. She's my friend."

Michael's face registered shock. The chair clattered to the floor at Claire's feet, and the bottle lowered back to Michael's side. He mouthed words but couldn't say them. Then shock gave way to outrage, and the words came back. Claire looked on the verge of tears.

"You want to run that by me again?"

I cleared my throat. "I said she's my friend, and my coworker. She's done nothing to hurt you. So leave her alone, please." I felt a hand touch my shoulder.

"Gabe," said Muriel, "Do you know what that is?"

I looked from Claire, who was cowering against Theresa, to Michael, to Muriel. "I know who *I* think she is," I said. "Why don't you tell me who *you* think she is?"

Muriel shook her head. "We can't say its name," she said. "That empowers it. But I can tell you it's not one of us."

Michael turned back to Claire and raised the bottle. "Make that *wasn't* one of us."

Drunken minds wander, and as I watched the bottle trace a slow arc towards the ceiling, I wondered why fear paralyzes. I wondered how the Archangel of Judgment could hold an eons-old grudge against an editorial assistant who bothered nobody, and who cooed deliciously when kissed. I wondered whether I believed any of the whoppers I'd been listening to all night. And yes, as I beheld a murder that was about to happen whether I intervened or not, I wondered how this, too, would affect my chances of promotion.

Chapter 14

THE JUDAS KISS

And Satan entered into Judas, who was surnamed Iscariot, one of the twelve. And he went, and discoursed with the chief priests and the magistrates, how he might betray him to them. And they were glad, and convenanted to give him money. And he promised. And he sought opportunity to betray him in the absence of the multitude.

—Luke 22: 3-6

"Stop it," I said.

The room had gone deathly quiet, and my words sounded less like the voice of reason than a foghorn. When I was a kid, my typical approach to handling the school bully was to fork over my milk money, or my four-color clicky pen, or my new denim jacket, with a smile. The price of peace was always less than I was willing to lose teeth for. When my history lessons finally got around to Neville Chamberlain giftwrapping the Sudetenland for Hitler, I remember thinking, *now that's a man.*

Michael turned and looked at me again.

"Put the bottle down," I said, walking over to him and gently—as if I was ruffling a parakeet's feathers—placed my hand on the elbow of his raised arm.

The rage in his stare foretold weeks, perhaps months, of hospital convalescence for me. His labored breathing promised the use of painkillers and physical therapy. All of this I'd seen before, in the parade of bad-tempered stupidheads I went to grade school with. But now there was something new. Frozen for a moment with my hand on Michael's huge elbow, I saw his bared teeth and realized that having an earlobe bitten off was—for the first time in my life—possible.

"Please," I said.

"What possible purpose will that serve?" said Michael.

I'm Neville freakin' Chamberlain, buddy, I thought. *Kick my ass, rule the world… I don't care. Just leave me alone.*

The arm with the bottle lowered, and I heard sighs of relief.

"I think you guys should leave," said the bartender. He was standing about twenty feet away, looking relaxed and wiping a mug with a dishtowel. It didn't help my nervous state to realize that, had Michael charged me, the bartender would probably have stopped wiping the mug... and that's all.

"He's right," I said, taking the bottle from Michael's hand and placing it on the bar. "We better go."

With a rush of breath, Claire got up from her stool and ran to the back of the bar. Theresa shot me a chilly look before getting up to follow her. Kelvin remained seated, gaping, as he'd done throughout the whole episode.

Muriel and Raj had come up behind me, and together we guided Michael towards the door of the bar.

"Nice friends you have, Gabe!" called Theresa.

I looked over my shoulder to see Claire and Theresa huddled by the jukebox. It looked like Claire was sobbing. Theresa, on the other hand, looked about ready to smite the Sword of God all by herself.

"I'm sorry," I said. "I..." But the words wouldn't come, and the rest of the bar was looking at me as if my departure was the best idea they'd ever had. Shrugging, I followed my three "friends" out the door.

The fresh air seemed to calm Michael down further, and he seemed to laugh a little when Muriel said something to him I couldn't quite hear. I pulled Raj aside for a moment.

"Raj, how did I just get away with that?"

"With that?" he said. "With what?"

"Stopping Mikey," I said, surprised again that I was using the familiar version of his name. "You saw him. He was... Christ, I've never seen anybody that mad before. And..."

"And?" said Raj.

I sighed. "I never won a fight with wimpy resistance before. It's never worked," I said.

Raj shrugged. "He is sword. You are strength." He looked at me as if that were self-evident.

"A moron is what he is," said Michael, now approaching us with Muriel.

I met his gaze and saw that the anger was gone, replaced by something like disappointment.

"Mikey," I said, "I can't have you killing my coworkers. It's not nice." I looked at Muriel for support, but she merely looked down. If she was choosing sides, it wasn't apparent.

"Listen close, Gabe," said Michael, crossing his great arms and fixing me with a gaze that made me feel like a shrimp on a toothpick. "Because I'm only gonna say this once. I don't give a muskrat's ass who you work with. It's your life, you know? You chose this wacked-out plane of existence, and that's cool, and if we were stupid enough to chase after you, well... that's our problem. But..."

He uncrossed his arms and pointed at me.

"If I find out you're boinking that thing, I'll rip you apart. And if you think I'm kidding, just try me. Comprende?"

A chill jitterbugged down my spine. I looked at Muriel.

"Stay away from her, Gabe," she said. "Get another job, if that's what it takes."

I turned and walked away. I'd had enough of this circus a half hour ago, and now I just felt numb to the whole thing. Walking down the street towards the subway station, I could feel their eyes following me and knew they were talking. I couldn't care less. In the morning, I would find Raj and tell him I didn't want to see those crazies again, ever. And that I would testify if Claire were harmed after that ugly incident. If Raj ever wanted to go out for a beer again after work, he could sit on a hammer and spin.

I woke early in the morning and dressed for work quickly, hoping to be gone before my wife emerged from the shower. By unlucky chance, she was still awake when I stumbled in late the previous night with toxic breath and shaky hands, but I wasn't in the mood for talking and answered her questions with monosyllables. Of course, that sparked a blast of passive-aggressive sarcasm, and so began another fun hour of Let's Explore Why This Isn't Getting Better. I'd become so good at this by now that I kept my wife busy with pointless conversation almost effortlessly while I trudged into our bedroom, shed my clothes, and rolled into bed. It only took one mumbled "But why does that matter?" and a "And why do you suppose that is?" to keep her distracted long enough for me to fall asleep. It works beautifully every time. If I was greedy enough, I could market the cure for insomnia: The steady rhythm of dysfunctional point versus counterpoint.

The morning sun on my face felt like an accusation as I left my apartment, and I couldn't shake a vague feeling of guilt for the entire subway ride to work. My old boss had disappeared and I was doing nothing about it, even though I knew what happened... or at least, I thought I did. Wasn't there some moral imperative to make sure Oliver Barney and his goons faced justice? Walking through the front doors of Cathedral, I marvelled at how much worry I was devoting to three angel chuckleheads while the rest of my world teetered on an uncertain axis.

I was almost feeling better about everything when, right there in the hallway between Marcia's office and mine, I saw a poster that had been tacked to the wall. Written in black marker were the words EMPLOYEE OF THE MONTH. Below that was a crudely drawn smiley face, and below that was written the name of Rosie Peterson, the assistant director of Public Relations.

"Oh, no." I said, rolling my eyes.

"Ah, there you are!" said Marcia, coming towards me down the hall. She looked at her watch. "And only seven minutes late today. To what do we owe this honor?"

I expelled a deep breath. We hadn't been talking for more than three seconds, and I already had two things to bicker about.

"Can I have a little slack, please, Marcia," I said. "I had a rough night." Pointing to the poster, I said, "What's this?"

Marcia beamed. "It's part of my new morale-building program. What do you think?"

I looked at the poster. As I read it again, I imagined thunderheads building above us... everything was sunshine and roses right now, and it could stay that way if I wanted it to. Marcia could stay in a good mood, and there could be no hostility to start off a bad day. All I had to do was keep my mouth shut.

"Well, it's a great way to make everyone feel like they're working at Burger King," I said, watching her smile fade with a satisfaction I'm not proud of. Her face went stony.

"I take that to mean you don't like it," she said. "Is that because you think someone else should have won instead? Hmm?"

I bit my tongue. Rosie was a pleasant enough person to work with... a mother of three, she kept multiple photos of her kids in little herds on her desk. Interspersed among the photos were little stuffed creatures of indeterminate taxonomy... froggies wearing clown outfits, duckies with disturbingly human facial expressions, and—sigh—a four-inch-tall statuette of Jar Jar Binks. Decidedly less cute were the errors that infested the press releases she wrote. Misused homonyms. Apostrophes that appeared in the middle of words, signifying letters that weren't missing. Thirty-word sentences without a single verb. Marcia caught perhaps ten percent of these before handing the drafts to me for what she liked to call "polishing." I, in turn, shared the misery with the other editors. Some people would take issue with Marcia's selection of Employee of the Month... but I wasn't about to go there.

"Marcia," I said, "This kind of thing doesn't work in a company like ours. It will make people competitive and resentful... and that's only the ones who take it seriously. Others will be embarrassed by it. Eventually it will turn into a popularity contest, and those are best left to high school kids."

She crinkled up her nose. "Really, Gabe, jealousy doesn't become you. If you work well, maybe I'll put your name on the poster someday." And that was the end of that.

I went to my office and closed the door, hoping to take my frustrations out on some innocent author's manuscript. It only took about seven seconds for someone to knock.

"What?" I said.

The door opened and Theresa stepped in.

"Can we talk about last night?" she said.

"No," I said.

She closed the door behind her and glared. "You owe Claire an apology."

"I know," I said. "Can we get into this later?"

"That biker dirtbag should be in jail," she said. "I can't believe you were hanging out with him!"

As I struggled with a reply, Claire appeared behind Theresa and rapped her knuckle against the door frame.

"Hi," she said. Her hair was drawn back in a ponytail today, and I could see she was wearing her little green pendant earrings. They had a tendency to draw attention to her eyes, for some reason, even though her eyes were neither green nor even blue. I don't notice details like this on any other woman... even my wife.

"Hi," I said, hoping that I wasn't slipping into a moony stare. "Um, Theresa, could you give us a minute here?"

Before Theresa could reply, Kelvin's head appeared over her shoulder.

"Hey dude," said Kelvin. "You think that guy will sell me his Harley?"

I sighed.

"Well, tell him to think about it," said Kelvin. "Anyhow, that's not what I came down here for. Charles wants everybody down in the lobby."

"Now?" I asked.

"Yep," said Kelvin, and then he was gone.

I gave Theresa and Claire an exaggerated shrug. "Well, there you have it," I said, standing up. "We gotta go."

They both looked disappointed, and I tried not to hide my relief. I had no answers for them… at least, no answers that they'd believe. I'm not sure I had answers that I believed.

We walked to the main lobby, where most of the company had already gathered. No red stoles were visible, so apparently there were no promotions. Looking around at people's faces, I searched for clues as to what this was all about. Fear, for example, would indicate mass layoffs. Amusement would signal a celebration of some kind… a sales goal met, for example, or a bestselling book. But the faces around me reflected only blankness, and mild hostility, and a vague look of stupidity that all poorly managed companies seem to cultivate. In other words, it was business as usual.

Except, perhaps, for what was going on at the head of the lobby. A dais had been erected, and behind it stood Charles, a few of the major executives, some uniformed policemen, a couple of suits I didn't recognize, and — to my shock — Oliver Barney and his Gang of Six. My mind reeled with theories, the most disturbing of which had Barney trumping up charges against Charles and throwing our not-quite-beloved leader in jail.

"Silence, please," said Charles, raising his hands. "I have an important announcement to make."

Here it comes, I thought. The babbling in the room stopped.

"I'd like to introduce Mr. Conway here," said Charles, touching the arm of one of the suits I didn't recognize. "He's visiting us today from the Securities Exchange Commission, and he's discovered something very interesting." Charles glanced at Oliver Barney, who looked as if he'd rather be enjoying a nice spinal tap.

"Perhaps you're all familiar with Mr. Barney here," said Charles, motioning to Barney. "Mr. Barney has made quite a name for himself by breaking up the companies that he buys. In fact, I can now safely tell you that he nearly did that to Cathedral."

A rush of murmurs filled the lobby.

Charles continued, "Yes, our beloved company nearly fell prey to this pirate, and the only thing that stopped him from giving you all pink slips tomorrow was the fact that he broke the law in trying."

More murmurs. Charles's smug look told one and all that he was running the show here. Even the cops looked amused.

"That's right, everyone. According to Mr. Conway, this man was given material nonpublic information about our company for the purpose of trading in its securities. This is in violation of the Insider Trading and Securities Fraud Enforcement Act of 1988, particularly Regulation Fair Disclosure Rule 10b5-1 and Rule 10b5-2. Mr. Barney was given this information by several key –and, I should add, disloyal — Cathedral staff members. These people are standing next to Mr. Barney because that, too, is illegal. And so they will all be escorted from our premises by these fine, upstanding members of our law enforcement community. Their employment here is also terminated. So let's wish them bon voyage as they leave."

Pandemonium broke out. I knew Charles would use the information I gave him to thwart Barney, but I never thought he'd make a spectacle of it. And now, as everyone pointed and scratched their heads, the policemen began to escort Barney and the Gang of Six towards the front doors. Louise Dreyfoos was sobbing. Bobby Ortiz merely shuffled along with his head down. He looked sad and naked without his trumpet. Each of them walked out with a policeman in turn, one after another, and it wasn't until I looked at the last one in line that I realized that the Gang of Six was now a Gang of Seven. Suddenly I felt faint.

"Holy Mary, mother of God," I said to nobody in particular.

The last person in line was Marcia, sputtering at the cop next to her and looking bewildered. As I looked around at the crowd, I noticed a few people taking pictures. From somewhere to my right came a chorus of voices singing, "Na na na na, hey hey-aaaay, good-byyyyyyyye!" Peeking over the heads of the crowd, I saw that it was my editors, standing in a line and encouraging others to join in. Theresa and Claire had their arms around each other's shoulders, and they were grinning. Kelvin was energetically flipping Marcia the bird while singing at the top of his lungs.

"Stop that!" I yelled, but they couldn't hear me over the ruckus.

I looked back at the dais, where Charles, now standing alone, had both hands in the air in a hushing motion. The noise died down only after Marcia, the last in line, had walked out.

"Great things happen only because people make them happen," said Charles. "The reason why Mr. Barney's plan was thwarted — indeed, the reason why most of you still have jobs — is because one man had the courage and the morals to blow the whistle on this plot."

Oh, no.

"One man," continued Charles, "was fortunate enough to find out about this and put a stop to it before disaster could strike. That man," he said, beaming and pausing…

Please don't say it.

"Is Gabriel Marino, from our book group."

Wild cheers erupted, and as the sound of applause filled the room I felt hands slapping my back. The world swam before my eyes as I backed away from the stage, unable to say anything to the people swarming around me. Charles had taken my story and run with it, eliminating both Barney and Marcia in one stroke. She never saw it coming. Even though the charge against her was bogus, her reputation was trashed and she was now unemployed. I don't think my mouth closed for the entire time these thoughts whirled through my head. Obviously, Charles was snake enough to renege on the deal we'd made. But could he actually have fabricated evidence? Had I taken action—finally, after all this time—against the lesser of two evils, leaving the greater to rule over a corporate hell on earth?

I looked at Charles again and felt revulsion, then anger, and then something darker. *This is not the end*, I thought, clenching my teeth. *I don't care if I end up working in a car wash. I don't care if I wear a name tag for the rest of my life. There will be a reckoning for this.*

"This concludes our assembly for today," said Charles, gloating for a few last seconds before picking up some papers from the dais and turning to go. Then he paused.

"Oh, and Gabe?" he said, grinning an impish grin that indicated he'd "forgotten" this one last thing. "Why don't you stop by my office for a moment? I think we have a few things to discuss."

To my horror, whoops and cheers filled the room. "Way to go, Gabe!" yelled somebody I couldn't see.

I looked for my editors in the crowd but couldn't find them. From behind me a hand rested on my shoulder, and I turned to face Mitch Mitchell.

"Man, I bet you'll make VP for this," he said, shaking my hand. "Way to go."

"I... I..." I said... and that's all I said. Mitch's prediction was too horrible to contemplate. Yet I now realized that he was probably right. Charles's enemies were now vanquished, and the spoils were about to be distributed among the victors.

Just about everyone congratulated me before they left the lobby. The editors were delirious. I got a hug from Claire that nearly drove everything else out of my mind, but even that wasn't enough to stop the foreboding I felt as I began the walk to Charles's office. The betrayer awaited. So did my Judas kiss.

Chapter 15

A DEAL WITH THE DEVIL

Again, the devil taketh him up into an exceeding high mountain, and showeth him all the kingdoms of the world, and the glory of them; And saith unto him, All these things will I give thee, if thou wilt fall down and worship me. Then saith Jesus unto him, Get thee hence, Satan: for it is written, Thou shalt worship the Lord thy God, and him only shalt thou serve.

—Matthew 4: 8-10

I made a point of slamming the door behind me after I walked into Charles's office.

"You know," I said, "I don't like you any less than I did yesterday. But yesterday you were a haughty CEO who commanded some respect, at least. Today you're beneath contempt."

He smiled. "Why don't we go out for some lunch? We're having such nice weather."

"Eat this."

He walked around me to the door, opened it, and made an after-you gesture with his hand. "I think your demeanor will change when you see where we're going."

It was clear that he wouldn't be denied, so I walked with him without saying another word. As we passed through the halls and out the front door, people gawked and spoke in hushed voices. We wouldn't have attracted more attention if we'd herded a pack of mountain goats through the lobby.

We continued walking out the main door and down the street, with Charles humming to himself and me clenching and unclenching my jaw. I wanted to swat the giant windbag for what he'd done, and I wanted nothing in the way of gratitude from him. Still, I was also curious about what Charles's idea of a reward would be. Something told me I would get more than a free burrito for ratting out his enemies.

We walked into a ritzy place named Chez Chez, a place I often ignored on my way to seedier fare like Paco's. I'm never at home in these places: Nothing I've done in life merits anyone calling me sir, and when I show up at a restaurant, I expect the food I order to be piled high on my plate. Spare me the arugula and save the presentation for the art on the walls... if I walk away hungry, I feel ripped off. It may be nothing to be proud of, but I am a product of the same American indulgence that makes 7-11 stores sell tubs of sugar water that ebbs and flows with the phases of the moon. It's the same sickness that drove *Willy Wonka's* Augustus Gloop to drown in chocolate. Take my money if you must; just feed me.

"I bet you don't dine here often," said Charles.

"Not on what you pay me," I said, poring over the menu. "Hmm, now where's the Beef-a-roni?"

"Well," said Charles, unfolding his napkin and placing it on his lap with care, "I believe that's about to change."

I placed both elbows on the table, hoping somebody—anybody—would be offended by the faux pas. "I don't want your money," I said. "It's smeared with the blood of the innocent."

"Oh, relax. There are plenty of places in town that will hire a twit like Marcia."

"That's not my point," I said. "We had a deal, and you broke it. She did nothing to you, and you not only canned her, but also humiliated her in front of everyone. I hope she sues your ass off."

Charles took a sip of water. "Oh, I've taken care of that. She'll have no grounds. Trust me."

So that answered my question about falsified evidence.

I sighed. "You think I'm not familiar with this technique you're using? Taking someone to a public place, so that they don't make a scene?"

He shrugged. "Do you think I have bad news for you?"

Before I could answer, the waiter arrived. His tuxedo shirt was whiter than the tablecloth, and as he spoke, I noticed that his teeth were, too.

"Good afternoon, gentlemen. Welcome to Chez Chez. It's a particular pleasure to see you again, Mr. Ting. Would you like to hear the specials?"

I looked at the waiter and cleared my throat for a good yell. "I'm sorry, Charles! I don't care how much you pay me! I won't put an ice cube in my mouth and blow you while you call me your little penguin!"

Silverware clattered to tabletops around us. I heard a few hushed exclamations, followed by a man giggling.

The waiter looked as if he'd just been punched. "Perhaps you gentlemen need some more time. Here are your menus," he said, dumping them on the table and scurrying away.

"I didn't think you were capable of such vulgarity," said Charles, glancing furtively around the room.

"I can do better," I said. "Hire Marcia back, or I'll ask you how you got herpes from a Boston terrier."

"But why? You don't even like her."

"That doesn't matter. I want you to do what's right."

Charles sighed. "Very well. If you want to cut to the chase, we'll cut to the chase. You get Marcia's job, at... oh, let's say twice your current salary. What would you say to that?"

I was stunned. Visions of the future danced through my head: A car not speckled with rust. A home in a neighborhood where neighbors walked poodles. My daughter at an Ivy League school without any student loans. Charles's amused expression made me hate him more, but... he knew how to sing a siren song.

"You know what my current salary is?" I said. It wasn't really a question.

"The increase was effective yesterday." The smug charm was returning.

"And where is Marcia in all this?"

Charles smirked. "If not in prison, then somewhere near the Javits Center, holding out an empty coffee cup." He laughed out loud. "Oh, don't look so miserable. I'm sure her fellow Daughters of the American Revolution can offer assistance... if she can bring herself to ask for it."

I looked at my butter knife and wondered if anyone had ever stabbed themselves in this place before. I could do things with that money. There was my daughter's future to think of, and if I squirreled away enough I might start a small press of my own someday. I could also have a hell of a time in Vegas. My mind reeled at the thought of walking into a Nevada chicken ranch and announcing that I had more cash than I knew what to do with. And then, inevitably, my conscience woke up.

"I don't think I can do this, Charles," I said, the words coming out like a stale burp.

He smiled. "Not even if you get Marcia's office?"

That was nice. I'd have to disinfect everything inside it, of course, and maybe hire a shaman to drive out the goblins. But it was bigger.

"Oh," said Charles, toying with the pepper shaker in much the same way he was fiddling with me, "and you won't have to contribute towards the premium for your health insurance anymore."

I was speechless. It would be unfair, and possibly illegal, for Cathedral to do that. But it was also another nice chunk of cash, considering that my wife and daughter were listed on my plan.

"Charles," I said.

"Let's see," he said, drawing a finger to his lips. "There was something else... oh yes."

His eyes met mine, and I wondered if I looked like a boxer on the ropes. There was no feigning indifference now... he'd dragged me way beyond that. I knew it, and so did he, and as he delivered the last walloping haymaker I could feel something in me sag, then break.

"You get to name your own successor."

He leaned back, looking like he'd just told me I held the winning lottery ticket. I nearly laughed. This was supposed to win me over?

What was he thinking? Sure, I already had a candidate in mind—Theresa was the best in the barn, and there was no disputing it. Especially with Sally out of the picture. I could promote Theresa, then hire another editor, and then the team would be all set...

Sally.

The realization dawned on me at last, and Charles began to chuckle as he watched my face change. I'd told him about Sally's firing; he knew it was a sore point, and thus he knew which button to press. Given the chance, I'd have done anything to bring Sally back from the unemployment line... especially since my lame defense of her at her last stand against Marcia. And now he'd given me the chance... provided someone else hadn't hired her by now.

"Well?" said Charles.

A thought came to mind. "Charles, where's Jerry Lanville?"

The surprise on his face looked real. "I don't know. I haven't seen him in at least a week. Do you know where he is?"

I hadn't included Jerry's name when I identified the Gang of Six, so his reaction seemed natural enough. I breathed an inward sigh of relief.

The waiter came back. "Would you gentlemen like to hear the specials now?"

I sighed. "I'm not hungry." Rising from the table, I tossed my napkin on my plate and pushed my chair forward.

Charles remained where he sat. "You don't have to dine now if you like," he said. "But I'm afraid I require an answer now."

"Let me make a phone call first," I said. Then, noticing his look, I said, "Don't worry, I won't reveal anything about our deal. I just need to know something before I decide."

Charles handed his menu to the waiter. "Bring me my usual, Alphonse. If you please." He waited for the waiter to walk away. "This afternoon, Gabe," he said. "This afternoon or never."

"Fine," I said, and left.

The air seemed fresher outside the restaurant, and I sucked in gulps of it as I trudged back to Cathedral. I think I'm better at mental self-flagellation than most people, and as I crossed the street I whipped myself bloody. Yet there was some good to be found. Saving Marcia was a lost cause, of course, but I could undo a wrong by hiring Sally back. Theresa was due for a promotion anyway; in fact, I'd been worrying that this, on top of our recent friction with Marcia, would force her to scan the help-wanted ads. And I could use the cash. Oh yes, I could definitely abide that.

Entering Cathedral's doors, I chose the path to my office that would bring me past the fewest number of people. It meant tiptoeing past the cubes of some friends, but it was a busy day and they all seemed to have more pressing things to do. Reaching my office, I closed the door behind me, flipped through my Rolodex, and started dialing.

The phone picked up on the second ring, and with some apprehension I identified myself.

"Gabe! How the hell are ya!"

I smiled. "I'm okay, Sally. How about you?"

Five minutes of chitchat followed. Then about 10 minutes of me talking, as I filled her in on everything that had happened. Then, after some high-energy Q-and-A, I braced myself and asked my question.

"Huh. So Marcia is gone for good?"

"It looks that way."

"Well, I've got an interview on Friday but it's with a medical publisher. Shit, I can't even say methylisothiazolinone, let alone spell it."

I laughed.

"So," she continued, "this would be the same job as before?"

"Yes."

"At the same pay?"

"Actually, I can probably get you a little more, since this is a hire and not a leave-of-absence situation."

She was silent while she absorbed this, then spoke a number.

* * *

I debated with myself for the rest of the day. To an outside observer it would look like I got much done: I went to meetings, checked the status of our books with the editors, dropped in on marketing for as long as I could stand it, then returned to my desk to read for a while. In reality, I accomplished nothing. When no one was around, I whipped out a box of paper clips and arrayed them into two opposing armies on my desktop. Each clip stood for a reason to either accept the promotion or tell Charles to stuff it. Eventually I had an equal number of clips lined up in a standoff, so I replaced the clips representing the more compelling reasons with larger items like erasers and pens. More battle ensued, and when neither side gained an upper hand I let out a cry of frustration and smote the entire field with my fist. This, of course, sent most of my toys clattering to the carpet in front of my desk. Too late, I realized that Mitch Mitchell had been standing in the doorway for quite some time, and he now looked as if I were aiming a gun at him.

"It's... ah... hard to get good office supplies these days, isn't it?" he said.

"You're damn tootin'," I said, hoping I didn't look as demented as I felt.

He nodded, and that was the last eye contact we had for this encounter. "I, uh, just wanted to discuss this back cover copy with you, but... it's not urgent. It can wait. Yeah."

"Good," I said. Then, feeling appalled, I added, "Sorry."

He nodded again, then retreated back up the hallway. Sighing, I picked up the phone and dialed Charles's number.

"Yes?" he said.

"It's Gabe," I said.

"And?"

I hate you, I thought. *You are the absolute nadir of our species, the walking emblem of every knuckle-dragging beast that thinks success is only satisfying when it comes at someone else's expense. You and every living member of your bloodline should be packed into a rocket and fired towards the sun... it's the only way your darkness can ever be turned into light.*

"I'm waiting," he said.

My computer pinged, drawing my eyes to the screen. The CathMail icon was blinking.

To: Gabriel Marino
From:
Subject:
Re:

Don't!

Archangel

"You've got a deal," I said.

Chapter 16

A SAVIOR ASCENDANT

"And David rose up early in the morning, and left the sheep with a keeper... and went, as Jesse had commanded him; and he came to the trench as the host was going forth to the fight, and shouted for the battle."
—I Samuel: 17: 20

The next morning brought another Grand Ordination. With the entire company decked out in their red stoles, we committed mass sacrilege again as Theresa and I walked down the aisle. Three other people accompanied us, but those were paper promotions—Cathedral's management was infamous for tacking the word "senior" to a worker's title without assigning any new responsibilities. Of course, the word had meaning when it came to senior vice presidents and other members of the elite... but two of the other three people walking the aisle with me were now Senior Administrative Assistants. It was like being crowned King Crap of Turd Mountain, and I felt a little embarrassed for them.

Of five honorees, only I wore a long white robe. This was Charles's idea, since I was now a member of his executive posse. When I was a child, my mother forced me to become an altar boy at our church, Our Lady of Eternal Shame. The kind lessons of that institution were lost on the other Catholic boys my age, who gave me "The Boosh"—a ritual dousing of the head in a flushing toilet—every chance they got. The white was to them as a red rag is to a bull. After a few of these, I came to hate the robe so much that I quit, vowing never to humiliate myself that way again. Now, at the apex of my career, I was right back where I started from. All I needed was a Boosh to complete the picture.

Charles went through the usual theatrics, warbling about change for the sake of corporate progress. Then, once everyone was nearly asleep, he got to me.

"I think we're all familiar with Gabe's recent contributions to Cathedral," said Charles. Several people chuckled. "Through his master plan, Cathedral has risen to the forefront of educational publishing. That's a great accomplishment," he said, beaming at me like a proud dad.

It sure was, I thought, trying to look modest and grateful. *For Jerry Lanville. Anybody remember him?*

"Well, here at Cathedral, we reward great accomplishments. And so it pleases me to announce Gabe's promotion to Junior Vice President of Communications. Let's give him a hand, everybody!"

I didn't hear the applause begin. I was too shocked. There are good reasons why the word *junior* doesn't appear in most people's job titles... reasons that are similar to those prohibiting companies from making employees wear Pampers. There were no other junior VPs here, nor had there ever been. Perhaps the title was Charles's way of appeasing his other VPs, who were all older than me. It's hard to be threatened by a colleague whose title practically begs for a lollipop.

I sulked for the rest of the ceremony, wondering if I had to wear a beanie with a propeller from now on. Theresa was happy—and rightly so—with my old title of Executive Editor, and the senior administrative assistants... well, they made the most of the occasion. At least somebody had it worse than me.

After the congratulations and the cheers, the first thing I did as Junior Vice President was to pay a visit to Cathedral's Public Relations. Since these people now reported to me, a good start seemed important. They were probably disoriented by the rapid departure of Marcia, and it would be comforting for them to know that I would be a kind ruler. Of course, I'd *have* to be... I knew as much about P.R. as Marcia did about editing, so I wasn't exactly qualified to boss them around.

What I found when I reached their warren of cubes looked more like Washington's army at Valley Forge than a public relations team. Dazed people wandered around with shoulders slouched. Rosie Peterson was weeping quietly behind the army of fuzzy wuzzies and photos arrayed on her desk. Grave faces watched as I made my way to the center of their area.

"Hi everybody," I said.

They stopped what they were doing at once. Phone receivers clacked down. All eyes were on me with no one so much as breathing. Marcia must have ruled with an iron fist here, because a drill sergeant couldn't have shut this place up faster.

"Most of you know me already, but for those of you who don't..."

"We're sorry!" blurted Rosie, setting off another spasm of weeping.

I looked at her. "Sorry for what?"

She pointed to a stack of papers on her desk. "I was supposed to submit these timesheets ten minutes ago. But we didn't know who to give them to, with Marcia gone. Please don't punish us."

"Um... you're telling me that Marcia made you bring these to her by a certain time every day?"

She sniffed. "By 9:05. Whoever's late has their direct-deposit privileges taken away."

I sighed. "Okay, everyone, listen up. My first act as your supervisor is to take these," I said, picking up the pile of timesheets, "and put them where they belong." I leaned over Rosie's desk and slam-dunked them into the waste-paper basket.

Gasps and murmuring broke out.

"Your time isn't billed to anybody, so I see no reason to log it," I said. "From now on, the only people who will get their direct-deposit checks cancelled are those who waste my time with timesheets."

"Really!" yelled somebody near the back.

"And," I said, "I'm discontinuing Marcia's employee-of-the-month program. You guys are every bit as professional as my editors, so I won't insult you with condescending incentives." I punctuated the last two words by drawing quotations marks in the air with my fingers.

More murmuring. Now there were smiles breaking out.

"Thank God," said Rosie. "I was so embarrassed when Marcia put my name on that poster."

"Excuse me... Gabe?" said a woman I didn't know.

"Yes?"

She pointed at two keys hanging from tacks on a corkboard near Rosie's desk. They were chained to large wooden paddles, apparently to keep people from pocketing them. One paddle was blue, and the other was pink. A piece of paper was tacked to the board next to them, on which names and times were written. "Do we still have to sign out for rest-room keys? I mean, it's kind of embarrassing."

"Did she really make you do that?"

Everyone nodded.

I shook my head in disbelief. The policy of locking rest rooms was bad enough—I couldn't change that, given Manhattan's urban paranoia against letting "undesirable" people enter the premises to relieve themselves—but this was too much. I removed the keys from the board and handed them to Rosie. "Rosie, could you go find a locksmith this afternoon and make copies of these for everyone?"

Cheers erupted. I was beginning to feel like the liberator of a prison camp.

"That's about all I have to say for now," I said. "I'll meet with you individually very soon, so we can get to know each other and shoot the breeze. In the meantime, I look forward to working with you."

I turned to walk away, and was immediately embarrassed by the sound of applause.

"Gabe! Wait!" said Rosie.

I turned again. "Yes?"

"You forgot to lead us in the Pledge of Allegiance."

Jesus wept. "Um, why don't we add that to the list of things you don't have to do anymore," I said.

We were beyond applause now. The whooping and desk pounding could probably be heard on the other side of the floor. One man who had been watching me with desperate eyes now clenched his fists and closed his eyes, a bitter smile forming on his lips. To my horror, they began to chant my name, banging on their desks in time to each syllable: "Gabe! Gabe! Gabe!"

I waved at them and beat a fast retreat back to my office. It was unnerving. All I'd done was treat them like humans. Yet, to my horror, I had the inexplicable yet powerful feeling that these people were changed. All I wanted was a positive start, but these people were now legion of fanatics ready to fight a jihad. What had Marcia done to these people?

Scooting into my office, I tried to forget all this by immersing myself into e-mail. A few messages from accounting were on top of the queue—those went into the CathMail wastebasket with an emphatic punch of the delete key. There were three messages from Mitch about some crackhead marketing initiatives. I nearly responded to these after my chuckling subsided, then remembered that Theresa would be executing these items from now on. Forwarding them with some regret, I wondered if she'd enjoy Mitch and Jenna's messages as much as I did.

My phone rang. I was about to have my first call as junior vice president. Oh, the anticipation. I picked up the receiver.

"This is Gabe," I said.

Silence. Then, in a grating voice that sounded familiar, I heard "Hey, knucklehead. Long time no see."

I nearly dropped the receiver. "Ah, I'm sorry, I think you have the wrong…"

"Nah, you remember me. You was playin' peek-a-boo on the roof. Haya doin'?"

I didn't answer. I couldn't speak. The memory of that night had almost faded to nothing, and I'd have been happy to forget the running, the hiding, and the gun. Listening to this guy now, I *really* wanted to forget that gun.

"Never saw you that night," he continued, "so I been wonderin' how you been."

I'd begun to sweat. If he hadn't seen me that night, how did he know who I was?

"Ya know, that wasn't very nice, what you did yesterday. You must like embarrassing people."

I thwacked my forehead with my free hand. Of course. Thanks to Charles's stupid announcement, Barney knew exactly who led the hounds to his trail. There were photographers and reporters at the big exposé. If he hadn't already suspected it from our brief introduction in the cafeteria. God, that seemed like ages ago.

"So you're quiet now?" he said. "For somebody who don't talk much, you sure got a big mouth. My fatha always told me the quiet ones bite you on the ass when you're not lookin'." A wheezy sound came over the receiver… it might have been chuckling.

"Um… what do you want?" I said, my voice sounding like Kermit the Frog.

"Oh, I was just callin' to say hi. You and me, we're gonna get to know each other real well if you testify."

I swallowed. "If I what?"

"You know what I mean. Think about it."

It wasn't so much that I couldn't guess; I just didn't want to dwell on it. Knucklehead was Barney's hit man, or something… a brass-knuckle messenger. So if he was saying I shouldn't testify in a possible trial against Barney, it was clear that Barney wanted me to forget anything I might have heard or saw. I didn't have the courage to tell him I'd chatter away like an organ grinder's monkey if they put me on the witness stand, but I did manage to keep my mouth shut for the next five seconds.

"You hear me, knucklehead?"

"I hear you," I said. No agreement, no argument… just an acknowledgement.

"Good," he said. "Oh, by the way, if you wanna look like a VP, ditch that dog-puke tie." A click came over the line.

I looked around my office. My door was closed, and no one—obviously—was here with me. Turning to the window, I half expected to see Knucklehead's nose pressed against the glass. No one was there. Across the street, the windows of offices bustled with people at other companies doing their jobs. Could he have been watching me from there? I looked down at the tie I had on—a mauve paisley pattern with a tiny mustard stain near the tip. I sighed. Knucklehead may have been bigger and badder, but if he didn't like my tie when he killed me... tough noogies.

I tried to stay under everyone's radar for the rest of the afternoon, but the first lesson I learned as a junior VP is that this is impossible. On top of the usual people yanking me into their meetings—Mitch and his marketing stoneheads, Theresa and the editors—were the other vice presidents. This came as a surprise. The same executive dandies who deemed it beneath them to return my customary hellos in the hallways now wanted my opinion on everything. We were synergizing. Consensus building. Thinking outside the box. It might have been a thrill if I'd cared, but two title promotions in a month meant I was in over my head. And so I nodded my head a lot, and sided with the majority whenever I detected one, and silently wondered if anyone in the room thought I was a moron.

The meetings with the editors and public relations people went better. The PR meeting was a particular treat, since my only recourse was to allow Marcia's former disciples to keep doing what they were doing. As their boss, I couldn't admit my ignorance. So I got around that by asking them "How did we do it last time?" every time they raised a problem for me to solve. Then I would praise the staffer who found the solution, and suggest that they try that again. From the looks on their happy faces at the end of the meeting, it worked well.

It was late when the last meeting concluded, so I decided to go home. Hours of squirming and evasiveness and note-taking—the people at Cathedral who write the most during meetings are the ones who don't know what they're talking about—had exhausted me. Only half-conscious for the bus ride across the Hudson River, I nearly missed my stop, and when I lunged to ring the bell, I drove an elbow into the ribs of the old woman seated next to me. I apologized several times as I clambered down the aisle, but I still took three shots in the head from her handbag before I got off.

It was dark out. As the bus drove away, I looked up at the sky and saw only one star. The walk to my house was about a quarter of a mile, and as I began walking down the tree-lined suburban street, I wondered if any extraterrestrial life was staring back at me now, laughing at the beating I'd just taken. No one else was outside. It was quiet, a refreshing change from the clatter at work, but now I stopped and listened carefully.

Footsteps sounded behind me.

Startled, I resumed my pace. Possible explanations ricocheted around my mind: The person behind me could be another suburban commuter, headed home. It could be some guy walking his dog. No, wait... if that were true, I'd hear the dog. Okay, it could be some guy *looking* for his dog. Maybe it was a Hare Krishna so fanatical about mooching some change that he'd followed me home on the bus. Or the maniac with the hook for a hand, in that old legend about the murdered teenagers.

The notion was chilling, but not as bad as what I was most afraid of. Namely, the guy I least wanted to see on a dark street with nobody around.

Knucklehead.

The footsteps were getting closer. It was clear that I had to do something. Had he followed me home? I could hear breathing now, hoarse and irregular, as if the figure behind me was excited. Eager.

Evil.

My own breathing quickened as the fight-or-flight instinct took hold. My attacker would overtake me in seconds. I thought about running, but given my lifelong habit of running like a duck, he would catch me anyway, and I'd have no energy left to defend myself with. No, it was clearly time for a stand. A challenge of survival often brings out the best in a man, I thought, and perhaps it was finally time to ditch the Neville Chamberlain act and dish out some whoop-ass. *Yes*, a voice I rarely heard in my thoughts seemed to say. *It's time to fight.*

A shoe rasped against the pavement behind me, so close I could feel the vibration in the pavement. It was time.

Stopping short, I twisted my hips and shoulders as I pivoted on the ball of my left foot. I'd been carrying my briefcase in my right hand, and as I began my rapid turn, I raised it out and up. Time slowed as I began to whirl around like a top, the briefcase picking up centrifugal force as I brought it around in a mighty roundhouse arc. It was at head level when I finally turned to face my enemy, and as my gaze locked on the shadowy figure in front of me I lashed out, screaming.

Chapter 17

KISS THE FIEND

I adjure you, daughters of Jerusalem, by the gazelles and the hinds of the field, do not arouse, do not stir up love, before its own time.
—Song of Songs, refrain (2:7, first repetition)

"Hey!" yelled the shadowy figure, ducking the blow from my briefcase and backing away.

My arm continued around, sending me off balance and lurching forward. I hadn't counted on missing my target, and now the weight of my briefcase pulled me onto the front lawn and down to the earth with an embarrassing plop. Rolling onto my back, I sprawled on the grass and looked up at my attacker. I was beaten yet untouched.

"Just kill me," I moaned. "I suck."

"Are you okay, Gabe?" said the figure, coming out of the tree's shadow. The voice was higher-pitched than I expected, and as my eyes uncrossed and fixed on my assailant's face, I realized why.

"Hi Claire," I said, dropping my head back to the soft grass. If I could burrow down with the worms and the gophers...

"That was some fall you took," she said. "Why'd you jump at me like that?"

I sat up. "Wait a minute," I said. "What are you doing here? Were you following me?"

She shrugged. "Well, yeah. I... just wanted to talk to you today, but you kept jumping from one meeting to another. So I followed you to the bus."

I squinted at her, remembering Michael's warning. "Are you going to kill me?"

She laughed. "I thought *you* were going to kill *me* for a second there. Until you wiped out, that is."

I rose to my feet, dusted myself off, and picked up my bag. From behind me I heard a door open, and then a male voice said, "Hey, get off my lawn!"

I turned. A fat guy in a wifebeater T-shirt and Elvis Presley sideburns scowled at us, clutching a baseball bat.

"Sorry," I said, stepping back onto the sidewalk. We continued walking in the direction of my house.

"Goddamn perverts," said the man, and then the door slammed shut in a startling encapsulation of New Jersey's suburban hospitality.

As we left Elvis's house behind, I looked at Claire. "So why didn't you say something on the bus? No, come to think of it... why didn't you say something in the Port Authority? Or at Cathedral?"

She shrugged again, this time with only one shoulder. The gesture was somehow endearing. "I was nervous," she said.

"Really? About what?"

"Well, I've... never had this kind of conversation before," she said. "The kind we're about to have, that is. I hope."

I looked at her. "And what kind of conversation is that?"

"Well, why don't we have it, and then you'll see for yourself," she said. The coy smile on her face piqued my curiosity. And yes, it was beginning to turn me on.

"Oh-kaaaay," I said. "Since we've made it this far, why don't we walk towards my place."

"Are your wife and daughter home?"

I stopped again, feeling her eyes on me. "Actually, no." My wife had said something last night about taking the baby to her sister's, but I hadn't really been listening. She had a barracuda up her butt about something I said or did, and said I shouldn't expect her home tonight. Squinting, I tried to remember what this was all about, and how long she said she'd stay. How big *was* that argument? I should have paid attention.

"Oh," she said. She had the good judgment to be silent after that.

We reached my house and entered, limiting ourselves to small talk for a while. My embarrassment began when we stepped into the hallway, with its knee-high crayon drawings on the walls, and got worse when we entered the living room.

"Hmm," said Claire. "Nice decor. Is this Contemporary Dowdy, or Postmodern Slob Rustic?"

"It's home," I said, kicking a fettucine-stained T-shirt behind the couch. "If you don't like it, try the front lawn."

"No, it's nice. Really." She peered down at a framed photo of my daughter on an end table. "Awww," she said. "She's so cute. How come you never talk about her at work?"

I shrugged. "Dunno. I guess I like to keep work and home separate in my mind. Kind of like Wemmick in *Great Expectations*."

"Hmm," she said. "Wemmick was a caricature. What are you?"

"Something else. Are you hungry?" I said, turning back towards the kitchen. "I could fry us a couple of steaks."

She looked cheated, but nodded. She followed me into the kitchen, where I popped a couple of sirloins into a skillet and boiled a bag of Uncle Ben's Rice for the Desperate and some frozen veggies. We talked over some work-related subjects while I cooked, with her leaning against the kitchen doorway and me making a lot more fuss over the simple meal than was necessary. While feeling her up with my eyes, I noticed that one more button on her blouse had somehow come undone. My eyes began to make regular sorties between that creamy V of skin and her eyes... something that didn't bode well for my cooking. The beef was crackling in the pan, with little wisps of steam rising from the top. *That's what your soul's gonna look like in the afterlife,* a little voice in my head whispered. *Just keep it up, kid.*

As if she could read my thoughts, she chose the moment when I was flipping the steaks from the pan to our plates to steer the conversation back to dangerous territory.

"So I guess your friends don't like me much," she said, a mischievous smile on her lips.

It was like someone goosed me. Startled, I bobbled the steak but rescued it with a spastic lunge. "Well, they, uh..." I didn't know what to say. I looked around desperately for something to look at besides her. Steak. Frying pan. floor. Cleavage. Vegetables. Cleavage. Rice. "They told me some pretty wild stories," I said, chuckling. "That Michael guy, he's a real nut. Could you grab the wine?" I said, pointing at the countertop before hustling into the adjoining dining room.

From behind me I heard her say, "Freddie's Box o' Vintage Red. Wow, my favorite!"

"Don't knock it 'til you try it," I said. She followed me into the dining room, and together we set the table and sat down. As an afterthought, I got up and found a candle in the kitchen junk drawer. As I set it on the table and lit it, I marvelled at what a bad idea this was... then sat down to eat.

"So," she said, poking at a sprig of broccoli. "Are you going to answer my question?"

I sighed. "What those guys said about you was ridiculous. You would've cracked up if you heard."

She raised an eyebrow. "So you don't believe them?"

"Should I?"

Her eyes met mine, and once again their dark luster held me.

"We're not so different, you and I," she said. "After all, I'm a woman, and you're a man." She looked at my chest, and something in me stirred. "Does it really matter, then, what other people think we are?"

I stopped chewing my steak. "Please tell me you don't believe all that crap, too."

She shrugged. "We can change a lot of things in this world. We can't change who we are."

"Wait," I said. "This is weird enough without misunderstanding each other, so let's get explicit here." I looked at her, and all kinds of unwanted connotations of *explicit* danced a striptease in my head. "Those people I was hanging out with in the bar said I used to be an... an..." I felt ridiculous even saying it.

"An angel?" she said, as if it were the same thing as bus driver, or Republican. "So what? I was too, once."

I dropped my fork. "Ah, that's not exactly what I heard."

The coy smile returned, and it was so fetching I nearly forgot what a strange business this was. "Well, before I became something else. But that's ancient history. I'm neither of those things now."

I thought again about the steak frying in the pan.

"Would you please chew, or breathe, or something?" she said. "You look like you're dead."

I reached for my glass of wine and chugged it.

"You're not taking this well," she said.

"Well, how am I supposed to react?" I said. "I'm having dinner with Legion the Cutie Demon. Whoopee!"

She looked down. "Don't call me that. I wasn't him. I used to be your... I don't know how to describe it. Kind of like a protegé. Once."

"Oh, great," I said, rolling my eyes. "Did we make out in heaven, too? Or did I pop down to hell every once in a while for a quickie?"

"You're not being very nice," she said, and the look of hurt on her face surprised me more than what we'd been discussing.

"I'm sorry," I said, not sure if I was. "This is a little hard to take. If all this stuff is true—and I'm not admitting it is, mind you—then I don't remember the things you're telling me."

"Of course not. You fell on your head."

"Why does everyone keep *saying* that?"

She smiled. "Because that's how you got here, silly."

"But... but how do *you* know that? Weren't you underground somewhere, torturing dead war criminals or something?"

"The underground bit is just a metaphor. Believe me, we could see you. It was kind of like when you wiped out on the sidewalk just now, only more spectacular. If you remembered it, you'd be really embarrassed."

"Oh," I said. It was all I could manage.

She had a faraway look in her eyes. "Was that Uriel with you and Rafe?" she said. "At that bar?"

I swallowed hard. She knew the identity of a woman she'd never seen before. And she had referred to Raj by a name she shouldn't have known about. Hell, even I didn't call him that. Two more items on the growing list of things that didn't bode well for my career.

"She puts an M at the beginning of her name now, but yes... I think she's who you're referring to."

"She's so pretty," said Claire. "She always was a pretty thing."

"Excuse me," I said, "but... were you and Muriel female up in... you know..." I pointed at the ceiling.

She giggled. "I told you, the directional metaphors don't apply. No, we weren't female, just as you and Rafe and that big dumb sword weren't male. We just... were."

"Uh huh," I said. Maybe it was the wine, or maybe these kooky stories were starting to grow on me, but it was getting easier to play along.

"Do you remember," I said, feeling myself blush, "When you said you kissed me because you didn't want to know what it felt like never to kiss me?"

"Yes," she said.

"Did you say that because of... you know, my falling on my head and everything?"

She looked down at her plate. "When I saw you cross descension, it was the first time I'd seen you since the war."

"War? What war?"

"Oh, I forgot," she said. "You've read *Paradise Lost*?"

"Years ago, but… yeah."

"It's not a bad summary of what happened. Except the real thing was a lot less talky. I mean, jeez, Milton had the Morning Star babbling on like Charles."

"Ah," I said.

"Anyway, when I saw you fall, I wanted to be with you again. More than anything. And I figured if you guys could cross, maybe I could do the same thing. So I tried it. It wasn't easy to figure it out, but… here we are," she said, beaming.

"Crazy people," I said, looking at the chandelier above the table. "I'm surrounded by crazy people. I live with them, I work with them, and now I'm starting to sound like one."

She reached across the table and rested her hand on mine. Her touch was warm. Nice. "None of us are crazy," she said. "Especially you. You're still the same wonderful guy I remember," she said. "Only now you're a guy, of course."

My heart rate had increased again. "Are you telling me I'm the main reason you're here?"

I felt her hand give mine a tiny squeeze. "The only reason," she said.

"So if you're who you say you are, you're here to tempt me?"

She let loose a peal of laughter. "No! I mean, not the way you're probably thinking. I told you, I'm not what I once was."

"You're a demon."

"No! I'm a woman!"

"Same thing," I said. I never knew it was possible to be turned on and scared at the same time. "So, what will you be when your life eventually ends?"

Her laughter stopped, but the smile remained. "I don't know. Honestly. I've never done this before."

A new thought occurred to me. "Do you know why I came here to begin with?"

She looked surprised. "The others didn't tell you?"

I shook my head. "That's why they followed me. They said I came down here for a reason, but it I left in a big huff and didn't tell them what it was."

"Well," she said, now playing gently with my fingers, "If you believe your scripture, you and I haven't spoken for thousands of years. So I'd be the last to know."

I looked at her, admiring the graceful line of her cheekbone. There's a passage in Ecclesiastes that I always found amusing in my childhood catechism... something about a woman's conversation being like a burning fire. It wasn't funny now. She made me desperate to know what my supposedly angelic self was up to, coming down here. "Incola ego sum in terra," I said, feeling lost as I said the words... and not because I didn't know what they meant, or where the thought had come from. "Non abscondas a me mandata tua."

She smiled, and leaned closer to me. Twin stars of candlelight glinted in her eyes, and the hand that was holding mine now rose to caress my cheek. Her touch was so light I could barely feel it.

"Don't worry, my wanderer," she said. "You're not as lost as you think."

Our eyes locked again. I could barely breathe. What I wanted to do next was an abomination. It was an affront to the higher being that created me. It was an act of betrayal that would destroy my marriage and scar my wife and me for the rest of our lives. It was the metaphysical equivalent of a short circuit whose consequences I couldn't even imagine. It was a black mark on my soul in the neverending scorekeeping of heaven and hell. And it was expressly forbidden by Cathedral's *Policies and Procedures Manual.*

"This is a bad idea," I said, leaning forward to meet her.

"I know," she whispered, and then our lips touched.

There was no holding back after that. Dishes and forks clattered to the floor as our bodies came together on the table. As garments came off one by one, our sighs became the west wind as we composed our own personal Song of Songs; only in our version her hair was not like a flock of goats streaming down from Gilead, and her teeth were not like a flock of ewes come up from the washing, and her breasts were not like clusters of the vine. Nor, for that matter, were her eyes like the pools in Heshbon by the gate of Bath-rabbim... and her nose, as I kissed it tenderly, did not remind me of the tower on Lebanon that looks toward Damascus. I did not liken my lover to the steeds of Pharoah's chariots. Her hair was not like draperies of purple, and as far as I could tell when my face was buried in it, there was no king held captive in its tresses. The buds in the garden did open, however, and the pomegranates certainly blossomed, and we did share the fresh and mellowed fruits we'd kept in store for so, so long. And when it was over and the twin fawns lay down in the night, I slept...

But my heart kept vigil.

Chapter 18

THOU SHALT NOT KILL

Whoever strikes a man a mortal blow must be put to death. He, however, who did not hunt a man down, but caused his death by an act of God, may flee to a place which I will set apart for this purpose.
—Exodus 21: 12-13

The next morning's commute to Cathedral was a quiet mix of exhilaration and shame. Claire had left some time before dawn, probably fearing my wife's return… but when I awoke no one was there at all. On the ride in from home, my head ached from the death match between guilt and lustful remembrance. What was I thinking? It was wrong, and I knew it... but I'd like to think that my supposedly rough trip from heaven to earth was an extenuating circumstance. If I could blame everything else on my previous lives, then this wasn't much of a stretch.

Slinking into my office an hour late, I dropped my briefcase behind my desk and ruffled through the pile of papers on my desk, hoping that anyone passing by would assume that I'd been there for quite a while. Sneaking a look at my monitor, I noticed my CathMail icon blinking. Three messages awaited me.

To: Gabriel Marino
From: Charles Ting
Subject: Meeting with Legal ASAP
Priority: URGENT

Get down to my office as soon as you can.

This was interesting. I wondered what he wanted.

To: Gabriel Marino
From: Charles Ting
Subject: Where Are You?
Priority: URGENT

GET DOWN HERE NOW.

Uh oh. If this was the second of three messages, I really didn't want to know what the third one said. I hesitated, then clicked.

To: Gabriel Marino
From: Charles Ting
Subject: You'll Be Fired in 15 Minutes Unless...
Priority: URGENT

...you're sitting in my office getting us out of this mess you made.

My eyes goggled. Looking at my watch, I saw that I had about 45 seconds to make it to Charles's office.

It was impossible to make a left into the hallway at high speed, so I bounced off the wall as best I could and bolted down the hall. Someone said hello as I whizzed through the editors' section—I couldn't tell who, and I didn't answer. It was regrettable that I made incidental contact with three people on the way to Charles's office, and I would need to apologize to Rosie later for knocking her bagel to the floor, cream-cheese-side-down, but there were more important things to worry about. I just wish I knew what they were.

Reaching Charles's office, I threw the door open and staggered in. He was reading a document behind his desk. One of the chairs before his desk was occupied by LaShonda Higgins, our senior legal counsel now that Louise Dreyfoos was behind bars. She was wearing an imposing lawyer suit, and looked stern. LaShonda was a genuine stress puppy, the kind of professional that lives a miserable existence behind a desk without crises to yelp about and people to bite on the ass. It's difficult to tell when a stress puppy is happy, unless you actually catch them chewing on a coworker's carcass. It was a shame she worked in corporate law... she'd be a great prosecutor.

"Would you close the door, please, Gabe?" she said.

I did. "What's the problem?" I said.

Charles looked up from his desk. "The problems," he said, "are these two documents. I've read them nine times while we've waited for you, and I still can't believe what they say."

I sat down next to LaShonda, whose gaze made me feel like a shoplifter.

"What documents?" I asked.

He leaned back in his chair and brought his fingertips together, as if he was holding an invisible ball.

"Do you remember an author named J. Pennington Stubbs?" he said.

I considered for a moment. "The name's familiar. Why?"

He smiled. "I think this will explain things better than I could." He reached across the desk to hand me a newspaper clipping.

Local Writer Dies in Bizarre Pork Chop Incident

By Tom Spicer, Staff Writer, *The Greenwich Courier*

J. Pennington Stubbs, a resident of Greenwich, died yesterday in a tragic incident that police are calling "a possible suicide." The body of Stubbs, a psychometrician who designed standardized tests like the SAT and GRE, was found in the early afternoon by a neighbor stopping in for a visit.

According to Malone's reconstruction of the event, Stubbs, a former employee of Educational Testing Service in Princeton, New Jersey, was despondent over a letter sent to him by an editor at a Manhattan publishing company. In an apparent suicide note left on the deceased's kitchen table, Stubbs blamed the editor for crushing his dream of being a published author and for "failing to understand the secret codex found in the grids of multiple-choice tests."

According to Stubbs's daughter Mona, Stubbs was a fan of conspiracy theories. "He had a wild opinion on just about everything... UFOs, the Kennedy assassinations, the popularity of professional wrestling, you name it. But he was a nice guy. He didn't deserve that nasty letter he got."

According to sheriff Malone, Stubbs leashed his two Great Danes, Scylla and Charybdis, and took them into his back yard at about 2PM. While holding two pork chops in one hand, Stubbs tied the ends of the two leashes around his neck. Then, at some point between 2:10 and 2:45, when his body was found, he threw the pork chops in opposing directions, causing the dogs to bound off after them. The leashes snapped taut when the dogs reached the end, breaking Stubbs's neck instantly and nearly decapitating him.

The body was discovered at 4:00 by Stubbs's gardener, Harley Floyd. "Oh, man, it was horrible," said Floyd. "I was stoppin' by to fertilize the petunias, and there he was, lyin' dead in the grass. There's still a flat spot. Want to look?" he said, pointing to a spot near the fence that enclosed Stubbs's property.

"I knew his book got rejected and all, but damn!" continued Floyd. "His wife showed me the letter he got. What a shame. That editor must be a real jerk."

Funeral services for Stubbs will be handled by the Lowenfeld Funeral Home on Dearborn Street.

After finishing the article, I took a moment to get my hyperventilation under control.

"Charles, the letter I wrote wasn't that bad."

"Oh really?" said Charles, leaning forward to hand me another document. "Perhaps this will refresh your memory."

I looked at the document. It was a copy of my letter to J. Pennington Stubbs, regarding the manuscript entitled *The Secret Semiotics of SAT Testing Grids*. Reading the letter again, I felt sick. It was that bad.

I sighed. "You're telling me this guy lynched himself over a rejection letter from me?"

LaShonda cleared her throat. "No, Gabe. We're telling you that Mr. Pennington's immediate family hired an attorney and are demanding a large amount of compensation."

"They what?"

"LaShonda and I got off the phone with them an hour ago." said Charles. "They're expecting us to call back with our reply. This mess you've gotten us into could be very, very expensive."

"But what did I do that was illegal? I mean, maybe I was in a bad mood when I wrote that letter. But the book sucked, Charles. That was indisputable."

"We didn't do anything wrong," said LaShonda. "Unless, of course, you wrote more of these letters to Mr. Stubbs. I don't know what else you might have said to him, but his family's attorney says there are two items of concern. One is the intentional causing of emotional distress."

"That's ridiculous!"

"Again, we won't know that until you tell us what you did," said LaShonda. "And you'd better start talking, because they're also talking about involuntary manslaughter."

"But... I didn't kill him! I just sent him a wiseass letter! How could I know he'd lynch himself with dogs? I mean, who does that kind of thing?"

Charles cleared his throat. "LaShonda and I are of the opinion that this won't stick in court," said Charles. "The whole thing's ridiculous, and when we call the Stubbs family's attorneys back, we'll use those very words." He leaned forward and laced his fingers together on the desk, looking like a vice principal lecturing a student. "But I have to say I'm disappointed in you, Gabe. Each of my executives has his own style in communicating with the public, but I've never seen anything this unprofessional."

He held the copy of my letter up. Clearly, this was my cue to be humbled. I considered several responses, and was about to say something... but then I realized an important point. I turned to LaShonda.

"This isn't about rubbing my nose in a mistake, is it? They want money."

"Very good," she said. "You figured that out all by yourself?"

"How much do they want?"

She eyeballed me for a moment, then offered a rare smile. "Two hundred million dollars."

Suddenly it felt like a golf ball was caught in my throat. Cathedral was a sizable company, but it wasn't Microsoft. A hit like that would... well, it would deprive my daughter of her hassle-free tuition, for one thing. For another, I would probably have to wear a sandwich board that read, "Will work for food."

"That would finish us," said Charles. "We have no parent company with deep pockets, and we blew our reserves when we bought Happy Test Prep last year."

LaShonda's face returned to its gargoyle expression. "Failure is not an option, Charles. Stubbs's legal counsel isn't stupid enough to take this to court. Unless, of course, Gabe has given them the means to do so."

She turned to me again, and her scowl would curdle cream.

"Is there anything else I need to know about this letter? Was there any more correspondence between you and Mr. Stubbs?"

I shook my head.

"Did you ever talk to him on the phone?"

"No."

"You didn't know him personally?"

"Nope."

"Has anyone else on your staff written to him?"

"Uh-uh."

"Has he submitted other manuscripts to Cathedral? Perhaps to another editor?"

I shook my head again. "I was executive editor at the time. If he sent us another manuscript, I'd have known."

She considered this for a moment, then turned to Charles. "I think we're in the clear. There was only one letter between us and

Stubbs. And although we didn't use very diplomatic language, we can hardly be blamed for the writer's actions."

I wondered about that. In my experience, it was hard to foresee how authors or prospective authors would react to criticism. The conversation always got tense when I broached the subject of changes to a manuscript. Even the most delicate overtures often led to a shrieking contest between them and me. Taking them out to lunch sometimes eased the pain, but even that didn't stop some authors from throwing food. Of course, it wasn't always this ugly. After a while, an editor learns that people who spend every waking hour banging words into a machine—night after night, year after year—can't separate the personal from the professional. You learn what to say to prevent jags of crying or teeth marks bitten into your forearm. And when they say they take criticism well, you don't challenge them. Ever. Yes, I understood what happened to J. Pennington Stubbs. His death was ridiculous, but the pain behind it was real. A writer doesn't expect an editor to burn down his life's dream and dance in the ashes. And yet... how could I expain this to LaShonda and Charles? Who would believe that what I had done was less an act of petty sarcasm than a war crime of my profession? That my intentions—smirky and venial as they were—didn't matter?

LaShonda was piercing me with her gaze again. "Is there anything else I need to know?" she said. I could swear she was salivating.

Yes, I thought.

"No," I said.

"Well," said Charles with a shrug. "I guess that's it, then. LaShonda and I will deal with the matter for now. No need for you to stick around for this."

"Right," I said, getting up and trying to hide my haste in walking out the door.

The walk back to my office was marred by encounters with several people I wanted to avoid. Mitch wanted a projected marketing budget for next year, and I redirected him to Theresa's office. Rosie asked for direction on a thorny P.R. issue—apparently a reporter had been calling with questions about the Gang of Six fiasco. I told her to tell the truth.

"But... it's not my job to tell the truth."

I sighed. Public relations people were second only to philosophers in fabricating distinctions between truth and lies. Both could look you in the eye and say that the world as you knew it was all wrong. Even worse, they do it with passion and conviction. This is why I tried not to work directly with P.R. people before I was promoted. It was also why I never drank with philosophy majors in college. Yet I understood that there were media issues involved here, and it wouldn't do to have Rosie make pubic any information that would embarrass Cathedral any further.

"Tell you what, Rosie. From now on, when you talk to this guy, limit yourself to yes-or-no answers. Even if he asks open-ended questions, answer him with either yes or no. I'll leave it to your discretion as to which word to say for any given question. How does that sound?"

She considered this for a moment, her face gradually assuming an expression of wonder.

"That's... great! I'll be talking to him, but I won't really be talking to him. I think you just invented a new P.R. technique, Gabe!"

"Well, just don't name it after me," I said, and continued my retreat to my office.

Ah, silence. Sitting at my desk, I closed my eyes and let my mind wander back to the lustful mischief of last night. Sensory details floated through my memory, lulling me into a bliss that was shattered first by a pang of guilt from my conscience, and then by the ping of CathMail.

To: Gabriel Marino
From: anonym7441@invisiblemail.com
Subject: Meet me today

Gabe,

Meet me on the southwest corner of 51st and 5th today at 1:15pm sharp. It's important.

For most people, getting an anonymous message directing them to meet somebody somewhere would be exciting, at the very least. Right now, however, this kind of thing ranked somewhere south of pulling gum off my shoe. Yawning, I wondered which of my insane new friends was toying with me as I sifted through some more e-mail.

When the appointed hour came around, I ducked out the door and caught an uptown 6 train. As I entertained myself by reading the advertisements for hemorrhoid laser surgery and the ongoing cartoon adventures of Julio and Marisol waltzing through the world of HIV awareness, I allowed myself a moment of contentment. It was nice to get out of the office at lunchtime... I'd been bolting down too many tuna salads on rye in between meetings. Getting off at 51st Street, I ascended the stairs and paused at the top, allowing the sun to warm my face.

I walked west towards the designated rendezvous, enjoying the reverie until a nasty idea occurred to me. What if today's mystery liaison turned out to be Knucklehead? Would he kill me right there on the corner of 51st and 5th, with half of midtown milling around on their lunch hour? Probably not, but even if all he wanted was some friendly conversation (my mind wandered off on a tangent here—what would friendly conversation with Knucklehead be like? An endless recitation of sports scores? A half-hour's worth of penis jokes?) I wanted no part of it. Yet I couldn't just bail on the encounter, since it might be Michael or some other Internet-impaired angel trying to tell me something important. I stopped at the corner of 51st and Park to think the situation over. It didn't take long before I had a plan.

I rushed into a nearby Modell's Sporting Goods and bought myself a Yankees cap, some cheap sunglasses, and some of that black tar that ballplayers smear below their eyes to reduce sun glare. The cashier gave me a funny look when I put the cap on and smeared the tar over my upper lip. I gave her one back as I donned the shades, smiled, and walked out of the store. Thus disguised, I was now free to approach the designated intersection without the fear of being recognized—I could either find my mysterious friend and start a conversation, or walk away undetected. I'm not often this clever.

Approaching the corner of 51st and 5th, I slowed my pace and scanned the mob of office workers and tourists. No one I knew seemed to be around. People dodged and weaved around each other, the tourists stopping to gawp at nearby St. Patrick's Cathedral as the office workers brushed past them. Right on the corner, a clown wearing a sandwich board was yelling at anyone who would listen. Since the scene didn't look particularly dangerous, I edged closer to the corner and looked around for my mysterious friend.

"Free Tibet from tyranny!" yelled the clown. "Give Las Islas Malvinas back to Argentina!"

I broke off my search to look at the clown. Dressed in purple polka-dotted overalls, a spinning bowtie, and the largest, reddest afro wig I'd ever seen, he looked frustrated that no one was listening—that is, as frustrated as anyone can look with a painted smile on their face. The front of his sandwich board read, "Toodles the Activist Clown," and when he turned the back read, "Think when you laugh, stupid." I rolled my eyes. Some people never learned that the best way to be ignored in Manhattan was to make a spectacle of yourself.

Leaning against the post of the streetlamp, I faked a yawn and gave another look around. People rushing here. People jostling there. And still the clown kept yelling at everybody in sight: "Awaken, proletariat! Apathy sucks! Stop electrocuting bunny rabbits!" He got in my way as I tried to look north on Fifth Avenue, and as I craned my neck he stopped and squinted at me.

I made as if I was gesturing to someone behind him, but he was undeterred as he shuffled towards me in his big clown shoes. Every muscle froze as I wondered what to do. Was he crazy? Curious? Or worse, a hit man hired by Oliver Barney who'd seen through my disguise?

The clown cocked his head as he looked at me, then smiled a real grin through his makeup.

"Hi Gabe," he said, in a deep, familiar voice. "Remember me?"

I looked carefully at the eyes behind the painted mask. They didn't jog my memory at first, but then I made the connection between the voice and the blue-gray eyes, and as my jaw dropped to the streetcorner the clown's features seemed to realign themselves beneath the paint. It was improbable... no, it was impossible.

The clown standing before me was my former boss, Jerry Lanville.

Chapter 19

THE BOOK OF SECRETS

And the Lord God commanded the man, saying, Of every tree of the garden thou mayest freely eat: But of the tree of the knowledge of good and evil, thou shalt not eat of it: for in the day that thou eatest thereof thou shalt surely die.
—Genesis 2: 16-17

"It's great to see you," said Jerry. "You look good!"

"Thanks," I said, trying not to stare at the paisley pants. "You look... ah... different."

Jerry's grin widened. "Sorry. I couldn't mention this in my e-mail."

"*You* sent that message to me?"

Jerry the Clown nodded. I reached out to the lamppost for support, feeling woozy all of a sudden.

"Jerry, I thought you were dead."

He grabbed my arm. "Ssh. Let's talk over there." He nodded towards the doors of the office building on the corner. "With my clown outfit and your black-eyed Yankee look, people will think we're acting out a skit or something. I don't want to be noticed."

Allowing him to lead me through the doors and into the large lobby of the building, I removed my sunglasses and the hat. Jerry remained in clown guise. People were still milling around us, but the lobby was quieter and less crowded.

"Jerry, where have you been?" I said. "The last time I saw you, you were..."

"They let me go. I managed to convince Barney and the others that our 'disagreement' was a misunderstanding, and that I was on their side all along. I wasn't, of course. Not with what I knew."

"So what happened?"

He looked around again, apparently to make sure no one was listening. "I contacted the SEC about the whole scheme. I didn't leave out a single detail; they got copies of documents Barney hadn't seen yet."

"So... that was you who blew the whistle on them? I thought it was Charles." I told him about Charles and the staged perp walk in Cathedral's lobby.

He chuckled. "So that's who the other informant was. They told me another informant stepped forward, but they wouldn't say who. I think I can take most of the credit, though." He smiled broadly. "My information was better, and I had more of it."

"But Jerry, where have you been all this time? Do you have any idea how weird things have been since you disappeared?"

He glanced again over his shoulder, then leaned towards me. "Witness protection program," he said. "I run a little store out in western Jersey that sells costumes and equipment for magic acts. It's a lot of fun, actually. Who'd have thought that people actually bought rubber dog turds? I just wanted to let you know I'm okay, and that I won't be coming back."

I blinked. "You got the witness protection program just to get away from Knucklehead?

"From who?"

I explained my history with Barney's foul-mouthed henchman. It might have been my imagination, but Jerry's face seemed to pale beneath the white clown makeup.

"So they know who you are?" he asked.

I nodded. "Apparently. Charles must have told them."

He shook his head, a look of consternation on his face, and grabbed my shoulder. "Gabe, do you have any idea how dangerous these people are? Barney has a lot more resources at his disposal than this one man with a gun. And not all of those resources are... well, normal."

Now it was my turn to look around. "What do you mean?"

"He's into the occult, or something. I don't know if he's running some kind of satanic organization or what, but... the man is scary. I've seen evidence of it, what I know is probably just the tip of the iceberg. Don't tangle with him or his people. I'll see if I can get you the same protection I got."

I looked at Jerry in wonder. The man I once reported to was in the prime of both his life and his power. This was a man of proven ability, a natural leader with charisma and courage... yet here he was in a clown outfit, running scared from a boogeyman locked in a jail cell. It made no sense, unless...

"Jerry, what... um, evidence did you see, exactly? We're not talking about Knucklehead anymore, are we?"

He did another 360-degree search, and this time he saw something he didn't like.

"I have to go, Gabe. I've said too much already."

"Wait a second. You've gotta tell me this. What's up with Barney and Knucklehead? What's worse than getting chased around the office by a guy with a gun?"

He started walking away. I reached out and grabbed his arm, turning him to face me again.

"I need to know," I said. "Things in my life aren't exactly normal, either."

He looked at me with desperation in his eyes. "Fight for a united Ireland! Stand up for Falun Gong! What's wrong with you people?"

He pumped a fist in the air at some people who stopped and stared, then marched towards the door. "Wake up! Your carbon footprint is stomping out your future!" He turned back to me one last time.

"You can see it in his eyes," he said, then rushed out the doors to the sidewalk. I tried to follow, but a cluster of people in suits got in my way, and by the time I made it out the door, he had left the sandwich board on the sidewalk and was running down Fifth Avenue. He was looking back every few steps, like a man pursued, yet I didn't see anyone following him. It scared me to see him this way. It was conduct unbecoming an executive.

The creepy feeling stayed with me for the subway ride back to Cathedral. All things considered, the devil walking the earth was just another line on the list of disasters that started after my first promotion at Cathedral. Yet this latest warning—dubious as it was, coming from Toodles the Activist Clown—didn't sit well. Maybe it was the lack of sleep, or maybe it was the cumulative effect of reality eroding from beneath me... I don't know. One thing was certain though: I wouldn't be looking Oliver Barney in the eyes any time soon.

Returning to Cathedral, I stopped in on the editors to see what was going on. Theresa was lecturing Claire on a split infinitive she'd missed in some manuscript, and I thought about intervening... but didn't. Theresa's tone may have been a shade too condescending, and her argument certainly wasn't as absolute as she thought it was, in a time when the phrase "to boldly go where no one has gone before" was permanently imbedded in popular culture. And it seemed wise to let Claire fight her own battles, if I wanted to avoid office gossip.

Sally called me over to her cubicle on my way back to my office.

"What's up?" I said.

She pointed to a manuscript on her desk. "I've got the next big one right here. It's gonna sell like a mofo."

"Is that so?" I said, raising an eyebrow. "What's it about?"

She shook her head. "You won't believe it. It's a guide to surviving the modern office environment. It didn't seem like it had a lot going for it for the first 20 pages... I mean, come on... how oversaturated is this market right now? The next thing you know, Martha Stewart will be writing one of these."

"Okay. What's so special about this one?"

"Like I said, you're not gonna believe it. According to this guy, most office conflicts these days are caused by—are you ready for this?—angels and devils who've come down to earth to infiltrate the corporate infrastructure."

Suddenly my tongue felt coated with sand.

"Huh?" I said.

"I know! That's what I thought, when I first picked it up from the slush pile. But you won't believe how involved this gets! He's got an explanation for everything! Jams in the copy machine? Devil at work. Big spike in your 401k plan? Angels. It's ridiculous!"

"Sure is," I said, feigning indifference. "Throw it out and move on to better things."

"No, wait! This could be big if we position it as a goof. We could write some sarcastic cover copy and hire a cartoonist to do some funny illustrations. Then all we'd have to do is book the author on Oprah, and blammo! It sells and sells and sells."

"Sally," I said, wondering what the restrained panic on my face looked like, "We can't publish every crackhead manuscript that comes in. This isn't our demographic. Send him a rejection letter." I thought of my meeting with Charles that morning, then added, "A polite, nicely-worded rejection letter, please."

She sighed. "Okay. But for the record, you're being wimpy. And stupidheaded. This could be big! Hell, I'd buy it."

"Well, you may think it's funny, and I might too, but it doesn't necessarily follow that everybody else will. It's urban office humor. People between the coasts won't relate."

She rolled her eyes. "It won't matter. They don't buy books anyway, unless it's *Chicken Soup for the Soul* or *The Farmer's Almanac.* It'll still make millions."

"Sally," I said, picking the manuscript up from the desk. "Please. Just write the letter."

"Okay, okay. But where are you going with that?"

I smiled. "Just making sure you don't run with this any farther than you already have."

This got me a curious look from her. I ignored it, turning and walking back to my office. What gave me the heebie jeebies was the possibility that people might find out how right the author was. This manuscript was going in my lower file drawer and staying there. The idea made me feel like a corrupt politician, but who knew what would happen if *this* saw the light of day? Did this author really know what he was talking about? It was one thing to read the story I've been wanting to read since all this craziness began. It was quite another, though, to yell it through a megaphone like Toodles the Clown.

On an impulse, I picked up my phone and dialed Raj.

"M.I.S.," he said.

"Raj, it's Gabe."

"It's Gabe. Hello!"

"Raj, by any chance have you heard of a writer named..." I scanned the cover page of the manuscript. "Phil Joel?"

"Joel. No. Why?"

I was itching to say it. Here we go, I thought. "Because he knows about us. He wrote a whole manuscript about it. I've got it here on my desk." A feeling of despair washed over me. I had just used the pronoun *us*.

I heard Raj clear his throat, and when he spoke next his English was markedly improved. "You're serious about this?" he said.

"I'm looking at the manuscript right now."

He was silent for a moment. "This could be bad."

"I know. That's why I'm keeping it in a locked drawer."

"No, that's... not exactly what I meant. I need to contact the others."

"Um," I said, wondering who he was talking about. Then I remembered. "Not those two. They're insane."

"I'll get back to you," he said, and hung up.

Here comes the cavalry, I thought. *Now we're screwed.*

Immediately after I placed the handset down, CathMail started dinging like a pinball machine. Several messages flooded my inbox simultaneously. Surprised, I clicked on the first one.

To: Gabriel Marino
From:
Cc: Rajput Patel,
Subject: BURN IT!

THAT SNITCH I CAN'T BELEIVE SHE'S HERE AW SHIT GABE BURN IT BURN IT BURN THAT BOK NOW. SORRY MY TYPNG SUX BURN IT NOW

ARCHANGEL

To: Gabriel Marino
From:
Cc: Rajput Patel,
Subject: Re: BURN IT!

Gabe: Rafe told us about the manuscript. I'm glad you realize the implications of publishing such a work, but Rafe is right when he says there are other things to consider. Don't burn it. If Michael's (possibly rash) reasoning is correct, then having another "co-worker" from the old days here may not be such a good thing. You may not remember, but she's something of a tattletale. Are you certain this isn't a joke? Because if it isn't... we're in trouble.

Michael: Easy on the caps lock, please. You're giving me a headache.

Rafe: You were the last to cross. Did Jophiel see you go? Did she follow you? Or could this author's name just be a strange coincidence?

Archangel

A few more messages followed this one, but I stopped reading to consider a few curiosities. First, the speed with which Raj and his posse communicated was impossible... yet there it was. The first message was clearly Michael's: The spelling and grammar were definitely in character. The second was from Muriel, the brains of the group, if not its leader. All of them seemed to have an issue with identifying themselves in e-mail, but they sure did love to write. It was interesting to see that Raj was identified by name... but then again, he had a CathMail e-mail address, so anything cc'd to him from the outside would show that. Thinking about this was making me crazy.

To: Gabriel Marino
From:
Cc: Rajput Patel,
Subject: WTF?

HELLO? ANYBODY WITH AN OZ. OF COMMUN SENSE OUT THERE? BURN THE BOOK AND MAYBE THE BIG GUY WON'T FIND OUT DO IT NOW sorry uriel about the caps I suk at this burn it gabe

archangel

It was too much just to watch all this. Summoning all the chutzpah I could muster, I started typing.

To: Rajput Patel,
From: Gabriel Marino
Subject: Re: WTF?

Hi everybody,

The book's not a joke: It's right here. Is it true there are more us down here? And what's this news about getting in trouble? I'm a little fuzzy on the rules. We never resolved these things in our last conversation, did we? Your psychotic bottle attack didn't help, Mike.

Oh boy. I'm using the words *us* and *we*. Somebody shoot me.

Just out of curiosity, what kind of trouble are we talking about here? I have a feeling community service won't cover it.

I began to type my name at the end, then stopped and deleted it. What the hell, everyone else was doing it. I might as well join the fun.

Archangel

To: Gabriel Marino, Rajput Patel,
From:
Subject: Re: Re: WTF?

IF THIS IS JOPHIEL WE R SO SCREWD IF U DONT LIKE THE CAPS EAT ME I CAN BE PISSED IF I WANT 2.

ARCHANGEL

To: Gabriel Marino, Rajput Patel,
From:
Subject: Re: Re: Re: WTF?

Michael: Your attitude is not improving the situation.

Gabe: Keep the book under lock and key for now. And try not to read it... odds are it has just as many inaccuracies as facts. Remember, this version of Jophiel is imperfect. We need to contact her and find out what her intentions are. Until today, I thought we four were the only ones here. But if she followed us, there's no telling who might be behind her.

Rafe: Could you take care of this? You were closest to her before. I'm hoping that she might be more persuadable, now that she's here.

Archangel

Reading Muriel's last message, I wondered what "more persuadable" meant. It would be interesting if Raj's bond with her—whatever it was—took a different form now that they were a man and a woman. More visions of Claire came to mind. Nothing angelic about that.

A knock sounded at my door. Looking up, I saw LaShonda standing there with Charles's head bobbing over her shoulder.

"You have a minute for us," she said, closing the door behind them.

"Why yes, thanks for asking," I said, not even trying to fake enthusiasm.

They sat down. Charles looked contemplative, while LaShonda was wearing her standard look of annoyance. Neither said anything for what seemed like an overly dramatic pause, and it dawned on me that something else on my agenda for the day was going horribly wrong.

"I'm disappointed in you," said Charles.

"I'm sorry to hear that," I said. "I take it you're here to beat on me some more over the pork chop affair?"

LaShonda slowly leaned forward, speaking each word as if she was spitting out a piece of food she didn't like.

"Our conversation with Mr. Stubbs' attorney did not go as we hoped. We denied all responsibility for his death and refused to pay any settlement."

"Sounds okay so far."

Charles motioned to LaShonda not to speak. "We thought they'd fold when we called their bluff. But they're going to pursue this. Ridiculous as this whole pork chop thing is, they're trying to bring this to trial. So I want to make one thing clear before the real nonsense begins."

He stood up, approached my desk, and leaned over it so that his face was inches from mine.

"You got us into this mess," he said. "I expect you to cooperate with LaShonda to get us out."

Halitosis blasted my nostrils as he spoke. He and LaShonda were trying to be intimidating, but his bad breath was the most immediate threat to my well being, and as I leaned back in my chair, I tried not to cross my eyes. On any other day, the prospect of my CEO barking at me with his lawyer in tow would have been terrifying. But now, with God apparently ticked off that I flew the coop, the devil's henchman looking to kill me, and a clown trying to whisk me off the grid for my own good, it was hard to care about the legal claims of a suicidal writer. What could I tell Charles that he would actually believe? That his former right-hand man called himself Toodles these days? That his immortal soul was probably toast?

"Charles," I said, eyeing the manuscript on my desk, "If it comes down to my being subpoenaed, I can only say the truth. And rest assured, the truth will set us all free."

Chapter 20

NOTHING BUT THE TRUTH

The Law of the Lord is perfect, refreshing the soul; The decree of the Lord is trustworthy, giving wisdom to the simple.
—Psalm 19

The deposition requests arrived a few days later, signalling a new phase of our fun with law games. Charles's door fanned open and shut, causing the people sitting near it to start a betting pool on whether each visitor would leave looking terrified, furious, or dazed. I put down $5 on one of LaShonda's visits, hoping the two of them would fight like wolverines. Unfortunately, Charles's secretary later informed me that LaShonda departed his office looking merely grim. That could have meant a number of things, since Charles had that effect on many people.

I had a friend within the state court system, a jovial but ambitionless civil servant. He was one of my more interesting pals from college, a tubby dude in a John Deere baseball cap who could thread a conversation from college basketball to "Ode on a Grecian Urn" to the properties of quarks within a minute's worth of conversation. Clerical jobs can be a magnet for people like this. For every drone sucking oxygen in a cube, there's half a genius who wants the time and the freedom to just think about things. Neither type does their job better than the other, since drones are drones and the minds of the geniuses are usually somewhere else between nine and five.

When I asked my friend how long we could expect to wait before a trial, he snorted. "Any other time," he said, "it would be months. But right now it's like everybody's taking the Golden Rule seriously. It's weird. Landlords are being nice to their tenants. Surgeons aren't leaving clamps inside patients. Bosses aren't firing employees... except at your place. I dunno what's going on in the criminal courts, of course. I mean, hey, what's a day in Brooklyn without a stabbing. But we've got hardly any civil suits with everybody acting so *civil* lately. So unless your lawyer's hot on stalling tactics, your case will probably slide through here like buckwheat through a goose. Kafka would hate this crap."

I relayed this information to LaShonda, who dismissed it with a snort. Or maybe it was a growl. It was hard to tell with her.

"I could take this to court right now and win," she said. "It's stupid. Stubbs's lawyers are even stupider. If they want to postpone, well, whatever. It's up to the judge. But frankly, I don't care either way."

So ended my attempts to help.

I was deposed by Stubbs's lawyers a week later, which wasn't a big deal because LaShonda stomped all over most of the questions before I could answer. When all the squabbling was done, all the lawyers had were the facts that I worked for Cathedral and wrote the letter they waved at me. The seven words I was allowed to say were nothing special, and even I felt disappointed when the deposition ended and LaShonda yanked me from their office, a puppy on a leash.

The subpoena surprised nobody, and soon after it came I found myself in LaShonda's office being prepared for a trial.

"Don't say anything dumb," she said, crossing her arms on her desk and fixing me with that mean stare.

"Um, thanks," I said. "I don't suppose you could be more specific?"

"All right. Use yes or no answers whenever possible. Keep it short. Don't volunteer information that hasn't been asked for. Smile. Be polite. Don't pick your nose, burp loudly, or giggle for no apparent reason. Don't look at me, because the jury will think I'm coaching you." She shrugged, then raised her hands.

"That's it?" I said.

She nodded.

"But... don't you want to practice with some questions and answers? I mean, what if they ask me something... I don't know, potentially damaging?"

She yawned. "They won't. This probably won't even get past the settlement conference. And if by some miracle we do go to trial, their case will crash and burn no matter what you do. Have a nice day."

I opened my mouth to say something, but she'd already picked up her phone and dialled a number. So I got up and left. Halfway back to my office, I was confronted by a human roadblock. Theresa, Sally, Kelvin, and Claire stood in a line, arms crossed and frowning.

"Hey, guys," I said. "Do I have to pay a toll to pass, or something?"

No one smiled.

"You're withholding the truth," said Theresa, pointing at me.

I looked at her finger. "Everything I know is a lie. Don't take it personally."

"We want the manuscript," said Sally. "And we want to know why you're acting so weird about it."

"Me?" I said, bringing a hand to my chest. "What are you talking about?"

"Come off it, Gabe," said Theresa. "You're hiding something. Sally told us about the manuscript with the ghosts and devils in it. Why didn't you just tell her to reject it? And why didn't you let me handle the situation?"

"It's nothing, guys," I said, trying to squeeze past them. "The book cracked me up, and I wanted to show it to a friend of mine before I gave it back to Sally. That's all."

I attempted to squeeze between Theresa and Claire, and as I slid deliciously past Claire, I looked into her eyes and saw... feigned curiosity? Amusement? I'd have given my next promotion to know.

They followed me back to my office, clamoring the whole way. I had to close the door behind me to find peace, and even then I had to push against Kelvin as he cast aspersions on my parentage through the open crack.

"Just a peek, man. Please?"

"No," I said. The door closed, and that was the end of that.

* * *

The settlement conference was held at the state courthouse a week before the trial date. I wanted to attend out of curiosity, but Charles and LaShonda quashed that idea right away.

"I won't say anything," I said. "I promise. I just want to see."

"We said no," said LaShonda. "By now, their attorneys have evaluated the weakness of their case and they're probably ready to give up. At worst, they'll take some chump change and call it a victory. But with you in the room, all bets are off. You're a wiseass, and you're a little eccentric, and you'll be a loose cannon if you're there in the lion's den with Charles and me. So go back to your office and do... whatever you do all day."

This stung. "You know, LaShonda, you're not exactly the nicest person I've met either."

She gave me a rare smile. "Flattery will get you nowhere, sugar. Now get out of my office and let me do my job."

Of course, later that afternoon, I had a pretty good idea how the settlement trial went when they came back, called me into Charles's office, and told me that I should make myself available on the trial date.

"Wow," I said. "Good thing I wasn't there to fuck up the settlement conference, huh?"

"Shut up," said LaShonda.

I felt giddy.

"I expect you to conduct yourself well," said Charles. "This is still a ridiculous situation, and there's no way on God's green earth that we're paying those lunatics a dime."

Looking around at the stuffy decor in Charles's office, I sighed. "You know, Charles, I'm spending way too much time in here. Your taste is starting to rub off on me. Can I panel my office in oak, too? And I'd like one of those nifty credenzas."

He looked at me strangely; then comprehension crept onto his face like a particularly ugly turtle. "Are you asking for some kind of a bribe?" he said.

I smirked. I didn't really want panelling or anything else from him, other than the expression he wore now. "Never mind," I said. "I'll be there for the trial, and I'll tell the courtroom exactly what I did, which was pretty much nothing. Happy?"

"That will do," said LaShonda. Her mouth opened to speak again.

"I know," I said, holding up a hand. "I'll get out of your office."

* * *

Time seemed to zip by after that. The editors still hounded me about the manuscript locked in my desk drawer, but the questions gradually turned into sullen looks, and then into a vague chilliness in our day-to-day meetings. I tried to ask Raj about the manuscript again, but some crisis or other seemed to hold him up. I hoped to hear something more from Michael and Muriel, but he was closemouthed about them, too. They were busy, he said. I got no more than that.

When the day of the trial finally came, I left home early and met Charles, LaShonda, and just about everyone else from Cathedral's legal team at the courthouse. Charles and LaShonda were already involved in a pretrial conference in chambers, probably making the plaintiff a final offer of $1.95 to quit bugging us. They soon came back looking puzzled. There was no settlement to be reached, even though the plaintiff's case was looking cheesy as ever.

We filed into the courtroom and took our places. I half expected the place to look like something out of *A Few Good Men*, or at least resembling Charles's hyperoaked office, but the acid green walls and fluorescent lighting didn't lend themselves to flights of fancy. In fact, if it weren't for the elevated judge's chair and the lawyers' tables, the place could be mistaken for the DMV. I sat down in the second row next to Charles and read the graffiti on the bench in front of me while the open statements droned on. The Stubbs family's lead counsel was a pipsqueaky guy with a shock of red hair. I'm sure there are plenty of young-looking attorneys on the New York bar, but this kid looked as if he'd skipped a few grades in school and was now practicing while his classmates from kindergarten were toiling through high school.

As young as he looked, though, the kid was brutally professional as he painted his verbal picture of Cathedral for the jury. We were a symbol of corporate America gone haywire. We were greedy (I counted three uses of that word in his monologue), arrogant (five of this one), uncaring (four, if you counted two uses of *callous*), and irresponsible (just once, thankfully). We were weird. We hired people like me, which I suppose was an accusation that could have gone somewhere if he'd expounded on it, but he didn't. My attention flagged after 10 minutes of this. As he wound up his statement, I picked with my fingernail at the words "Fuk U" carved into the wood of the bench in front of me.

Then LaShonda's opening statement began. This was much more to my liking, since it lasted for only a minute and had one point to make: J. Pennington Stubbs was insane. Her task completed, LaShonda returned to her table and sat down.

It was time for Stubbs's attorney to call his first witness.

"Plaintiff calls Gabriel Marino," he said, looking not at me but at the jury.

I rose, flinching a little as my left knee made an embarrassing but painless popping sound.

"Remember your preparation," whispered LaShonda as I passed her table.

"My what?" I whispered back. The look on her face would melt iron.

I walked to my designated chair, where I was met by a court clerk holding a Bible. Placing my hand on it and raising my other hand as instructed, I listened as she asked me if I swore to tell the truth, the whole truth, every last bit of the truth, all possible configurations of the truth, and a lightly battered fricasee of fresh truth with a side order of sincerity.

"Yep," I said.

"Mr. Marino," said the judge, peering down at me from his perch, "The proper response is 'I do.'"

"Right. I knew that. I do," I said.

Suddenly a feeling of almost overwhelming clarity came over me. The clerk took the Bible away, and as I sat down I felt... great. The sleepiness that plagued me during the opening statements was gone, and now a curiously refreshing feeling came over me. Peace reigned. The vague feeling of trouble had gone away, and I wondered why I'd felt nervous about this day. After all, I was a decent, good person at heart, and could only tell the truth. The rest would sort itself out. I smiled as the redheaded lawyer eyed me from his table.

"Good morning," he said.

"Howdy."

"Would you state your name for the court, sir?"

"Sure," I said. And then, utterly without thinking, the next words spilled out of my mouth. "I am Fortitudo Dei."

Before anyone could react, I recoiled in horror. Where did that come from? Chuckles and muttering drifted from the seats behind the lawyers' tables. The readheaded lawyer rolled his eyes and looked annoyed.

"This isn't a joke, sir. Would you please answer the question honestly this time?"

"Sorry," I said, marvelling at my newfound sunshiny mood. "I meant to say that I'm Gabriel, one of four Archangels before the throne of God."

Rustling and chuckles broke out from the assembly.

"Mr. Marino," said the judge, "We have a full day ahead of us, so if you don't mind, cooperate with Mr. Hardy and answer his questions."

"I apologize," I said, wresting control of my thoughts. The words were just appearing in my head. I couldn't fight them, because they felt so good to say... I hadn't even considered saying anything else. Was the oath causing this? Or the Bible? Or the conjunction of the two? Silently cursing Raj for not warning me, I looked around the room for some kind of help. No one seemed to know yet that I was trapped, but they would. Soon. Because I now realized that, in all my childhood catechism classes, I didn't recall a single time when an archangel lied. Or withheld information. Or said anything in the Bible that didn't foretell some earth-shaking occasion.

"Are you all right, Mr. Marino?" said the judge.

"I'm fine," I said, wiping the sweat from my forehead. I looked at him with eyes that didn't feel like my own, and for a second I thought I saw two of him. Then I looked at LaShonda. The dreamy feeling was coming back, and thinking was getting harder again. *Get ready, LaShonda,* I thought. *Because if Hardy asks the right questions, I might uncork some things the world has never heard before.*

"Good," said the judge. "Then state your name, please. Your real name."

I froze.

With happy clarity, I considered the two answers, and with the last conscious thought I could possibly summon, I spoke.

"My name is Gabriel Marino."

And then I surrendered... to the consciousness that seemed both alien and familiar; to the inevitability that some mighty big changes were about to happen; and to the triumph and anger in knowing that heaven and earth could not keep me silent now.

Chapter 21

THE WRATH OF GABE

Blessed be the Lord, my rock, who trains my hands for battle, my fingers for war... touch the mountains, and they shall smoke; Flash forth lightning, and put them to flight, shoot your arrows, and rout them; Reach out your hand from on high—Deliver me and rescue me from many waters, from the hands of aliens, whose mouths swear false promises while their right hands are raised in perjury.
—Psalm 144

"Very well," said Hardy. "Now that we've established who you are... what's the name of the company you work for, Mr. Marino?"

I told him. The words felt like cotton candy on my tongue.

"Okay. Can you tell me whether or not you were working for Cathedral on..." he reached for a paper that was undoubtedly the letter I'd sent to Stubbs, then cited its date.

"Yes, I was."

"And what was your job title at that time?"

"My title was executive editor." I held back a chuckle. Once, when I was a kid, my dentist let me breathe nitrous oxide through a mask while he drilled a cavity in my molar. The giddy feeling that came over me then was much like what was happening now.

"I see," he said. "What's your title now?"

"Junior Vice President of Communications."

Hardy gave me a smile like an alligator's. "Well, congratulations on your promotion."

"Thanks." Sugarplums began to prance in my head.

"So tell me, what were the duties of your office while you were executive editor? Ah, Mr. Marino? Still with me? What did you do all day, Mr. Marino?"

I stopped admiring the striped pattern of his tie. "Well, I liked to sit in my chair and imagine all kinds of practical jokes I could play on my boss. You know, thumbtack on the chair, anonymous gift subscription to *American Pederast* magazine... that sort of thing. Never actually did them, of course. I also cut my toenails at my desk with the door closed from time to time, and fantasized about sex approximately 27 times a day."

A furrow appeared between Hardy's eyes. "That's very nice, sir. Now would you mind telling us what Cathedral paid you to do while you held that job title?"

I thought for a moment. It wasn't easy. "Well, I managed the day-to-day operations of my editorial staff, of course, and coordinated their work with that of other Cathedral departments. I bought manuscripts. I was also the primary liaison with Greenlawn Press, our publishing partner. Those were only my managerial responsibilities, of course. When I was acting as an editor, I had duties that required a whole different mindset."

"I see," said Hardy. "Well, why don't we start with the duties, and then we'll get to the mindset."

"Okay." God, that tie of his was interesting. It was like a Rorschach pattern. At that moment, a line of little duckies waddled behind their mom towards Hardy's breast pocket.

"Mr. Marino? Your duties, please."

"Yes. I read manuscripts, took authors out for expensive and awkward lunches, hired freelance illustrators, assigned proofreaders to... look, this is really boring stuff. Wouldn't you rather hear about the mindset? It's a lot more relevant."

Hardy gave me a piercing look, then shrugged. "All right. Let's hear it."

"Well," I said, knowing it was bad to explain too much but not really caring, "Editors are a little nuts, to be honest. We're hard-wired to seek and destroy bad communication. We wreck conversations by correcting people's grammar. We can't have lunch in a restaurant without looking for spelling errors on the menu, and when we find them, we gouge them out with salad forks. So naturally, people who work in this profession often develop certain... behavioral oddities."

I looked briefly at LaShonda, who was repeatedly drawing two fingers across the throat and mouthing something that looked nasty. Hardy, on the other hand, was looking like he'd found a $100 bill on the street. I decided that I liked Hardy.

"Is that so?" said Hardy. "Could you describe those, please?"

"Sure," I said, happy that he asked. "Cathedral's editors are book editors. For most people, discourse is a means to an end in their everyday jobs. For us, communication itself is a holy grail. Listening to most people talk is like hearing a grand piano being used as a battering ram. And reading what most people write makes us want to choke someone. We get all worked up over things that no one cares about, and we hold everyone who doesn't love language in contempt. We're a bunch of batshit, loonball kooks, and our fanaticism is rivaled only by people who yell and wave pamphlets on the subway." I couldn't remember the last time I enjoyed myself this much. I'd wanted to say these things for a long time... it felt like ages, and Hardy seemed genuinely interested.

"Your honor, can we have a recess?" said LaShonda.

The judge looked at her. "We've only been in session for twenty minutes."

She pouted, then sat down again.

Hardy was fighting back a smirk. "Ah, you were saying, Mr. Marino?"

"Right," I said. "We're a little nuts, you know. We pore over William Safire's column, hoping to catch him making an error. We got wedgies in grade school because we wore eyeglasses first. You know what that contempt does to a kid, Mr. Hardy?"

"Your honor!" said LaShonda. "Mr. Marino needs a break. He didn't sleep well last night, and he... may not know what he's saying."

The judge turned to me. "You okay, Mr. Marino?"

"Just peachy," I said, beaming back at him. "Thanks for asking."

LaShonda whimpered, then shut up.

"You were saying?" said Hardy. "What does that contempt do to a kid?"

"Oh, man... it manifests itself in all kinds of ways. Arrogance sets in, but we disguise it with a veneer of sociability. Things like feng shui start to become obsessions. We get compulsive about trivial matters, like socks on the floor. Or the number of ice cubes left in a tray before it's refilled. This freaks out our spouses. They don't complain much, though, because all that repressed intellectual hostility turns us into sexual tyrannosauruses at night."

"Mr. Marino," said the judge, "I have to draw the line here..."

"*Now* you draw the line?" barked LaShonda. "Now?"

"Sorry," I said. The courtroom had begun to take on the appearance of a child's coloring book, all smiley faces and rainbow colors.

"But your honor..." said Hardy.

"Ha!" I said, pointing at him. "See? You started a sentence with a conjunction! Grammar primers state that you can't do that. Do you know why, Mr. Hardy?"

Hardy shook his head.

"Damn. I was hoping you did, because I sure don't... yet I've had to enforce it every time. Starting a sentence with a conjunction doesn't obscure the sentence's meaning. Nobody gets hurt if you begin a sentence with *and.* Yet it's in the primer, alongside more logical rules like the ones prohibiting misplaced modifiers. Editors decide which rules apply to their work and which ones don't, and for the rest of their careers we are the ruling ayatollahs in a linguistic reign of terror. We have to be. Because—whoopsie, I just broke another rule—nobody else cares. Nobody!"

"I see," said Hardy. I could practically smell the smoke from the gears grinding away in his head. "So tell me, Mr. Marino, did you write this letter I'm holding up for the court to see?"

"I don't know," I said. "Could you bring it closer, please?"

He did. It was my letter to J. Pennington Stubbs, in all its laser-printed glory.

"Yeah," I said. "That's one of mine."

"Do you remember what you said in it?"

"Pretty much, yes."

"Very well. How would you characterize the tone of your writing in this letter?"

I smiled. "I was being a wiseass. So sue me. Whoops!" I feigned surprise, bringing my hand to my mouth. "You already did."

"Knock it off, Mr. Marino," said the judge.

"Hmm," said Hardy, reading the letter again. "I'd have to agree. Can you tell me, Mr. Marino, why you chose to be so harsh?"

"It's simple. The book was an affront to my editorial sensibilities, so I... well, I guess you can say I threw an intellectual temper tantrum in that letter. The sarcasm hides it a little, I guess, but not much."

Hardy nodded. "You said the book was bad, Mr. Marino. How was it bad? Were the author's ideas somehow faulty?"

"Let's put it this way: A good metaphor for quality writing lies in the cars of a freight train. Each car has a specific purpose, and they are all linked together as a united whole. There's no limit to the amount of ideas a writer can convey, as long as he designs the train of words to move smoothly down the tracks. We think of trains as ugly, industrial necessities. I say that's not fair to the trains: They can be quite elegant in terms of design. Mountains have been moved with trains, Mr. Hardy. So have the world's most important ideas."

"Eloquently put, Mr. Marino. Would you characterize Mr. Stubbs's manuscript as such a train?"

"No," I said, smiling. "He sent me a bunch of cabooses linked with bubble gum."

"I see. How was his grammar?"

"Stinkarooni."

"And his punctuation? How was that?"

"Random, at best."

"Hmm. Well... was his spelling any good?"

"Not bad, for a nine-year-old."

Hardy smiled. "Wow. Sounds like you had a real quality control problem there. I bet that manuscript got you all riled up."

"Objection!" yelled LaShonda.

"Sustained," said the judge.

"No, it's okay," I said. "I don't mind answering. It *did* make me angry." LaShonda was making strangulation motions with her hands, but there was no stopping me now. "If we publish enough works like Stubbs's manuscript, we legitimize crackpot ideas and reward lousy scholarship. I hate that. It makes me crazy."

"I see," said Hardy. "And were these thoughts in your mind when you wrote the letter to Stubbs?"

I smiled. If this was what it was like to have righteous fire flowing through my veins, this angelic stuff wasn't so bad after all. "Every last one of them," I said.

"Did you care, at the time, about how Mr. Stubbs would receive that letter?"

"Are you asking if I cared how the letter would get into Stubbs's hands, or do you mean to ask if I cared about how he'd feel when he read it?"

"Er... the latter, please."

"Right. Well, to be honest, I was hoping to irritate Mr. Stubbs."

A small flurry of talking swept through the benches behind the lawyers' tables. LaShonda was being restrained by two other people at the table. Hardy looked like a little kid on Christmas morning.

"Really? And why was that?"

I shrugged. "Well, I suppose I could have been more civil. Most people I know would have been nicer about the whole thing, and that includes the editors I work with. I'm sure Stubbs was a nice guy. But an editor can only put up with so much bad English before something snaps. I didn't mean to hurt him. He was just... well, intellectual roadkill."

Hardy looked at me with undisguised joy. After a few rapid breaths, he blurted, "Mr. Marino, in your estimation, are you good at what you do?"

"Ob—" said LaShonda.

"Sustained," said the judge.

"No." I said. "I mean, I'm a pretty good editor, but I'm terrible at managing. Sometimes, when I tell somebody to do something, I'm actually amazed that they do it instead of flipping me the bird. I'm also pretty spineless... I once let my boss fire someone on my staff because she mistook a cartoon snake for a penis."

The noise from the audience grew louder.

"Um, did you say..." said Hardy.

"Yep," I said. "And I won't even get into the bit about black men having green pubic hair. But speaking of colors..."

"Stop it! Objection!" yelled LaShonda, thumping the table in front of her.

"Overruled," said the judge. "This I want to hear."

"Cool," I said. "Like I was saying, I once allowed our bonghead marketing department to design pink covers for all of our books. Well, okay, wait a second... I *did* resist, but caved later because my boss liked the color."

"Wow," said Hardy.

"And... oh, wait! You've gotta hear this. Another time, during a staff retreat at one of those touchy-feely seminar places, my staff and I dropped our boss on her head during a trust exercise."

"I'm sorry to hear that," said Hardy with a big cheesy grin.

"Yeah, well... it wasn't as bad as the time a biker friend of mine threatened one of my subordinates with a broken bottle, while I just sat there sipping beer."

"I bet," said Hardy.

I laughed. "That was before I tried to bash that same subordinate in the head with my briefcase. You should have seen it... a big ol' roundhouse swing. Missed her, though."

"Her?" said Hardy, eyes goggling.

I looked over to the Cathedral table. LaShonda was sobbing.

Hardy shook his head, then turned to the judge. "No further questions, your honor. I think I've got everything I need."

He sat down, and the judge looked at LaShonda. "Ms. Higgins?"

LaShonda was no longer being held back, but she was looking at me with a homicidal hunger. Her bugged-out eyes would have been comical had they not been directed at me. "Mah-mah-mah," she stuttered. Her glare never wavered.

"Ms. Higgins? Do you need a drink of water or something?" asked the judge.

"Mah," she said. Veins pulsed on her forehead.

I looked at Hardy's table. He and his assistants, who looked even younger than he did, were stifling giggles.

"Mah... Mr. Marino," LaShonda finally said. She looked demoralized, and totally out of breath.

"Yes?" I said.

She stared. "Oh, forget it," she said, plunging her face into her hands and looking ready for the straitjacket.

I looked at the judge, a big huggy bear in a smart black robe. "Am I done now?"

He nodded. "You're dismissed."

"Okay." Smiling, I stepped down and walked away from the bench. The jury looked at me wide-eyed. They looked like a joyful garden of sunflowers. Waving to them, I made my way to the center aisle but walked past Charles instead of sitting down next to him again. I didn't even look at him. He wasn't visible through the singing moonbeams.

I walked up the aisle towards the exit, vaguely aware of people around me talking and pointing. I didn't care. They seemed like Lilliputians to my Gulliver, and it was time for me to go. There was no rational explanation for the triumph I felt: Some part of me was aware that I'd said some horrible things on the witness stand, but it wasn't a big part. Or a happy part. It was dawning on me that my happiness wasn't just a mood or illusion—it was buttressed by a mighty conviction that I had accomplished something I'd wanted to do for longer than that griping little part of me realized.

The air in the hallway was cooler and fresher, and I breathed in deeply as I left the doors to the courtroom behind me. They clicked closed behind me, and I waited for them to bang open again. One step, two steps, then... bang.

"Where do you think you're going!" yelled Charles.

I turned to face him.

"I've done what I set out to do," I said. "I think I'll go see a movie now, or something."

His face looked like a pulsing strawberry. "Do you know what's at stake here? What the hell is wrong with you?" Spittle flew from his lips.

The dreamy feeling I'd had since taking my oath was beginning to dissipate, but Charles's voice still seemed to echo across a long distance.

"Nothing," I said. "Something was wrong with me before, but I think I'm okay now."

The incomprehension on his face was comical, and yet... sad.

"What was that rant all about? We're supposed to be making *them* look like idiots, not us!"

I shrugged. "That was your agenda, not mine."

"And what was your agenda, exactly?"

Ah... the magic question. Until he asked, the answer wasn't clear. Back in the courtroom, I hadn't really questioned the purpose behind my actions... just acting felt good enough. Speaking those words to Hardy felt like being released from a dungeon after years of imprisonment. You don't question why you look at the sky and sigh for minutes on end. You just do. Now, however, the intoxication of that release had given way to a clarity of mind that was equally alien. But wow, was it nice.

"I want Stubbs's family to win this case, Charles," I said, using the same tone of voice I'd use to discuss the weather. "I want them to win big, and I want them to win ugly. And when they slam-dunk this company of ours, I'm planning to kick back and party."

"But... but... *why*?" he asked, his arms outstretched in a gesture of bewilderment.

To my surprise, as I looked back at him, the clarity vanished. Something still eluded me.

"I don't know," I said.

"How could you not know? You just dragged a multimillion-dollar company to the brink of extinction, throwing the careers of everyone you work with into disarray, and you don't know why you did it?" His voice boomed down the long corridor, turning all eyes to us. He looked ready to punch me.

I shrugged. "No."

"You're, like, stupid or something, aren't you?" said a voice from behind me.

Turning, I saw a teenaged girl standing there in the hallway. She wore fashionably ripped blue jeans and a T-shirt bearing the likeness of some dreadlocked singer. A long, red ponytail flopped off the right side of her head, and it was tinged in black at the ends. Impossibly large gold hoops dangled from her ears, and they slowly rocked as she cocked her head a little at me. She was smirking, and her nose was scrinched up, as if she was beholding someone distasteful. She popped her chewing gum bubble and wrapped the pink ribbon around her index finger.

"Hi," I said. "You... know something about this?"

She rolled her eyes. "A lot more than you do, *Gabe*."

My mouth fell open. She'd said my name the way most people say *asshole*. I could deal with being addressed this way by a perfect stranger, but I had no reply ready for a snotty teenager.

"And who might you be, miss?" asked Charles, with a tone of disrespect I agreed with for once.

She sighed. "My name's Phil, buttwad. Phil Joel."

Chapter 22

GABRIEL'S TRUMPET BLOWS AGAIN

Then the sixth angel blew his trumpet, and I heard a voice coming from between the horns of the altar of gold in God's presence. It said to the sixth angel, who was still holding his trumpet, "Release the four angels who are tied up on the banks of the great river Euphrates!

—Revelation, 9: 13-14

"*You're* Phil Joel?" I said.

"Yeah," she said. Then, catching my look, she added, "It's short for Philomena. My parents, like, cursed me for life when they named me."

"Shouldn't you be older?"

She smirked. "I'm what I'm supposed to be. You, on the other hand, are in *such* big trouble."

The door to the courtroom banged open again, and three people emerged... the three people I least wanted to see at that particular moment. They stopped when they saw us, and did not look pleased.

"Aww," said Michael, rolling his eyes and gesturing dramatically to Muriel and Raj. "It's Little Miss Irritating."

"Sword!" yapped Phil, clapping her hands together. "And light! And messenger!"

"Hello Jophiel," said Muriel. There was a softness in her eyes that the frown couldn't hide.

Charles's gaze ricocheted from one person to the other. "Who are you people?"

Muriel spoke first, cutting off Phil.

"We're old friends of Gabe's," she said.

"I can't believe you're all here together!" said Phil, crossing her arms. "You've just made my job, like, totally easy! You're *so* screwed!"

"You know how easy it would be to swat you down the hall?" asked Michael. "There must be a sale at Abercrombie you're missing."

"Michael," said Muriel.

"Go ahead and hit me. I'll tell him that, too," said Phil, crossing her arms.

Michael drew back as if to slap the girl, who merely thrust her chin forward and pointed to it. Michael hesitated, lowered his hand, and muttered something I couldn't quite hear. The girl turned to Muriel with a big grin.

"Mikey still has issues with women, I see."

"You have a few issues of your own, my dear," said Muriel. She rested a hand on Phil's shoulder, smiling.

"Wait a minute!" said Charles, glaring at me. "Why did you stick the knife in our backs in there? Why, in God's name, did you do that?"

Phil rolled her eyes. "What a putz. Isn't it, like, obvious?"

"Shut up, snitch," said Michael.

"Bite me," said Phil.

"Wait," I said. "Keep talking, Phil. What do you know about this?"

She smiled. "You were pissed, is all. This guy set up a company based on greed and blasphemy. You were watching, and it got worse and worse, and finally—oh, this is *so* against the rules!—you came down here to open a can of whoop-ass on the whole thing."

My mouth fell open. A vague feeling of deja-vu came over me, as if Phil had described some forgotten antic of mine from childhood. Yet I didn't remember anything from my supposed glory days: No wings, no choirs and harps, and certainly no obsessive peeping at Cathedral from behind a bank of clouds. Surely immortal beings had better things to do than monitor the business world. But then again, here these people were. And as weird as Phil's story was, she was right about one thing: Cathedral pissed me off. It had done so for a long time now, and if my outrage crossed unknown planes of existence... well, there were harder things in the world to believe.

Muriel shot her a warning glance. "That's enough, Phil."

Charles's head swivelled wildly throughout the exchange. Finally he held up a hand.

"Would you all excuse us, please? I'd like a word with Gabe in private."

"No," I said. "I think I know what you're going to say. And I don't mind if they hear it."

"Fine," growled Charles, crossing his arms and puckering his lips like a child about to cry. "So be it. Gabriel Marino, you're fired."

A feeling of sweet release washed over me. "I certainly am," I said. "I'm a holy-rolling, company-destroying, righteously incompetent son of a bitch. I'm fired, all right... but you're the one who got burned."

I turned to the assembled pack of crazy angels. "You guys wanna help me clean out my desk?"

They looked mortified. Then, suddenly, Michael roared with laughter.

"This isn't funny," said Charles, his eyes flicking nervously to Michael. "I have countless friends in the publishing industry. The only place you'll get a job from this day forward is a lemonade stand."

I thought briefly of my wife and daughter, living in the shadow of a mortgage and three years' worth of car payments. It's said that the good Lord always provides. I don't know about that, but he does love a good leap of faith.

"Whatever, Charlie," I said. "Maybe your friends in high places can help you build a new company after this one crashes and burns. Only next time, try to do it without the blasphemy and stupidity."

I stopped and looked over my shoulder.

"Don't make me come back," I said.

* * *

The journey back to Cathedral took several hours, since Michael was in the mood to celebrate and dragged us to his favorite bar for a drink or two. Generally, I'm not fussy about my waterholes in the city... I enjoy fern bars and dives equally, but this was the kind of place that left a greasy residue on your fingers. Dark, smoky, and replete with banged-up motorcycle decor, it had a Wild West danger to it. From dark corners eyes watched Muriel, which was bad enough, but they also watched Phil. I don't even want to contemplate the chances of Phil walking out of there if she'd walked in by herself.

We sat in a booth and tried to blend in as best we could... an illusion not helped by Muriel's trip to the bathroom in search of a paper toilet seat to drape on her bench.

A pitcher of Budweiser ("It's Bud or my ass, pal... your choice," said the bartender, an Ernest Borgnine lookalike with cauliflower ear) began to make this feel like a celebration for everyone except Phil, who griped about the Shirley Temple we ordered for her and sulked the entire time. The rest of the conversation was frustrating. I wanted to pump Phil for details on everything that happened before I "fell on my head," but there were too many topics of conversation. Michael crowed over my newfound "balls," banging on the table each time he repeated something I'd said to Charles in a Clint Eastwood imitation. Phil alternated between trying to shut Michael up and scolding me for just about everything I'd done since birth... and before it, too. Muriel peppered me with questions about what I would do for a living, now that my kamikaze attack on Cathedral was over. Raj had stayed behind at the courthouse... he wanted to see how the court case unfolded, and promised to update us later.

The bickering continued as we took a cab back to Cathedral. Night had fallen while we sat in Michael's death bar, and by the time we finally walked through Cathedral's front doors it was about 8:00. It was quiet in the hallways, and oddly dark... usually there was at least a handful of people wasting a nice evening here, but most of the offices were dark. As I walked down the hall towards my own office,

I peered into the few offices that were lit and saw no one. It was almost as if the few workaholics who could always be found here had decided, en masse, to go home.

"Hey Gabe," said Michael from behind me. I could hear the footsteps of the others behind him. "I'm not likin' this."

I turned back to him to smirk. "Well, you're the one who wanted to see where us pencil-pushers work all day."

He didn't smile. "I wanted to see where you work. Not where you die."

Muriel stepped forward, placing a hand on Michael's shoulder. "Gabe, something's wrong here."

I sensed it too. It wasn't anything I could see or hear... it was more like the vestige of a sense I once had. It was like something out of a bad horror movie, which would have been funny had my scrotum not relocated itself near my kidneys.

I walked into my office.

"Hey, knucklehead," said the man sitting in my chair, half in the shadows.

I froze. Michael came up behind my right shoulder.

"Was that you who just said that, or... aw, man, I shoulda known." said Michael.

The man in my chair remained seated. "Nice ta see ya again, Mikey."

"Gabe," said Michael, visibly stiffening, "Please tell me that Knucklehead doesn't work here. Please."

I craned my neck to look at Michael. "That's really his name?"

"The translation's a little off," said Muriel from somewhere behind us. "But yes, that's more or less it."

"What's going on?" shrieked Phil from out in the hallway. "Is that who I think it is? I can't see!"

"Well, ain't this cute," said Knucklehead. "A nice guys convention."

"You don't belong here," said Muriel.

Knucklehead grunted, by way of laughter. "Like you do, cutiepie?"

"You're *talking* to him?" said Phil. "Oh, that is *so* wrong. Wait 'til he finds out about this."

"Shut up," said Michael.

Knucklehead grunted again. "She's still yappin' like a Chihuahua?"

"Shut up," said Michael, this time to Knucklehead. "I'll take the tattletale over Morning Star's little pet any day."

Knucklehead stood up. "I'm gonna kick your ass," he said.

Michael stepped around me and crossed his big arms. "Nope," he said. "You and Lucy boy together, maybe. But he ain't gonna do much sitting in a jail cell, is he? Gabe took care of him," he said, clapping me on the shoulder. "Now I'm takin' care of you."

"Yeah," I said, cursing my voice as it broke into a nervous half-squeal in the middle of the word. Blowing the whistle on the Gang of Six was not a macho accomplishment by any measure, but if the devil got thrown in jail as a consequence, it might impress Knucklehead. I was outgunned here, but I could still bluff.

Without warning, Knucklehead rushed forward and gave Michael and me a hard shove. I staggered back, caught unawares, and collided with Muriel. Michael's back plowed into both of us, and as we all fell backwards I could hear Phil squawk. We all fell like dominoes. Looking up at the ceiling, I saw Knucklehead take a mighty leap over us into the hallway. Something dark was in his hand... something I might have recognized as a gun if my brains weren't rattling around like the insides of a mariachi.

"Ow!" shrieked Phil. "Get off me!"

Michael and I rose and, after helping Muriel and the pouting Phil to their feet, we started off after Knucklehead. He'd run in the direction of Cathedral's front entrance, which would take him through the editors' area and Accounting before he reached the lobby and the exit. Rounding a corner, I was surprised to see him huffing down the corridor only about ten yards ahead of us. Apparently our tough guy didn't run marathons.

We'd almost overtaken him in Accounting, with Muriel and Phil following close behind, when the sound of laughter stopped us in our tracks. Even Knucklehead stopped, startled by the unexpected noise. Looking towards the far end of the room, I was horrified to see my editors and my P.R. staff climbing down from the Tar Bar. Some of them had beers in their hands, and as they descended they looked at us with curiosity.

Knucklehead glanced back and forth from them to us, then towards the main doorway to the street. He did indeed have a gun in his hand, and now it rose towards my face.

"Dominic!" he bellowed, and now I could hear footsteps outside the doorway. Apparently Knucklehead had reinforcements coming. I turned to look at the angels behind me and my staff on the other side of the room. With a sickening certainty, I realized that all eyes were on me. The air was charged with impending violence. I looked into the eyes of the editors and P.R. people, and saw fear, confusion, and God only knew what else. But I also noticed, with mounting terror, that no one over there was looking at Knucklehead or the angels. They were eyeballing me.

All of them.

Knucklehead saw it too, and as he turned his head to give me a questioning look I made a decision. If this battle was really going to happen—if the forces of good and evil were about to lock horns in the Accounting section of Cathedral, Incorporated—then our odds of winning would never be better than now. My battalion was on the field, with Knucklehead's still out of sight. The time was ripe to strike. All my little war needed was a command... a heroic word or gesture to start it all.

The footsteps drew nearer. Knucklehead remained where he was, waving the gun back and forth at the two groups opposing him. It was time.

Raising my hand, I pointed at Knucklehead and the door and looked at the editors and P.R. people.

"Help," I whined.

It was the war cry of a milquetoast, and I was immediately ashamed, but it had the desired effect. With a startling yell, the editors, P.R. people, and angels charged forward just as three burly guys in dark clothing burst through the door. The pounding noise of the door caused Knucklehead's gun arm to jerk, and the weapon discharged with a deafening roar. The dark-clothed guys were carrying guns too, but now the Cathedral people were upon them, and as the close-quartered brawling began I didn't hear any more shots.

What followed was the weirdest spectacle I'd ever beheld at work. My staffers, charged with a rage I'd never seen them show before, slapped and scratched and gouged at Knucklehead and his thugs, who tried to keep together in the fighting but were gradually separated in the confusion. I watched in horror as Rosie Peterson, in conduct unbecoming a middle-aged teatotaler, threw a Scotch tape dispenser at one thug's head while Kelvin, after failing to get the guy in a headlock, bit his ear. Another thug leveled his gun at Michael, only to have it knocked from his hand by Theresa, who accomplished this with a forehand swing of a stapler. She then brought the stapler to the thug's temple with a backhanded flourish. I could hear the mechanism click as she made contact. It must have stung.

Keeping my back to the wall, I watched the melee erupt before me but did not join in. Something felt wrong. Looking around at the swinging limbs and flying office supplies, I saw a spot in the middle of the riot where there was no motion. Claire stood there, motionless, still holding the beer she'd brought down from the Tar Bar. Seemingly immune to the kicking and shoving around her, she remained where she was... a human eye in the small hurricane of violence. Her eyes flicked from one individual fight to another, and sometimes I saw anger and other times fear. She didn't seem to know what to do. As she looked around the room her eyes finally met mine, and the fear I expected to see was not there. She was small in stature, but something in her posture suggested a fierce power being held in check. A punch was thrown in front of her, temporarily obscuring her from sight, but when she reappeared from behind the thug's arm she was giving me an imploring glance.

I looked away in time to see Sally deliver a chopping kick to one thug's groin. His gun hit the ground first, followed quickly by his body. Another thug was down a few yards away, draped over a desk while Phil delivered rapid but ineffectual slaps on his back, yelling, "You don't BELONG here! You don't BELONG here!" over and over. Another gunshot sounded from somewhere on my left, and I looked just in time to see Muriel sneak up behind the thug, reach around his face with her hand, and plant an open canister of rubber cement squarely over his nose. Climbing up onto his back, she kept one hand over his mouth while the other squashed the can against his face. It didn't take long for the fumes to have their effect, and when the thug got dizzy and began to lurch, Kelvin launched himself at the thug in a flying tackle that would have been heroic if it hadn't knocked both the thug and Muriel against a bookcase.

Of the dark forces, only Knucklehead remained standing. My staffers, bleeding from noses and assorted scrapes on their arms but otherwise appearing uninjured, formed a circle around Knucklehead and Michael as they squared off against each other. Knucklehead's gun, like those of his three companions, was on the ground somewhere. He didn't seem eager to retrieve it, though, raising his hands in a boxer's stance against Michael. Michael responded in kind. They'd wanted this brawl since they first saw each other—it was a conflict as old as anything in creation—and everyone seemed to sense that as they formed a ring around the combatants.

Knucklehead feinted, then Michael took a roundhouse swing that missed, and then they were all over each other. With arms locked, they grappled and stumbled about the room, overturning chairs and kicking fallen Rolodexes across the floor. No one joined in as they fought, and as I looked from one warlike face to another I realized that Claire was nowhere to be seen. This was odd, but I had no time to wonder because the next flurry of rabbit punches brought the two warriors uncomfortably close to where I stood. Knucklehead had gained the upper hand, spinning Michael around with a crushing haymaker, and as Michael staggered back I sidestepped into the doorway of Bobby Ortiz's old office.

Wary of anyone sneaking up behind me, I stole a glance over my shoulder. The office had been undisturbed by the riot... in fact, it didn't seem as if anyone had touched anything since Bobby was led off by the cops. His books still lined the shelves, and his trumpet—polished and gleaming as ever—rested on his desk.

A brief counterattack by Michael pushed Knucklehead into the entrance of Bobby's office, blocking my exit and freaking me out momentarily. Knucklehead responded with a savage punch to Michael's face, and as the sound bounced off the walls I saw a vacancy in Michael's eyes. He was done. People were crowding behind Michael now, trying to see over each other's heads but still not touching him. Knucklehead launched a grazing jab at Michael's eye, but succeeded only in grazing the side of Michael's head due to a last-minute flinch by Michael. Frustrated, he buried his other fist into Michael's abdomen, doubling the big angel over and leaving him wide open for a final, decisive blow.

It was coming, and everyone knew it. Yelps and screams sounded from the room behind Michael, and Muriel, who had elbowed her way to the front, now fixed me with a searing look.

"Do it now, Gabe," she said.

"Do what?" I said, raising my palms. Yet I sensed that some part of me knew what she was talking about.

Knucklehead's arm began to rise again, slowly.

"Oh, for God's sake," said Muriel. "Would you please do it before it's too late!"

Knucklehead's arm was nearing its apex.

Panicked, I looked around for a solution—any solution—to present itself. Only books and papers stared back at me. That, and

Bobby's trumpet, shining oddly in the light spilling in from the hall. I reached for it, thinking for a moment that I might get away with bashing it over Knucklehead's head, but as my hand closed around it I noticed Michael's head rise. Quickly bringing the mouthpiece of the trumpet to my lips, I took in a quick breath through my nostrils and blew. Hard.

The resulting note was true and clear. I don't know much about music, but it sounded like a C and it didn't waver, sputter, or fade. My third-grade music teacher would have been proud, because the one-note song I played was enough to catch the attention of Knucklehead, whose head snapped around. His face wore a look of disbelief.

Before he could turn back to finish the beating, Michael's fist shot up and made hard contact with Knucklehead's jaw. The clacking sound of teeth made me wince, but the effect was much greater on Knucklehead, whose hands now clasped around his jaw. Another driving punch from Michael, and he was doubled over. Now it was Michael who was about to finish the fight, and finish it he did with a walloping smack that knocked Knucklehead senseless to the ground.

The next thing I remembered was whooping in the hallway. Michael was exhausted, but as he huffed and puffed he grinned at me. I caught quick glimpses of people hugging each other as they danced around in the hallway, and for a moment I was appalled at the celebration of such savagery. Then Muriel came into the room and hugged Michael, and as she turned to hug me I saw Phil bound up to Michael and nearly knock him flat with a squealing bear hug.

"I knew you could do it," said Muriel.

I pulled away from her and rolled my eyes. "I didn't do squat. He did all the work," I said, jerking a thumb at Michael.

"No," she said, looking at me with affection. "Believe it or not, you did what you've always done. It just... doesn't look so good in this world."

I was about to complain about this, but then I noticed a figure pushing through the excited crowd. It was Raj, and damn, did he look happy.

"Gabe!" he yelled, elbowing past Theresa. "Good news!"

"What happened?" I said.

He flashed the thumbs-up sign. "The case is over! We won!"

I sighed. "Raj, that's *bad* news. I wanted the Stubbs family to win that case, not Cathedral."

If Raj's grin got any wider, it would split his head in two. "Yes! Stubbs family win! Four hundred million dollars!"

"Damn," said Michael.

"I don't believe it," I said, leaning against the doorway for support. So the original demand of $200 million had been awarded... and doubled. Man, the jury must have really hated this company. Good for them.

"Yes!" said Raj, and now he was hopping from one foot to another. "The judge say that any company who hires man like you deserves all the punishment it can get!"

My smile faded. "Um, thanks Raj. I don't think I need to hear any more."

Muriel squeezed my arm. "Remember what I said. Your actions here aren't easy to understand."

"Yeah," I said. "I know."

Raj looked around at the room, noticing the blood, bodies, and overturned furniture for the first time. "Hey... what you guys been doing?"

Michael was craning his neck over the staffers, looking back towards the vanquished forces of evil. "Uh oh," he said.

"What?" said Muriel.

"There's one left. That little demon bitch Gabe's banging," said Michael. "Where'd it go?"

We looked around the room. There was no sign of Claire. We picked through the maze of upended furniture, but only the unconscious bodies of Knucklehead and his posse were on the floor.

Then an idea occurred to me. I looked at the ladder leading up to the Tar Bar. At the top, the trapdoor was open, revealing a patch of night sky.

"Guys," I said, "this last fight is mine."

Michael looked up at the trap door, then back at me. "Let's take it out together."

I shook my head. Muriel moved towards me.

"Gabe, I really don't think this is wise."

I smiled. "Remember what you said?"

She looked thoughtful for a moment, then nodded. And so, without exchanging another word with my newfound brethren, I ascended the ladder.

Chapter 23

ARMAGEDDON

Set me as a seal on your heart, as a seal on your arm; For stern as death is love, relentless as the nether world is devotion; its flames are a blazing fire. Deep waters cannot quench love, nor floods sweep it away.
—Song of Songs, 8:6

I paused near the top of the ladder, afraid of what awaited me up on the roof. This was the first time I ever considered the possibility of being murdered by a coworker, much less a demon who had the hots for me. I looked up through the trap door. It was a still night, with no clouds to block the stars lighting the darkness. Very well, I thought. If this is the last thing I see before my death... well, some have done much worse.

Emerging at the top, I saw that the Christmas lights adorning the oversize beach umbrella had been left on. It was quiet and peaceful. Claire sat with her back to me, in a folding chair she'd brought to the far edge of the building. If she heard me come up the trap door, she didn't show it. I sighed, steeling myself, then moved towards where she sat.

"Hi," she said, when I was about ten feet away.

I stopped. "Hi there." A slight breeze picked up, playing with the outer fringes of her hair. "It's, ah, pretty nice out tonight, isn't it?"

"Yeah," she said, without moving.

I took another step closer and shoved my hands in my pockets... a gesture of affability that was pretty stupid, considering she was facing in the other direction. "So...um... we were just wondering where you snuck off to."

Her head turned halfway towards me. There were no horns or fiery eyes... just Claire. "Yeah," she said. "Sorry about that. It just... got a little too intense down there."

I faked a laugh. "I know what you mean."

She smiled in profile, then turned back to the limited view of the river.

"Hey," I said, "Would you mind if I sat with you for a bit?"

She gestured to the spot next to her. "Sure."

I pulled one of the folding chairs from the stack by the umbrella and set it up next to hers. Trying not to look her in the eye, I stared out at the river for a while.

"The company will cease to exist soon," I said. "I caused it, sort of. And I got fired for it. So I guess I'm not your boss anymore. Which is good, because I don't think I was ever much good at it."

"You were better at it once," she said, chuckling. "But you're right. I liked working for you, though."

"You didn't fight us," I blurted out, immediately regretting it. Was there any point to ruining the moment? Was another fight really necessary?

"No," she said, and the lilt in her voice made me look at her this time. It was hard to read her expression, but there was no violence there. There wasn't much of anything, really—no mischief, no attraction, and no happiness.

"You really are beautiful by moonlight. Did I ever mention that?"

She smiled again and looked down. "I think it might have come up in the past few weeks."

"Yeah. I was just checking. So... why didn't you fight us, Claire? It sure looked like you were going to, for a while."

She sucked in her breath. "I almost did," she said, exhaling sharply. "You'll never know how close it was. But I just... couldn't. Not against them." She looked out at the river some more, then shook her head. "No, that's a lie. It's you I couldn't raise my hand against."

She was looking at me now, and in all my life I never wanted to kiss a woman more. Her dark eyes held mine without a hint of reproach for her failure, tiny glints of moonlight lighting the way to a love that portended all kinds of catastrophe.

"I'll be in a lot of trouble when get back to where I came from," she said.

I laughed, and this time it was real. "Me too," I said. "Jophiel's keeping a rap sheet that predates my birth."

"She's still a pain in the ass, isn't she?"

I nodded. "I feel like I've known her for a thousand, long, annoying years."

She looked up at the sky. "It's funny how life turns out... how changed we are when we move through this world. She's almost cute, with that little attitude of hers."

"Tell that to Michael. He's about ready to duct tape her mouth."

She giggled. "I miss you guys sometimes. Now that I'm here, that is. I'm not sure if I did... you know, before."

"Well," I said, wondering if it were really true, "I'm sure they miss you a little too. Even if they do want to pulverize you right now. I guess it wasn't always like this between... you know, your kind and ours."

"And the future? What about that?"

I bit my lip. The question was pointed, and I had no idea whether she meant the future of heaven and hell or the future of her and me. I thought I was clear on the latter point, but oh, the dancing starlight in those eyes...

"I don't think there is one," I said, swallowing hard.

"No?" Her voice had a tinge of resignation, as if she'd known the answer but hoped for something different.

"No. Good will always be good, bad will always be bad, and... I'll always be married," I said.

"Always?" she said, and now there was a ghost of a smile.

"Oh, no," I said, shaking my head. "Don't even go there."

"What about later? *Much* later?" she said, raising an eyebrow.

Now there was an idea. Yet, after what we'd done, I wondered if there'd even *be* an afterlife for her or me. Still, if there was...

"Maybe," I said, and nearly cracked up when her other eyebrow rose. "I promise you nothing, mind you. Just... maybe. That's all."

She shrugged and turned back to the river. If she was hiding a grin, I couldn't tell. Suddenly I felt more than a little guilty.

"I should be getting back home now," I said. "There's a lot I have to account for, and I'm not sure where to begin."

"Yeah," she said, and just like that, I could feel the moment pass. I knew that I'd want it back later. We sat for a moment longer, and then I stood to leave. She began to rise as well, but I placed my hand on her shoulder.

"Wait," I said. "At least for a little while. They're probably still... excited down there. Let me herd them towards home, and then you can go down that ladder when they're gone."

She waited for me to reach the ladder and start climbing down before saying, "Did you ever think that maybe you should protect them from me?"

I looked up in surprise. A wry grin was on her face, and I laughed, but suddenly it felt like someone poured icewater down the back of my shirt.

"I guess not," I said. "But while we're on the subject, you're not going to do anything... you know... *bad* while you're here in this world, are you?"

The grin never faded.

"I promise you nothing," she said.

Some verbiage the author wanted us to print

AUTHOR'S NOTE

Some readers will undoubtedly find it jarring to see the Holy Bible quoted so often in a tale replete with profanity, greed, sex, crime, and other vices. They may also be upset that I curled the tenets of Roman Catholicism into sacrilegious, 230-page pretzel. If any of those readers made it this far in my book (I'm guessing they haven't, but who knows?), I apologize for any hurt feelings. My tale was written to amuse, not to offend. The story made me do it.

An earlier version of *Gabriel's Fired* appeared as a serial novel at the now-defunct literary web site *CaféMo.* My heartfelt thanks go to its proprietor, Maggie Balistreri, whose decision to green-light that project eventually led to this book. Her constant encouragement during the writing of the first draft made all the difference. I will also shamelessly plug her hilarious *The Evasion-English Dictionary* (Melville House Publishing), since it taught me something about language while cracking me up.

I also thank my friend Dave Gosse for serving as my first reader. His expertise and good judgment vastly improved the story. I'm also grateful that, despite my griping, he stuck to his guns when he knew he was right. It's annoying when friends do that, but it's also invaluable.

Huge thanks go to you, Gentle Reader, for buying this book. If it made you smile, it was all worthwhile.

He wouldn't shut up until we printed this, too

ABOUT THE AUTHOR

Richard Christiano is an English teacher who resides in central New Jersey. After earning degrees from Drew University and Felician College, he squandered his education on a staggering variety of professions: He has been an editor at an educational publishing company, an account executive at an international advertising agency, a collator, warehouse thug, forklift operator, truck driver, market research interviewer, and writer. This is his first novel.

Questions? Comments? Anecdotes?

E-mail the author at dogberry415@yahoo.com

http://christianobooks.webs.com/

Made in the USA
Middletown, DE
26 November 2022

16069134R00136